Natalie Blazou
P9-CCW-173

ONE WORLD
A GLOBAL ANTHOLOGY OF SHORT STORIES

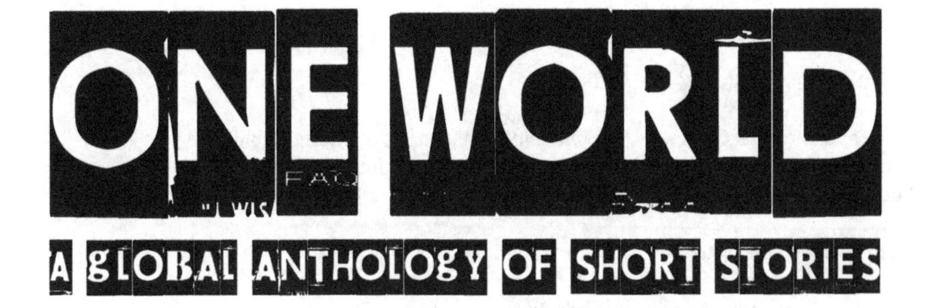

New Internationalist

First published in 2009 by
New Internationalist Publications Ltd
Oxford OX4 1JE
newint.org

Reprinted 2010, 2012, 2014, 2015.

Front cover image: Victor Ehikhamenor (Nigeria).

Edited for New Internationalist by Chris Brazier.
Designed for New Internationalist by Alan Hughes.

Printed by Lightning Source.

British Library Cataloguing-in-Publication Data.
A catalogue record for this book is available from the British Library.

Library of Congress Cataloguing-in-Publication Data.
A catalogue for this book is available from the Library of Congress.

ISBN: 978-1-906523-13-8
(ebook ISBN: 978-1-906523-76-3)

INTRODUCTION

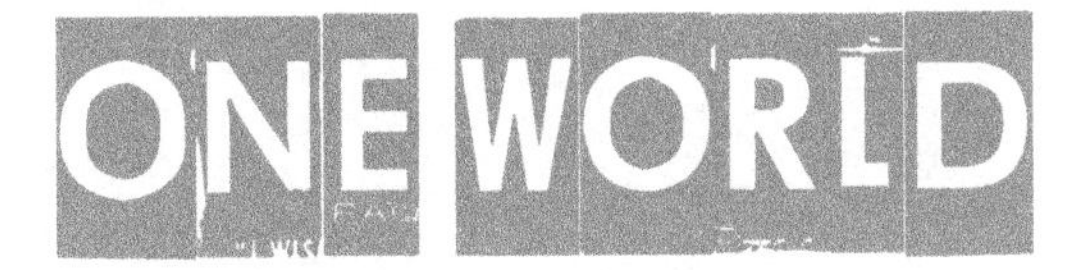

THE CONCEPT OF One World is often a multi-colored tapestry into which sundry, if not contending patterns can be woven. For those of us who worked on this project, 'One World' goes beyond the everyday notion of the globe as a physical geographic entity. Rather, we understand it as a universal idea, one that transcends national boundaries to comment on the most prevailing aspects of the human condition.

This attempt to redefine the borders of the world we live in through the short story recognizes the many conflicting issues of race, language, economy, gender and ethnicity, which separate and limit us. We readily acknowledge, however, that regardless of our differences or the disparities in our stories, we are united by our humanity.

We invite the reader on a personal journey across continents, countries, cultures and landscapes, to reflect on these beautiful, at times chaotic, renditions on the human experience. We hope the reach of this path will transcend the borders of each story, and perhaps function as an agent of change.

Welcome to our world.

Ovo Adagha & Molara Wood
for the One World group of authors
October 2008

CONTENTS

ELAINE CHIEW MALAYSIA

LENG LUI IS FOR PRETTY LADY

EVERYONE SAYS I'M lucky; lucky, because Mrs Kong likes to give me her old clothing, dresses she hasn't worn since the 1980s and her old underwear. Most of them don't really fit me, the bras have strings trailing from the torn lace and the dresses are too formal for scrubbing the kitchen floor or clambering up on top of counters cleaning shelves. So, with the dresses, I sometimes cut them up to use as dishcloth since Mrs Kong thinks store-bought dish-wipes are an unnecessary household expense. Or I give the dresses to my friends when I see them in Central Hong Kong on Sunday. Maridel, with arms sectioned like pink lotus roots and hips like the soft underside of a pear, says to me, "I don't want your frumpy housecoats, Alina, freebie or no." "You're lucky I offer them to you," says I. She shrugs and pulls up these cords she's sewn with finesse onto her fake suede shoes to make them look like boots. "Those boots make you look like 'ho'," I say. She smirks, "Ain't it look like *Pretty Woman* though?" She knows I'm a big fan of that movie.

No, I can't say I'm as lucky as everyone seems to think, at least not compared to Maridel. Her *taitai* doesn't get up till two in the afternoon, being a nightclub singer, and only comes home in the wee hours, so Maridel can protest all she likes, but we all know she goes to bed at ten. So I've said before to Luya and Febie, our luck is entirely determined by the kind of job or mood your taitai holds. If she has a bad day, you have a bad day too.

Luya, with her Palmolive-glossy hair, likes to disagree. She has opinions on everything. She says that if you're better educated than the other 140,000 *amahs* here, your employer inevitably sees your worth and will treat you better. As if she's a Chinese antique – stare hard enough, maybe you can see the value of a moldy cracking piece of wood. She says it may even be the staircase to a better job, maybe as a restaurant hostess or an office assistant. She's mental, having this kind of *bahala na* attitude about everything. Me, I've got myself an English literature degree from university in Manila and look where it has got me. What's the difference between me and Febie, who can barely speak English? We both get up at six in the morning to get the children to school, we cook and clean all day, and then we have to hear the harping from our taitais, "*Aiyaa*, why you no clean behind door stump, look here, balls of dust big as *yu dan*" ('fish balls' – I've learned a lot of spoken Cantonese, that chicken-scrawly writing in the newspapers that makes life in this city one giant mystery) or "You big stupid egg, you boil chicken until you can poke at flesh and it spring back." I have to bite back reply, "No, Mrs Kong, chicken dead, you can poke but it no spring back."

Mrs Kong looks at me suspiciously, so I know she knows I have a good education and speak better English than she does. Luya's dead wrong on this one – if you are better educated, your taitai thinks you're acting superior, and she's waiting to pounce on your mistakes and make sure you know your place. Stacking my pillow against my arm at night, I don't think about what Luya told me, that she's heard about José out with some girl, or Abuela kneeling for me daily at Santa Ana or three-year old Juanita looking at pictures I send home and saying "Mama?"

No, I think about how to survive every day with Mrs Kong.

❖ ❖ ❖

Febie likes to call me 'Leng Lui' – Cantonese slang for 'pretty lady' she picked up from the street vendors in Mongkok. But I'm not cheap like Charina or Fredahlia who cruise for gringos with white skin like sharks at tom-tom clubs in Wanchai. Charina and Fredahlia are no better than prostitutes, I tell Maridel. "They got style," she says, "learning how to smoke cigarettes and doing the hip-hop." Who cares if they can swing their hips and smile their secret smiles in the hopes of piggybacking one of those sharks who will whisk them away to America or London? Would you sell your soul just so you can have a chintz drawing room or fake Oriental vases or stainless steel hobs or a game room with dead stuffed animals hanging on the walls?

No, I stick to my movies. Ling-Ling and Sdever share a DVD player and after *Thomas The Tank Engine*, I sneak in a few minutes of *Pretty Woman* or *An Officer and a Gentleman*, all these romances that Mrs Kong buys and watches with subtitles of chicken-scrawly writing, slumped in the living room with curtains drawn, chain-smoking and wearing her owlish tortoiseshell frames, crying into her Oolong. Each movie takes me a long time to finish because I get only ten minutes a day, but it makes the expecting doubly sweet. Lots of time in between washing dishes and peeling onions to daydream about myself in the movies. Febie often says I got the face. Sometimes I can even see myself speaking lines in front of a camera. "It's not that far-fetched," I say to Luya and Maridel, who hoot with scorn. But what's the harm of daydreaming in the boring routine we face every day? It's like those edges that hold a jigsaw puzzle together or the pages within a book cover. I watch these romances and I dare to dream that when I return to Manila, José will come greet me at the train station, daisies in his hand and our daughter beside him. Is that so far-fetched?

My lot could be worse. It could be like Eliza-Eunice who got spanked in the head with a frying pan because her employer thought she'd stolen HK$32 from an ashtray – Eliza-Eunice who died in the hospital a week later from a blood clot in her brain caused by a concussion. Even if her employer rots in jail, who do you think is the loser? Lucky for me, Mrs Kong isn't really too much into using an apparatus to give one a whipping. She likes the knuckle maneuver, a sharp and hard rap to the side of the head. Mr Kong hardly seems to notice I'm around.

But what we fear most is losing our jobs. We have two weeks to find a new job before getting deported. As Maridel tells me, it was explained to her by this Australian she was seeing, "youu knoaw, a conundroom?" If we get fired, we can't get a new job unless we have a discharge letter from our old employer, and call me dumb, but unless you have an employer who has a conscience where amahs are concerned or who is just plain nice, you'd be a fool to think you can get that discharge letter. Now that's a real 'conundroom'.

❖ ❖ ❖

The Kongs are a bit funny. The kids are normal enough: Sdever likes to chew on cotton buds, Ling-Ling operates on her dolls with scissors. Mrs Kong drinks White Russians in the afternoon and insists it's only milk. Sometimes she has her cronies over for mahjong and amidst the clack-clack of those short tiles, I can hear her complaining tones to these bejeweled ladies in faux fur, as if life has kidnapped her and demanded a ransom.

Mr Kong is a branch manager for HSBC. Sometimes, he works late, though I don't know why, since the branch closes by five. When I first came to work for the Kongs, I was impressed by what a dapper little man Mr Kong was –

clean-shaven, suit neatly pressed, shoes shined to a dull gleam, and he washes his hands 10 or 11 times a day. Until one day when I glimpsed him cutting his toenails and emptying the clippings into a plant sitting on their bedroom windowsill. When next I went to water it, I lifted the fronds and there at the base was a mountain of toenail and fingernail clippings.

Lately, he has taken to putting a turnip next to his bedside lamp. I found it one morning and puzzled, replaced it in the refrigerator. Later that evening, Mr Kong strides into the kitchen, which he never comes into, opens the refrigerator, takes out the turnip and walks away with it, but not before I see the expression in his eye – furtive and creepy. Before bedtime, I espy him speaking to it, sitting on the bed in his neatly ironed pajamas with his feet firmly flat on the mat. His words are unintelligible, but his chest puffs out and his shoulders straighten – perhaps he pours his heart out to the turnip, since he and Mrs Kong don't speak much beyond tidbits about the children. When I tell Maridel, she laughs like a wild woman, "What, he talks to a turnip? Why a turnip?"

Mrs Kong hardly notices, or maybe she simply doesn't care. She's flirting with the young man who tends the Chinese medicinal shop down on Sai Yeong Choi. He shows her dried deer-antlers and they both giggle with hands over their mouths. Taking out a brown oblong piece that looks like a finger, he whispers something in her ear – Mrs Kong flutters her eyes and turns dragonfruit red. He turns to me suddenly and says in English loudly, "Penis. This penis." I feel pity for Mr Kong, because he works hard and tries to be a good father. But Sdever only gurgles at him with a slack jaw. Again, I wonder if the boy has brain damage, because only an idiot has a crooked mouth like that; Ling-Ling ignores him completely, intent on her toy musical instruments, her dolls or her drawing pads.

But soon things heat up. Hot as you can boil an egg on the pavement and Mrs Kong gets all dolled-up. She tells me she's going to the medicinal shop to get some soup ingredients. "I can go, Madam." She waves her hand dismissively, slings her purse over her shoulder, stops to check her lipstick in the hallway mirror. One hour later, she's still not back. The nursery calls about Sdever. Then the school calls about Ling-Ling. I tell them she's coming. I put the chicken where I've been pulling out small white quills from the pink skin into the water-filled sink. I'm uneasy, but maybe they're just chatting. Who does hanky-panky in daylight?

When I get to the shop, the iron-grill door is padlocked. No-one in sight – the shop is brown and murky, still as a crocodile slumbering in hot swampy waters. The ceiling fan has been left on, whirring silently like helicopter blades. On the pavement I squat and wait 10 minutes, 15 minutes, 20. No sign of Mrs

Kong. Maybe she isn't here after all. Maybe she came and has gone on to the Park N' Shop opposite. I fan myself with an old newspaper, thinking about Sdever, probably sniveling scared, and Ling-Ling, who hates being the last to leave school. Angry, I jump up and through the grilled iron-bars, I shout, "Mrs Kong! Mrs Kong!"

She emerges half-dressed, hair askew, her lipstick smeared. "It's you," she says, accusingly.

I'm not the one with my petticoat down my legs.

"What you doing here, huh, Alina?" she demands, pulling her dress over her camisole – in her haste, slotting buttons into the wrong eyehooks. The young man is behind her, cigarette dangling, wearing tight briefs and a white singlet damp in patches.

"I'm sorry, Madam," I say, "but Sdever and Ling-Ling..."

Mrs Kong cuts me off, saying something in rapid Cantonese to the young man. He comes forward and unchains the padlock, smirking, his eyes tiny slits against the sun.

Mrs Kong comes outside and grabs my arm. "Let's go, you stupid egg." She marches down the street, half-hauling me as if I've done something wrong. "You don't say nothing about this to anyone, you hear me? Or I fire you."

❖ ❖ ❖

But Mr Kong must have sensed something's different. Maybe he too sees Mrs Kong's smiles in the mirror, her fuller lips, her swaying hips. Suddenly, she seems as bouffant as her hair. The next evening, Mr Kong is again with his turnip – at first it seems he's whispering to it, then looking closer, I see him kiss it. Not just kiss, but his tongue flicks in and out.

"Sir?"

He drops the turnip like a hot chicken-bun.

"Your tea, sir?"

"Uh... not right now." He picks up his turnip, looks at it, melancholy-like. But his tone is gruff. "Where's Mrs Kong?"

"She's at Mrs Chin's for mahjong."

"Aah... yes, I forgot. The kids?"

"Asleep, sir."

"Good. Bring my tea, Alina. I'm tired now."

When I tell my Sunday group about Mr Kong's tongue-ing of the turnip, they split their sides.

"Really?" Febie asks, eyes wide and mouth open.

Maridel says, "He probably need those deer antlers, maybe then he don't need to practice on a turnip."

Luya shakes her head, "I'm glad I don't work for a Chinese taitai. They're cruel and weird."

To the fact that if I tell anyone, Mrs Kong would fire me, Maridel says, "That's no threat. Spill the beans and I fire you," she mocks in her best Cantonese accent, surprisingly sounding just like Mrs Kong. "Peel potatoes wrong and I fire you. Sweep room bad and I fire you."

"Yeah, what you know about that," I say, "your taitai only sweeps once a year."

Luya pats me on the shoulder, *"Até,* nothing bad happen to you now, you lucky because you know their secrets."

❖ ❖ ❖

The afternoon visits to the medicinal shop and Mr Kong's turnip abuse continue. I finish more romances, one movie per sitting. *Pretty Woman,* a few more times. Out in the living room too, with curtains drawn, sometimes drinking White Russians. One evening, while changing the water in the vases, I ad-lib the lines to *Pretty Woman* in the hallway mirror, the part when she talks about being a princess trapped in a tower. Suddenly, in the mirror, I see Mr Kong watching me. But he doesn't watch me like the gringos do in Central, openly, lewdly. Mr Kong watches me with one scary eye in between the hinges of the door to the kitchen.

Then, one afternoon, as I come in from mopping the outside terrace, Mrs Kong is standing in the lobby with a packed valise.

"Madam?" I ask.

"Call Mr Kong in office to pick up chillen, Alina. Cook them omelets for dinner. I don't want Ling-Ling stay up too late. If chillen cry, tell them I call them from Phuket."

"Phuket, Madam?"

"Yes, I go vacation. I be back next week."

"But does Mr Kong know where you're going, Madam?"

"No, but he no care anyway." She laughs bitterly and then, I'm alone with the chillen.

I've never called Mr Kong at the office before. Trembling, I say, "Mr Andrew Kong, please," as soon as a female answers in rapid Cantonese. I breathe a sigh of relief when, instead of interrogating me, she simply says, "Wait just a minute."

When Mr Kong comes on, the words stick to my mouth like pellets.

"Hello, anyone there?"

"Mrs Kong, sir. She's left for Phuket."

"Who's this?"

"Alina, sir."

"What's the matter, Alina?" His voice is sharp with surprise.

"Mrs Kong, sir, she's left for Phuket. She say she come back next week. She ask you to pick up children. But she gone, sir."

There's only silence from his end.

"What time?" he finally says, sounding tired and I like to think, gloomy. But not angry, so maybe I won't get hit with a frying pan.

"She left at four, sir."

"No, I mean, what time do I pick up the kids?"

"Oh, five, sir. Five-thirty latest."

"Damn it, it's ten to five."

❖ ❖ ❖

There's a lot of bawling that night, little Sdever sniffles even when asleep and there's a trail of yellow mucus down his cheek. Ling-Ling throws all her dolls at me and I pick them up and put them in the treasure chest. She repeats this tantrum while Mr Kong sits in the kitchen with his newspaper, but I notice he's on the same page still an hour later. When it's finally time for Ling-Ling to go to bed, I see her dolls scattered around the floor – all their heads have been neatly scissored off.

Over the next few days, I do what I can for the Kongs, who all look amputated, as if missing an integral limb and can only hobble from place to place. Sdever will not eat, even though I try to entice him with the stir-fries he likes. I boil Mr Kong his chicken medicinal soup. Ling-Ling says she wants to write Mrs Kong a letter and mail it to Phuket. I give her pen and paper, she comes out with a drawing of a giant squid sucking up the sun. "What's that?" I ask. "Phuket," she says. Mr Kong continues to massage his turnip, slowly, deliberately, his eyes watching me. At night, I worry about José; I try not to think of him being out with another woman, but my mind keeps filling with images of Mrs Kong in Phuket with that young man from the medicine shop.

❖ ❖ ❖

It's been ten days and there is no Mrs Kong. That night, I ask Mr Kong, "Are you going to try to find her, Mr Kong?"

Mr Kong looks up from sipping soup. Since Mrs Kong's departure, he has insisted I take dinner with the family. These dinners are awkward silences, only the tinkle of the soup spoon against the tureen, the children in bed, me and him watching the bark or fungus or dried tofu swirl around the milky brown liquid; occasionally, a chicken neck bobs up when I use the ladle. Now he looks at me as if I've just spoken to him in Tagalog.

"If she comes back, she comes back." He heaves a sigh full of dust.

"But maybe you should call her." I look pointedly at the Phuket number scrawled in big letters across the calendar hanging atop the spice rack.

"She's on vacation. She does not want to be disturbed. You know how she is if you disturb her when she is doing something."

Yes, bang, bang, a quick whack to the head, I know. But I don't say this, I purse my lips instead. "What will you do if she doesn't come back?"

He drops his spoon and holds his head in his hands. "I don't know, Alina."

He looks so sad and confused, I'm embarrassed for him. "Erm… how's the sesame chicken I made for you?"

"I can't think about food," he groans. He looks up, eyes glistening like watermelon rinds. Suddenly, his hand is on my arm, a pale milky claw. "We don't need Mrs Kong, Alina."

I react in alarm and drop the spoon, the liquid scalding him. He draws his hand back quickly. Afraid, I scrape my chair back and make to grab the dishcloth made of Mrs Kong's old dresses to wipe his hand dry. This time he reaches again for my hand and he doesn't let go. "Alina, listen to me, it took me a long time to get up the courage to say this. God knows, I'm much older than you, and I'm married with children. It's a bit sudden, but just give me a chance, you'll see that it can work."

My mind struggles to match the words I've just heard to their unbelievable meaning.

"Sir?" Trembling, I try to yank my arm away. Months later, I'll remember the tortured pose we were in: I, half-risen from my chair, one arm reaching for the dishcloth and the other being pulled back by Mr Kong, while he holds on for dear life, still sitting down, soup dribbling down his chin, and the only word that comes to my mind is "Stuckey".

"Alina, I've mulled over how best to put this, how to convince you of my intentions. Do you know how I sometimes stay late in the office? It's because I'm afraid of letting my feelings show, of not being able to control myself."

I renew my struggle to get free at this.

"But it seems I can't help it. Your face torments me every day. I find myself practicing what I'll say to you in the office. At home, my fantasies overwhelm me – you and I could be the ones in Phuket now..."

"At home?" I ask stupidly, but some hidden knowledge is struggling to reveal itself to me.

"Yes, many times I thought you'd suspect – the way I was practicing my overtures. Haven't you heard me rehearsing my speech to you?"

This rehearsed rant that sounds like a bad canton movie?

"Haven't you seen me practice so I wouldn't be inept?"

The word comes to my lips unbidden, "Turnip?"

"Yes, my darling, that turnip is you."

A wave of disgust, profound and dizzying, uncoils inside. "Sir, let me go. I insist, please." I wrench my fist away, only to have him rise from his chair and grab me around the waist.

"Oh Alina, we can be such a comfort to each other. Especially now."

"Stop it. Let me go. Sir. Please." Stuckey, Stuckey, Stuckey, my mind chants. Struggling desperately, my mind hovers over the choice between mute submission or being fired.

"Together, Alina, we'll make happiness happen."

"Sir, you're upset, but..." I can't finish because Mr Kong's mouth is on mine, and his tongue is a lizard peeping through a crack in a dry wall.

I manage to twist away and, just as I've seen them do in movies, I move my knee upwards in one swift motion, making hard contact with his nether parts. He doubles over, cupping his crotch, and lets me go. Stuckey, Stuckey, Stuckey! I bring my elbow down between his two scapulas, as if perfecting a karate chop, and as he jerks one hand up to reach around his back, lifting up his face, I pull my fist back and pop him one in the eye. Our tussle up-ended the dining table and the soup tureen lurches and tips over as the liquid sloshes down onto Mr Kong's naked feet. He yelps, keels over and curls on the floor like dried shrimp.

I brush at the trailing wisp of hair on my forehead. Looking up, Mrs Kong stands in the doorway sporting a tan, her mouth agape.

❖ ❖ ❖

Pandemonium begins with a 'P' for police. Their radios crackle back and forth. Mr Kong holds an ice-pack to his eye (one can easily see his feet are none the worse for wear, it's just drinking soup, *ah sueh,* I say, but PC Chan's head bobs vigorously as he listens to Mrs Kong). She smokes and draws up a complaint. She doesn't look at me when she tells PC Chan I've been plotting to be Mr Kong's mistress ever since I took up employment with them.

"All these pretty amahs behave like prostitutes," he says, and his eyes on me are cold and murderous. When they lead me away, I turn to him and say, "It's just like the movies, I'm in the movies now."

❖ ❖ ❖

Spend one night in a Hong Kong cell, the walls are cement cinderblocks without windows, and the bars remind me of the cages Abuela kept her prized roosters in. I sleep on a cold cement bench, and there's no blanket. Deep in the night, my heart aches to hold my little girl, and I cry out to José. But he cannot hear me now. I sing softly to myself, ballads my Abuela taught me when I was little, and the sound of my own voice makes me scared.

The next morning, a police officer calls my name and opens the cell-door. Afraid of where he's going to take me next, I hang back on the bench, my eyes wide and my breath coming heavy. "You're free to go." His voice bounces around the cell.

Outside in the main booking room, I see Mrs Kong in a silvery dress, smoking. She looks at me quick, then she turns smartly and heads out the door. "Hurry up, you bad egg. You give me enough trouble last night, now I have to pay your bail. I take out from your salary, you understand?"

What I feel is bitterness, sudden, piercing. I don't feel grateful. She has all the power. I should be happy I'm not going to jail but I don't feel relief. The station door is open, and the humid air outside blows in. It smells sweet and clammy. The police officer hands me my watch. I can see he's wondering why I don't take it.

In her car, Mrs Kong says, "Sdever won't eat when I feed him. Ling Ling behave like wild monkey." Finally, Mrs Kong looks at me, her face with make-up looking like a Chinese porcelain doll. It's what I see in her eyes that suddenly looms up close like a shadow on my heart – a wildness, a grasping – and I realize she's so lost without me. I am the jigsaw piece hooking her family together. It's now I begin to understand.

Elaine Chiew lives in London, England with her husband and two children. She was a corporate securities lawyer before becoming a full-time mother and writer. Her fiction is published online and has most recently appeared in *Hobart* (the Games Issue), *Alimentum*, Better Non Sequitur's anthology, *See You Next Tuesday 2* and selected for Dzanc Books' *Best of the Web 2007* anthology. 'Leng Lui is for Pretty Lady' was first published in *Storyglossia*, Issue 27, and was a Top 25 Finalist in the Glimmer Train Short Story Award for New Writers.

KELEMO'S WOMAN

WE HEARD ABOUT the *coup d'état* on television. The 20-year-old British sitcom dumped on our Third World audience was zapped off like a page flipped by an impatient hand. Martial music interrupted our lovemaking and snatched us back down to earth. The tight rhythm of our bodies jolted, and Kelemo prised himself apart from me with a desperate urgency. Bold, block letters across the screen spelled out "Newsflash."

"What?!" Kelemo's eyes popped wide in shock. I should say I was shocked, too, but the coup was not unexpected. At least I didn't think so. A wave of public disaffection had been rumbling against our rulers for some time. The way I saw it, something had to give. And this was it.

Our country's coat of arms filled the small screen. The motifs looked like they had been painted on by a brush dipped in runny palette, thanks to the old television set whose color definition had long lost its sharpness. The coat of arms faded away to reveal an army man whose skin was rendered a pink-dotted brown on our screen, his uniform turned into an unflattering blue. Our flag hung limp, downcast next to the goggled general, whose halting rhetoric informed us that we were now under martial law. The Army Ruling Council was being constituted to govern and to set a timeline for return to civilian rule.

"Civilian rule? Not if they can help it." Kelemo flopped back onto the pillow. "The army will want to sit this one out for years and years." He propped himself back on one elbow, the better to see the rising dictator on television.

A nationwide curfew had been imposed, the general intoned in a wooden voice. Any miscreants or saboteurs seeking to destabilize the nation would be arrested or shot on sight.

"Miscreants? We are in for it now, for sure." Kelemo buried his face in his hands. "Now the spectacle! The spectacle of ordinary citizens criminalized into saboteurs before our eyes!" Kelemo's eyes darted around the room. "This is the worst that could happen. Politicians were corrupt, but the army can only be worse. Soldiers belong in the barracks, not in government!" He pointed in frustration at the screen. "How can this, this goon, say that the army is doing this for the country's good? Who are they fooling? They are in this for themselves! See the Rolex on his fat wrist?"

The cover sheet peeled away as I slinked up to Kelemo. I let my breasts caress his back as I curled around him. It usually worked, but not this time. He sat up impatiently and planted his feet on the faded black and white of the chequered linoleum floor.

"Civil society must rise against this nascent tyranny. We have to lobby the international community, force them into taking a stand. We must agitate. Strategize. The struggle begins here and now. No time to waste. All right-thinking people have a duty to resist this."

It was beginning to sound like the speeches Kelemo delivered on podiums at rallies ringed by the police, their teargas and batons ready. The one thing missing was his signature pose with fist in the air like some god invoking mortal anger, to galvanize people into believing they were comrades with one societal vision. I knew it all well. The hiding underground, the imprisonment without charge, the dicey, precarious life we had lived in our four years together. A life to which I was vicariously sentenced. I had grown weary of it. We were lucky to have had some peace and quiet of late, lying low in this rented room, sharing inadequate kitchen and toilet facilities with others in an overcrowded tenement building. I avoided contact with the walls always, to keep the old curling paint from flaking onto my clothes.

But now Kelemo's activist zeal was rising again. It had never died away, no. And this time, the implications for our lives were even more unpredictable.

"Just don't start getting ideas," I said. "This is the army now, you know? The politicians just threw you in jail for kicks now and then. Soldiers are humorless; they will do much worse. I am tired of running, diving and ducking. And for what, to live in some rundown neighborhood in Nimke?"

"Soldiers are humorless; they will do much worse – your words, Iriola, not mine," Kelemo hissed. "At least we are agreed on one thing."

"But..."

"But me no buts, Iriola," he cut in. "This neighborhood, this community, has potential. I believe in this place, decrepit as it is. It has given us sanctuary. But it is rundown as you always remind me, not because of what you call our diving and ducking, but because of government mismanagement. You've not been able to get a job since university, not because of my activism, but because of unaccountable leaders who destroyed our economy, and you know it! This country is being run to the ground, and soldiers will only speed up the burial. You, me, and others like us, are going to have to fight – and sacrifice – to turn around the course of this nation!"

"But I've already sacrificed, Kelemo!" I cried. "Remember my mother?"

Kelemo looked away. "That's unfair, Iriola," he said softly. "She was like a mother to me, too. Remember that." Kelemo's late father and mother were activists. Personal suffering was in his blood; he'd become inured to it.

"I don't know that I want to do this any more, Kelemo. Let's just lie low. It's best that way." I avoided his eyes. It was a shameful thing to him, to strive for oneself alone. "Maybe they will hand over to civilians soon, and things can go back to normal. Let's just wait and see, eh?"

"You should know me better than that, Iriola." Kelemo shrugged my hand off his shoulder and rose brusquely from the bed. The soft, natural light from the window cast a silvery glow on his bare skin. His face had a severe aspect now, with determination etched in his features. He stood in front of the television, worked his jaw and racked his brain. Hands on hips, he listened intently, head cocked to one side while the general droned on. The sound faltered, and Kelemo banged the side of the television impatiently. The volume cracked up higher as the general rounded off his address. "God bless our dear motherland," the goggled one concluded. Our national anthem swelled out of the television and filled the room.

"Bastards!" Kelemo snatched his Y-fronts and trousers from the bedside chair.

❖ ❖ ❖

The countryside zips by in strips of rushing greenery on both sides of the road. The curfew has taken hold. Towns look deserted, their inhabitants harassed into their homes. And everywhere, the fatigued presence of soldiers. Hyenas in camouflage, they prowl to keep the nation compliant. The radio informs us that crack teams of military officers have been sent to scour locations suspected of harboring subversives. Nimke is one such location, and I am in the clutches of one crack team.

The army jeep gobbles the miles and subdues the potholed road that runs west to the state capital. There are soldiers in the seats behind me. Now and then, I catch the driver spying on me in the rear-view mirror. I hold his gaze steadily till he looks away, discomfited. I smile to myself and steal a quick glance at the senior officer in the front passenger seat. The brigadier has not looked back since we left Nimke.

A stream of news spews from the jeep's radio. New government structures are in place, and shadowy persons who now will steer our nation's destiny are stepping out of the anonymity of their barracks. Two decrees are announced. The constitution is illegal. New laws being made as though on the hoof.

Kelemo had been gone nearly an hour when the corporal kicked our door open. There were other activists to confer with, underground systems to be re-activated. It was war, and Kelemo saw himself on the front lines, to liberate our country from the military, to re-establish democracy, however flawed. He kissed me roughly. With one last look from the doorway, he was gone.

I rolled onto my back and studied the damp stains in the ceiling. My role in the struggle ahead was mapped out for me. I knew the drill. I would support as the loyal partner to the courageous, self-sacrificing activist.

There were many hardships in this activist life, but I was secure in the knowledge that the only thing Kelemo loved more than me was the motherland. We had a bond, he and I. I knew this, as did my mother.

Mother realized she would not live to see me wed Kelemo, and so on her deathbed she entrusted us to each other six months before the coup. Kelemo then left the hospital room in search of the administrative office to pay her medical bill. Mother drew her last breath while Kelemo was gone, and so he was not privy to her final words. They were never meant for his ears, anyhow.

"Iriola," Mother's voice was hoarse, her breathing labored. "You have no father, and now you will have no mother." She allowed a dramatic pause. "Iriola, this country of ours cannot be helped. No matter what the likes of Kelemo do, no matter the sacrifice, this country can come to no good. No good, you hear me?" Another pause. Her eyes burned into mine from sockets deep in her shrunken face. The light in those eyes tormented me with a vision of an end that lurked for me in some dingy hideout someplace. Mother spoke to steer me away from that end.

"Iriola, trust no one. Allow yourself to be pulled down by no one. I mean, no one. Don't be like me, slaving all my life to stand by men and for what? To die of a wasting disease before my time? Iriola, I beg of you. If the house is falling or the boat is sinking, secure for yourself a safe landing. A comfortable patch. Now you will have no mother. The person to watch over you, is you." Mother allowed herself another pause. A lasting pause.

We left the hospital and returned to our city flat, but there was no room for my grief. A stone on the kitchen window's outer ledge alerted Kelemo to collect a note written in code from a nearby canteen. Such tactics were part of his underground information system. I caught sight of my face in our hallway mirror while he was gone and quickly looked away, repelled by my reddened eyes, swollen from crying.

"What is it now?" I asked on Kelemo's return.

"Wait..." He raised a hand for silence and closed the door carefully behind him. One hand picked at several days' growth of facial hair as he deciphered the note. "Iriola," he said finally.

"Yes?"

Kelemo smirked bitterly. "Judge Bilando has dispensed his special brand of justice again."

"Bilando, that government stooge. What is he up to now? Whose head is on the block this time?"

"It's my head, Iriola." Kelemo drew a deep breath. "He has granted the police an arrest warrant."

I began to shake. "Oh God, not now." Kelemo caught me before I could slump to the floor.

"We'll have to leave this place. Tonight. The police will raid us by morning, and they won't take prisoners. It will be a show of force for the restive populace. They will claim I was shot while trying to evade arrest. You are not safe, either. We've got to get what we can get, and go."

"Noooo!!!" My cry was like an arrow through my own ears.

"Iriola, the neighbors!"

"Damn the neighbors! What about my mother?! I can't leave her in the morgue and run, Kelemo! You, you, you, see where it's led me? What about my mother?"

"I'm sorry, Iriola. I don't mean to put you through this, but it's better to be safe. What use are we to the struggle if we are killed? And you? You're no use to your mother dead. Think about it! She would want you to get away in these circumstances; she would understand. Listen to what I am telling you!" Kelemo shook me. He spoke in short, urgent bursts. "We have to go. A contact from my student union days will be by the harbor in an hour. We've got to be there."

I cried and cried, hitting Kelemo repeatedly on the chest. He grabbed my hands and held me tighter to him.

"Shhh," he soothed, "there's a safe house waiting for us in Nimke, a small town about 200 miles from here."

We fled under the veil of night from the harbor. The contact kept his dark glasses on the whole time we were there, but he genuflected constantly to Kelemo the activist leader. Three motorbikes zoomed out of the darkness at the contact's signal, the lights rendering me temporarily sightless. Kelemo got on behind the first moped rider, I climbed onto the second, and the contact jumped onto the third. We would be in time to catch the inter-city night haulage vehicles from the motor park. The city's lights shimmered upon the rippling waters of the harbor as we sped off.

In the back of a goods truck later that night, among lumpy sacks of cassava and rice, I found I could not sleep. Kelemo snored heavily while I lay my head on his chest and wept into the dark, musty air. I wished I had not had to go on the run with him, but where else would I go? My mother's old tenement room was no longer there. Her landlord made me collect her things during the final stretch in hospital and locked up the place because of unpaid rent. I had nowhere to go. It was Kelemo or nothing. I was his woman. Stars twinkled in the sky overhead, and Mother's last words came back to me. I wiped my tears and wondered how it would feel to be my own woman.

It was a month after we arrived in Nimke before Kelemo could organize the money to pay someone who paid someone to arrange a burial for my mother in the city. From the window of the Nimke safe house that turned out to be only a single dingy room, I looked down the winding alleyway outside and dreamed of the day I would see my mother's final resting place.

❖ ❖ ❖

Kelemo was one of the 'subversives' whose names were being read out on the corporal's radio as he advanced further into our room. The army man's boots stamped dirty imprints on the floor. I could hear the commotion as other soldiers rampaged through the tenement. I rose from the bed and held the cover to myself. The woman in the next room screamed at the top of her lungs and begged a soldier, *please, don't, don't, don't*. I heard the laughter as her cries were defeated into whimpers. No use begging hyenas, I thought. I promised myself that whatever would be taken from me, I would freely give, of my own will. The corporal's eyes traced a lusty line down the length of my body, and I allowed my cover-cloth to slip to the floor.

Later, the corporal led me through the temporary encampment of the local primary school. Past its low hedges roughly cut by the lone gardener with his machete in the sun. Past the classrooms whose outer walls had in time acquired the color of dust. Past the browning lawn of patchy grass tuft, red earth, and stone. On a normal day at recess the school compound would pulsate with the noise and chatter of scores of pupils. Now silence stretched its hollow fingers over the place as we made for the headmaster's office, over tire tracks freshly etched by army jeeps.

I stood uneasily to one side as the corporal stiffened in a salute to his superior in the headmaster's office. The headmaster's wife and two daughters were in a photo amidst notepads atop the big mahogany desk against which the brigadier leaned. The family were likely under curfew in their home by now. A man in his mid-forties, the brigadier looked too genteel for my usual image of a soldier. I could not imagine him in a war. He had a thin, well-groomed mustache over full lips, but was otherwise clean shaven and smooth skinned. His boots shone. They did not look like they had stepped on the grass outside.

"Sir! This young woman was found in premises believed to be the hideout of the activist, Kelemo Vela." The corporal was now at ease. "The subversive is at large, but we have taken his woman prisoner so she can help with our investigations into his whereabouts and activities. With your permission, she is to come with us to the headquarters, sir!"

The corporal saluted again. He threw a secret, reassuring half-wink at me as he exited the office. We had an agreement after all. I would give a routine statement at the barracks in the state capital and then go free. He could arrange it, if I would be his woman.

It was the brigadier's decision that I come with them in this jeep, the first in a convoy of five. No need to handcuff me, he instructed. His men obeyed.

❖ ❖ ❖

The corporal sits to my left, his helmet garnished with shrubbery like he's been fighting in some bush. Yet all he has confronted in this coup so far are the likes of me. The ridiculous posturing amuses me, but I discipline my expression into blankness. I remember his boast to another soldier in the school compound in Nimke. Unaware that I was already inside the jeep and could hear, they laughed on the other side of the canvas as he said in Broken English: "I just dey take the girl to go play with am. I go fuck am, fuck am, fuck am – and after that, I go drive am comot!"

I am the sexual plaything to be driven out once he is done with me. I smile. If only he knew, the corporal, that I view our agreement with as much derision as he. If he knew of my deal with his superior. A deal I negotiated at my shrewd best, on my knees, alone with the brigadier behind the closed door of the headmaster's office. The brigadier's fly was splayed open in front of me, and he gasped as he gave in to spasms. He touched the nape of my neck with such longing. His wedding band was cool on my skin.

He promised me everything I wanted and more when I rose to meet his eyes. I had a degree in Biology. I needed a job. I wanted to live safe and well. I had yet to see my mother's grave. No problem. The state's Commissioner of

Education had just lost his job, along with other top officials. Politicians, they deserved no better. A woman would be a progressive choice for the important post. A fresh young face untainted by the corruption of the ousted government. A good way for the military junta to reassure the masses, to show that soldiers in government can bring fresh ideas. The brigadier's family lived overseas. He was not in the habit of going drinking or whoring with fellow officers. His quarters in the army cantonment were spacious but lonely and could use a woman's touch. I always had a fascination for a certain caliber of officer, I had told him.

❖ ❖ ❖

More news on the radio. The driver turns a knob to increase the volume, so we all hear as the brigadier is named the new military administrator of the state. Soldiers cheer, and though his back is turned, I know the brigadier will be smiling. I am with a winning team. Army men roar in open jeeps behind us. They shoot repeatedly into the air in celebration.

"Are you all right back there, young lady?" the brigadier finally turns round to ask, when the noise has died down a little. I nod and lock eyes with him to affirm our pact. Then I lean back in the seat and close my eyes in relief.

More news on the subversives. Kelemo has been apprehended in a nearby town. My eyes remain shut, and I steel myself to keep from wincing. I focus on the motion of the jeep gliding me on to a new life.

I pray Kelemo survives. I suppose he will wonder why, when he learns about the choices I have made. But Kelemo was not in that hospital room when Mother breathed her last. And I always obeyed my mother.

Molara Wood won the inaugural John La Rose Memorial Short Story Competition (2008); and received a Highly Commended Story Award from the Commonwealth Broadcasting Association (2007). Her essays, reviews and short fiction have appeared in publications including: *Sable Litmag, In Posse Review, Drumvoices Revue, Humanitas, Chimurenga, Farafina* and *Per Contra.* She lives in Lagos, Nigeria, where she works as the Arts and Culture Editor of *NEXT,* a national newspaper.

MARTIN A RAMOS PUERTO RICO

THE WAY OF THE MACHETE

THE MACHETE

IT SURPRISED NO ONE, least of all the cane cutters of La Cuchilla, the day Juanito's father fought Scipio Armenteros, the town braggart and bully.

Scipio Armenteros towered over everyone in town, was the strongest worker and hardiest drinker. Tales were told about this man; for example, Scipio could drive nails through a board with his bare hands. He could lift a young bull on his shoulders and drink rum all day without losing consciousness. He could whip anybody in a fistfight – at arm wrestling, rum drinking or in a machete duel. There was talk that Scipio Armenteros had killed a man – served time in prison for it, too.

On the day that bully came to La Cuchilla, bad luck tagged along, slouching like a cowering dog.

❖ ❖ ❖

Josué Villafuerte said to his son, "Juan, will you go to the *colmado*?"

Standing on the porch of their house, the boy Juanito said, "What do you want, Papa?"

Josué gave his son a few reales. "Take the money. Go to the colmado and buy a pound of coffee, a dozen eggs, a pound of beans and three pounds of rice. Will you remember this?"

"Sí, Papa."

"Don't dally on the road," the man instructed in a firm tone. "Your mother needs the groceries right away."

"I won't," the boy assured him.

Juanito dressed plainly in baggy trousers and a homemade cotton shirt. He had skin the transparency of alabaster, in which blue veins stood prominent like tributaries. His achiote-red hair framed a face with deep-set brown eyes. And though he had a handsome face, with strong features and eyes moist like a puppy's, on it there was an expression of perpetual sadness.

The boy mounted Lucero, the year-old roan, one of two horses his father owned. He rode the horse bareback to the only grocery store in town by way of an unpaved road. It unwound for half a mile down and across the mountain slope where Juanito lived.

The morning air was cool upon the boy's skin. On another occasion he would detain his mount to savor the crisp country air with its fresh smells of dew on the tall grasses, wild marigold petals and flowering oak trees. He did notice something, however. In a clear patch of shimmering sky Juanito saw a buzzard gliding on updrafts, a sure sign of a dead or dying animal nearby.

When he finally arrived at the colmado, the boy dismounted and hitched Lucero to a post in front of the store. He saw other horses there – fine, impressive beasts with twitching flesh and flaring nostrils. The colmado was a modest structure: four walls of oaken boards, shuttered windows and a gabled roof made of zinc. The boards had been painted lime green, but the paint had since peeled, the roof red from rust.

Juanito liked to come here, either on errands or to buy candy.

He placed his foot on the front steps of the colmado and stopped. Coming from inside he heard booming laughter and voices like thunder. He recognized one voice, clearly above the rest: a deep, guttural basso – Scipio's voice. The boy hesitated. He had never seen the big man up close, remaining content to gaze at him from a distance, admiring the way Scipio cut cane, observant of every scythe-like swoosh and measured stroke of his machete.

Always Juanito had imagined the man looming as tall as a mountain, sweat-stained, imposing, dangerous. Someone to reckon with, consider and fear. More than a match for anyone, especially the cane cutters of La Cuchilla.

Inside the colmado the revelry increased like a crescendo. Juanito thought about returning home – now. But if he did, what could he tell Josué?

His mother needed the groceries to prepare the Sunday meal. That was a fact. She would surely punish him, for if Juanito failed to do this simple task, then the boy's father must go to the colmado. Josué would accept no excuses. And another fact, equally as important: Josué would not accept cowardice.

Hands shaking, the boy gritted his teeth and entered. He spotted the counter in front, the ceiling low, the gloom inside encroaching like an oppressive blanket. As if to strengthen his resolve, Juanito seized upon the odors of hanging smoked hams and beef, salted codfish and poultry feed in barrels. He saw pickled eggs in a huge open jar. And then an overpowering sensation of smells accosted him: cigar smoke and illegal rum. The latter – sweet, pungent – clung to his nostrils like sealing tar.

As the boy walked, the sawdust on the floor stuck to the soles of his bare feet, adding to his discomfort.

He counted four men in the colmado, smoking and drinking, their elbows leaning on the counter. The fifth man, wire-thin and hunched, labored wearily behind it. Juanito shuffled to the counter, clutching the coins in one hand as he grasped the waist of his pants with the other.

He recognized the tallest man there. No doubt about it, his sheer size gave him away. Scipio Armenteros.

From behind wire-rimmed glasses, the grocer leaned over the counter and said, "What do you want, Juanito?"

Head bowed, the boy said, "I w-want . . ."

He stammered, unable to complete the statement, and sweat scurried down his neck and back.

"Speak up," the grocer insisted.

"I--I want a p-pound of . . ."

"Say, Rosendo!" The grating voice of one of the men. "Serve us another round here. We're as thirsty as a dry well. Hurry up, hombre. Move that worthless old carcass."

The men drank straight rum out of tall glasses. Juanito guessed they would get drunk soon, if they weren't drunk already.

"In a minute," the grocer said. He turned to the boy. "Tell me what you want. You can see I'm busy today."

Juanito gulped, took a deep breath and mentioned quickly and without stammering the four grocery items Josué had asked him to get and in the exact amounts.

The grocer said, "You're such a smart boy. I'll have the groceries for you right away."

Though Rosendo said it with a crooked smile, Juanito didn't smile, his lips pursed and hands sweaty. He kept thinking that if he were to look up, where he wasn't invited, something bad might happen. What exactly he dared not guess. Just something... unexpected.

Juanito waited. He bit his lower lip and felt like a bird trapped in a cage, eager for escape or release. He stared at the floor and grasped the coins tighter, until his palm ached. In spite of the tension he sensed in the hollow of his stomach, he craved a closer look at Scipio Armenteros. To see for himself what all the brag was about. He dared not look or make a sound, however, for fear of what these men

– especially Scipio – might say or do. Just let the sweat collect upon his nose and upper lip and scurry like mice down his neck and the middle of his back.

Rosendo hurried with the groceries, which he brought in a paper bag. Juanito took the bag and paid. The grocer gave him change.

"Gracias," Juanito said, and started on his way.

"Boy. Yes, you."

Though they had been spoken normally, with no hint of aggression or meanness, the words exploded in Juanito's ears like thunderclaps. No mistaking it. Scipio Armenteros had uttered those words, his voice undeniably menacing.

"Turn around. Come here. I want a word with you."

Juanito turned. Though his legs felt like tree stumps, he dared not disobey. He moved.

"I've seen you around. You're Josué Villafuerte's son, aren't you?"

"S-sí," Juanito said, his voice a flutter.

"I want you to tell your papa you met me in town. Know who I am, boy?"

"S--Scipio A--Armenteros." He pronounced the name, head bowed.

"True. Tell your papa the cane cutters have told me about his reputation. Tell him I am good with the machete. The best. Tell him I want to see him, and that if he doesn't come to the colmado today, I'll tell the men he is a coward." Scipio leaned closer, his breath a pungent mix of cigar smoke and rum. "Understand, boy? A coward."

"S-sí," Juanito blurted. "I understand."

"Look at me, boy. I won't bite."

Silence. The boy raised his head and gazed squarely, without flinching, upon Scipio's brooding face.

"That's better. Am I so ugly that you can't bear the sight of me?"

"No, señor."

"Good. You look like a smart boy. Go tell Josué Villafuerte what I said. Every word. I'll wait for him here."

Juanito breathed, turned and ran. He almost dropped the bag of groceries as he bolted past the door and out.

❖ ❖ ❖

The ride home seemed to go on forever, the road burdensome like a stretched brown ribbon with no end in sight.

Juanito could not get the man's physical dimensions, the grotesque features of Scipio's face, out of his mind. His face was not unlike the mask of the carnival demon or *vejigante*: square on top and low-browed, unwashed and unshaved.

The bulbous nose hung pendulous over a pair of fleshy lips. The ears protruded forward like swinging doors. The mustache curled menacingly at each corner like a scorpion's sting. And the hair, plastered to his head, looked matted and dirty like an old mop. Finally a two-inch scar crossed Scipio's left cheek at a diagonal.

Though ugly enough to scare the bejesus out of a boy in broad daylight, Scipio's face was not his most disturbing feature. Juanito thought: his *eyes*. Set wide apart, their whites red from habitual drinking, Scipio's eyes seemed to explode from his face with a piercing blue luster that had struck fear into the boy's heart and jumbled his emotions.

The expression in Scipio's eyes – it harbored something evil.

Then the boy recalled another detail, no less important than the rest: Scipio's machete, honed and unused, its blade painted a dull red, leaning against the counter menacingly. In the hamlet the machete was both a tool and a weapon, and there was always the rumor of a fight.

Juanito figured that's what it would amount to – a fight – if he told his father that Scipio Armenteros waited for him in the colmado with an ornery disposition and a sharpened, unused machete. But the boy must tell because the braggart had called Josué Villafuerte a coward.

And nobody ever did that. Not in La Cuchilla, the hamlet known as "The Knife."

"Go in the house and fetch my machete," Josué instructed his son, "and a spade."

"What?" Juanito asked, bewildered.

"Just do what I say. Go."

Juanito went.

Dolores, the boy's mother, asked, "Why do you want the machete, Josué? Today is Sunday."

She stood on the porch of their two-room shanty, a young but frail-looking woman wearing a mended calico dress. She had loose coal-black hair and mesmerizing jade green eyes.

No hint of nerves showing, Josué looked sternly at his wife. "He challenged me, the fool. He wanted to test my courage. The cane cutters have bragged about me, told him I can fight. They always brag."

"You mean that man, Scipio Armenteros?"

Josué nodded.

"Surely you won't fight him?"

Josué straightened. "We had words. There were men there, *braceros* and other field hands, some of the landowners as well. Scipio said if I didn't fight him I wasn't macho. I told him I could fight him and win. No brag; it's a fact."

He paused, breathed. "Dolores, I'm no coward."

Dolores's eyes moistened. She wiped them with the back of her hand. When she spoke, her words were pregnant with apprehension. "You'll fight this man? He's bigger and stronger. Folks in town say Scipio killed a man. He'll kill you, Josué."

"Maybe. But maybe I can kill him first. He has never seen me wield the machete. If I kill him it will be in self-defense."

"How will we live without you?" Dolores protested. "The *zafra* will start soon. Who will cut the cane? Who will put food on the table?"

Josué placed a hand on her shoulder. "Juanito's almost a man. He's strong, reliable and hard-working. He will cut the cane."

"But—-"

"Don't worry, *mujer.* I'll be all right."

Before Dolores could answer, the boy came lugging his father's machete and a spade. He gave each to his father, and waited.

Josué thanked the boy. He stared into his eyes and said, "While I'm away, I charge you with care of the house. Look after your mother and sister. You have much courage for someone so young. I know I can depend on you."

"Don't worry, Papa. I'll look after them."

"I know you will, Juan."

Juanito felt proud because only his father called him Juan, a man's name. Everyone else said Juanito.

"Adiós," Josué said.

"Adiós," said the boy, watching his father leave and wondering if he were saying goodbye to him for the last time.

❖ ❖ ❖

Juanito worried. Inside the house his baby sister cried, probably wanting to be suckled. Or maybe she too had noticed Josué's prolonged absence. Dolores said nothing, which Juanito thought was odd. He waited on the porch, staring at the deepening shadows and yellowing sky.

Not a leaf fluttered or blade twitched; no nocturnal animals scurried. And only the baby voiced its discomfort.

"What do you think is happening?" Juanito asked. "Think they will fight?"

Dolores came and stood in the open door, framed like a Madonna with the infant cradled in her arms. She shook her head, sniffled.

"I don't know. I try not to think of anything bad happening."

"It's getting late. And Papa hasn't come home."

"Josué said that man, Scipio Armenteros, challenged him to a fight. He said Scipio didn't consider him macho."

The boy scratched his shaggy hair, picked a blade of grass from his shirt. "Scipio's always challenging someone. He likes to brag. Boy, does he like to brag."

"I worry every time your papa leaves the house with the machete. Even when he goes off to work. I worry he might come home maimed, or worse. If Scipio called him a coward, Josué will fight. Your papa doesn't brag."

"I know," Juanito said. "He left me in charge of the house. He told me to look after you and the baby. And I will."

Dolores smiled. "You have courage. A proud and brave little boy, in a man's world."

"Why would he take a spade with him this time, Mama?"

"I don't know." She bowed her head, her eyes again moist. "He has never taken one before."

Juanito noticed her concern. "Mama, I'm going into town to look for Papa. I'll take the other horse."

Dolores cuddled the baby. "Be careful, Juanito," she said as he left. "I don't want to lose you too."

❖ ❖ ❖

Like a dying ember the sun had begun to smolder beyond the cordillera by the time Juanito rode his father's mare into town. He asked at the colmado and Rosendo told him Josué Villafuerte and Scipio Armenteros went to the ravine to fight a duel.

Duel.

The boy did not recognize the word, disliked its sound but was certain of its meaning, because by analogy and implication the word must surely mean a fight.

Riding at a gallop, Juanito arrived at the ravine and saw the cane cutters there, an excited but disciplined throng.

He dismounted and approached, felt his feet sink into the soft soil of the ravine, his heart racing like a wild stallion's. Rippling water sounds greeted him, and on the branching trees the leaves rustled like doves taking flight. The tall elephant grass yielded, verdant and pliant, to the onslaught of the cooling breeze.

Strange, sinister: the wind brought with it the peculiar taint of blood. The odor struck with such force, Juanito almost reeled from it. Then the smell began to blend with the scent of water, as the men – speaking in hushed tones – parted on either side like a wave, breaching a path for him.

Juanito didn't believe he would find his father dead. Other people died, the *abuelos* or old people especially, but not his father. Then he saw and believed what his mind had rebelled against. His knees buckled but, like an obedient soldier, he irrevocably advanced, unwilling to permit the full force of the spectacle to weaken his reserve or dampen his resolve.

The fight had been wild, wicked and terrible. The boy had never seen so much spilt blood – it was everywhere, on the ground, on the grasses, on tree trunks – except during Christmas when pigs were slaughtered.

He had wondered why Josué had carried the spade. Now he knew. The men had used the spade to dig two adjacent holes in the loose soil of the ravine. Once stripped of his shirt, each combatant had climbed into his hole, filling it with soil so that it impeded movement from the waist down.

Seeing this now, the boy could not help but admire his father's seriousness. There was no joke in that man. Josué Villafuerte would never back down from a fight. Neither did he permit – once challenged – his adversary to do so. Either the challenger would feel intimidated and leave, or else he must fight.

The fight had been a contest to the death, a *pelea* of mythic proportions. No escape or retreat asked for and none given.

From the amount of blood staining the ground next to the body, and because his torso lay splayed as if in crucifixion, Juanito concluded that the braggart died first. Wounds and slashes were cut like roads deep into his flesh. Both of Scipio's ears, his nose and his left hand were severed. Even his head had come close to decapitation. The "O" of his mouth, filling with flies, appeared frozen in awe, and the lifeless eyes – their intense glow now extinguished – stared vacantly at the fading sky.

The weapon, Scipio's machete (plaintive and supplicant, pointing outward), rested next to his body.

Then Juanito looked at Josué, and saw his father's body had not been mutilated as badly, though it too had shed its butcher's bucket of blood. Scipio's blows, mighty enough to fell the thickest cane, had severed Josué's right ear and three of the fingers on his left hand but neither of his appendages. Multiple cuts and stab wounds, like war medals, adorned his father's arms and chest.

Juanito couldn't help but marvel at the sight he saw next: Josué's blood-soaked arm whose hand had somehow held on to the machete.

The machete. Juanito took the blade from his father's hand and regarded his well-defined and clean-shaven face. Rake-thin and wiry-muscled, Josué Villafuerte had been compelled to fight against impossible odds. So that only a fighter with raw nerve, metal fiber and undaunted courage could have finished Scipio off, or died trying.

Juanito's father was such a man.

The boy moved away from that scene without stumbling or shaking, with poise and as straight as an uncut stalk of Caribbean cane. He wanted to cry but didn't. Time enough for that at the wake, and later at the funeral. Time to think, also to remember. The cane cutters would respect him more – now that he had unwittingly enlisted into their ranks – if he bridged the tragedy with composure, courage and *cordura*. They would also see to the cadavers.

The boy looked at the machete. It had blood on it, Scipio's blood. No doubt Josué's precious blood on it as well.

The boy used a leaf from a banana tree and wiped the residue of blood from the machete's cutting blade. He noticed that its edge had hardly dulled, all 24 inches of steel honed clean, right up to the handle. He considered the machete, this tool which had served his father and his father's father before him. It would serve him.

Machete in hand, Juan mounted his mare and headed for home.

THE WAY

Not long after his father's funeral, when Juan Villafuerte turned 13, he spoke with the landowner to ask for his father's job. He carried with him the same machete Josué Villafuerte had used to kill Scipio Armenteros, which the boy had taken from his father's blood-soaked hand.

Had the hacendado not witnessed the duel, he might have refused the boy's request. But everyone in town – especially those who had seen two grown men fight to the death in the ravine – believed it to have marked a turning point, a watershed, in La Cuchilla. For important events since that day were referred to as occurring before or after "la pelea," The Fight. So the landowner agreed, and in this way Juan went to work in the same sugar cane fields as his father before him.

There were other boys working there, but most lugged water or carried food for the peons, while the really young ones were no doubt truants from school. Juan left school to work in the fields of Caribbean cane, and almost immediately regretted it.

Sun, sweat, sores: such was the crucible in which the cane cutters were forged. Even for mature men, no strangers to hardship and death, it was hard work. No less so for Juan.

Only two hours into the job blisters began to appear like blooming roses on Juan's hands. Cuts, too, which itched from contact with the blades of grass as he swung the machete. After a while the heat and humidity became insufferable. It was then he began to consider the task he had set for himself to be an inexorable burden not fit for boy or beast.

Dizzying was the sight of uncut cane, extending like a sea of gold in every direction. And the smell of ashes and burnt stalks permeated everywhere. He felt sweat ooze from his pores, salty when it reached his tongue and mouth. The sweat soaked his pants and stained his cotton shirt. Even the soles of his booted feet sweated.

On a clear patch of ground, under the canopy of an old mango tree, Juan wiped the sweat from his brow and rested.

One of the workers saw him sitting there and said, "Are you okay, boy? Want water?"

When Juan nodded, the cane cutter – a bronzed skin veteran of many zafras, his face weathered from the tropic sun – motioned for one of the water carriers to come forward. A barefoot boy brought Juan water. Juan took the ladle offered, dipped it into the pail, and drank.

"Not too much," the cane cutter cautioned him, "unless you want a bellyache."

Juan returned the ladle and thanked the boy. The water carrier smiled, two front teeth missing, and scurried in search of another thirsty throat to quench.

In a no-nonsense tone, the cane cutter said, "Better get back to work. It isn't midday yet, and you haven't laid out much cane. Won't do to let the *capataz* see you slacking."

"Sí, señor," Juan said.

The man helped the boy to his feet, then left.

Enthralled, Juan watched the more experienced men cut cane. He noticed they worked with the precision of a well-oiled machine, swinging their machetes without wasted motion, letting the cane fall in neat piles where it would later be picked up and carted to the mill for grinding.

Though it wouldn't be easy, Juan realized he must learn to work this way.

The late morning sun was always a factor. Its rays scorched the boy's head even through the woven straw of his hat. As if it were alive, the air pulsated with the sun's heat, and everything shimmered: the cane, the machetes, the bowl of blinding sky. The glare was great. Though he wanted them to move, Juan's feet felt rooted to the earth and would not budge. So how could he cut cane? From where would he get the strength and resources?

Conscious of the burden fate had decreed, aware of the responsibility he must bear (his own, and two other mouths to feed), Juan wanted to work but couldn't. His hands were sore, his limbs ached, and his heart beat as if it would burst in his chest. He shaded his eyes and gazed at the sun, heavy and oppressive overhead. The golden stalks swayed. The air vibrated. He felt faint. So he lay on the ground, in the shade, and soon dreamt.

In his delirium Juan saw a ripe field of cane, stretched out like burnished metal, ready for the harvester's hand. He saw two men in that field, fighting a duel to the death. One man, in his baggy trousers and rolled-up shirt, he recognized easily as Josué Villafuerte. The other man, who looked taller and heftier, had to be Josué's nemesis: the daunting Scipio Armenteros.

The men brandished their knives and wielded them like swords, sparks flying each time the machetes clashed. It was a haunting vision, provocative. Juan had never witnessed a machete fight, even in the hamlet of La Cuchilla where knife dueling was common fare.

The boy cheered for his father, but wondered how the man could possibly win. He knew fighting was useless because Scipio was stronger and meaner and had already killed a man. The duelers clashed – steel against steel – until something eerie happened. For no apparent reason the men ceased fighting and used their machetes to cut cane instead. They looked in Juan's direction, and encouraged him with hand signals to follow in their wake.

At first the boy was puzzled. Could they be asking him to join the fight, or cut cane? They waved persistently, and finally he understood what they meant. Both Scipio and Josué wanted him to fight, not give up: to cut cane.

Juan woke, refreshed. An unexpected breeze had dried his sweat. His limbs no longer ached, and his heart felt calm in his chest. Later he would eat what his mother had prepared, finish work, go home and rest. He understood what he must do; his fate need not be questioned.

The will to work came from his heart as well as his head. Josué Villafuerte and Scipio Armenteros had shown him the way of the machete: that the wielded blade could give life, as well as take it. Courage would come, day by day, with each stalk of fallen cane.

Juan Villafuerte raised his machete, blade catching the bright sun, and he cut cane.

A former educator, **Martin A Ramos** lives in Hormigueros, Puerto Rico. His short fiction has appeared in *Chiricú* (Indiana University) and *Latino Stuff Review*. His poetry can be found online at *The Cortland Review* and *Red River Review*, and has been published in *Dragonfly*, *Cyclo*Flame*, *Rattle*, and *Writer's Digest*.

PORCELAIN

THE PIECES OF broken pottery in the sand revealed themselves subtly. Marion tried to be patient, letting her eye pick out the particular shade of blue, dulled by a crust of sand and salt. She took small steps, eyes fixed on the ground, squatting for a closer look when soft color glimmered up from between the stones and shells. Mostly, it turned out to be nothing more than a mussel shell, the surprisingly pure blue of its inside margin tricking the eye. So far she'd only found five bits of porcelain.

She couldn't see the breakers from here. The beach sloped up quite steeply from the water, then flattened out into this broad stretch of sand before entering the low milkwood forest. Here, in a series of oval depressions, was where the high-tide debris of the Indian Ocean had gathered over centuries: cracked pieces of fine old porcelain along with rubber flip-flops and sand-frosted bottlenecks. Not a few old sailing ships had come to ruin off this part of the coast – Dutch, Portuguese, British, journeying eastwards or hurrying home, laden with fancy goods.

The china was dry and porous, the glaze worn off and the edges smoothed. The triangular shards held no trace of the fury of the waves that had shattered them. The pieces grew warm in her palm, and clicked against each other when she opened and closed her hand in time to her steps. She crouched to examine a piece of bone – slender and white, probably a gull's. Perhaps there were sailors' bones here too.

Standing too quickly, Marion was struck by a sudden dizziness, as if the world were surging backwards, or as if her own life had sped up for an instant; but it was only the cold wind quickening. She stood still, waiting for this little tremor, this moment of imbalance, to pass.

An observer would see a tall, voluptuous young woman with a pink-and-cream complexion, her coarse gold hair twisted up and caught in a tortoiseshell clip. Her cheeks were flushed and her brown eyes clear. The hands cupped around her finds were dimpled and pink and slightly blotched in the cold, and the tapering fingers delicate. Hers was not a modern beauty. Marion looked like the women carved on prows of old ships: the heart-shaped face, the creamy bosom, the small mouth with its rose-petal lips, the strong, classical nose. Looks that would have aroused admiration two or three centuries before. As if to enhance this impression, she was given to wearing layers of lace and corduroy, long dresses, blouses with low bodices to show off her neck and cleavage. They were impractical clothes for beach walking: the hem of her skirt was crumbed with sand, and the dark-red crocheted shawl draped around her shoulders was damp at one end.

The wind picked up, strafing her cheeks with sand so that she had to pull the shawl around her face. The other hand closed tighter around the porcelain chips. Then the rain came in a cold, loose curtain from the sea, damping down the sandstorm and wetting her through, tightening her clothes against her breasts and thighs. She started to trot towards the trees, skipping awkwardly in the damp skirt, gasping with pleasure. She was young enough for such moments of animal exhilaration to speed her along without warning.

Breathless, she peeked into her palm, where the blue-and-white china gleamed. The rain had washed the dullness off. It was bluer than new, as if the pigment were still wet and the glaze just applied in some faraway workshop. As if it did not know that it had been mortally damaged.

She allowed the squally wind to pull her up the beach and along the gravel road, towards the old wooden house that stood beyond the milkwoods. Pausing just before the veils of rain obscured the view completely, she saw, far out on the horizon, the faint suggestion of a ship – just a hint of tall masts, misty shreds of sails unfurling, palest smoke on pearl. Eyes closed, she put her head back and gave her neck and chest to the rain. When she looked again the ship had dissolved into cloud; but she stood for another minute or two in the downpour, staring out at the gray.

The wet steamed off her in the firelit house, where the walls were festooned with dry seaweed and strings of sea-urchin shells. Aunt Amelia was sitting in her swivel chair at the trestle table in the corner, gluing together the pieces of a fine porcelain vase. She scowled through her spectacles, which had mauve plastic frames that clashed with her brown eyes. Aunt Amelia had a special technique: she would construct an armature of chicken-wire, vase-shaped, onto which she would fasten the broken bits of Chinese porcelain with Prestik – a lark here, a pagoda there, two lovers on a bridge. So fragile, these ghostly vases, more air than porcelain. All around her, arranged on shelves and bookcases and tabletops and in big woven baskets on the floor, were other pieces and assemblages: piles of shards, cracked plates with triangular bites taken out of their rims, undone jigsaw puzzles of smashed china.

"I saw the ghost ship," Marion said, unwinding the damp shawl from around her neck.

Aunt Amelia held up her angled tweezer-tips and gave Marion a keen glance. "Did you really?"

Marion glanced into the round gilt-frame mirror on the wall. She understood at once what had given Amelia that apprehensive look. In the mirror she saw not her own face, but her mother's: high color in the flushed cheeks, bright hair darkened with dampness that could be rain or sweat, eyes glowing as if they were melting in her face. Celia's face. Marion quickly looked away.

"No, of course not *really*, Auntie A. It was just the cloud coming in." She went towards her aunt with her hands cupped together.

"Ooh, what have you got for me?" Amelia swiveled in the chair. She was in her late fifties, but with a body that was still strong: rounded and busty, like all the women in their family, but more compact than the others. Despite the rainy weather she was dressed as she always was, in a loose white short-sleeved shirt, khaki shorts and leather sandals. An outdoors woman: her calves were muscular and her biceps tight, beneath skin that was starting to crinkle from years of solitary beach-walking. Hair that had once been gold was graying now, cut short every month with the kitchen scissors by Auntie Belle. As a result it always looked a little tufty and irregular, with a wavering fringe.

Marion unclasped her fingers and let the chips of blue and white trickle off her palm and onto the table. They were still slightly damp.

"A good haul," Amelia said intently. The gleaming points of her tweezers picked out and separated the five shards, teasing them apart like a fussy bird's beak. One with a tight geometric pattern, mesh-like; two plain white; one white with a narrow double band of navy; and the last, the smallest, showing the roof of a tiny pagoda.

"Do they fit?" asked Marion.

"Hard to tell..." Amelia turned the pagoda fragment with the tips of the tweezers, flipping it over. "This one – possibly..."

Amelia was absorbed. Marion retreated to sit crossed-legged in front of the fire, watching her aunt sort through the pieces that lay heaped on the table and in the woven bowls at her feet. A few moments later, Marion heard footsteps behind her and felt firm fingers on the crown of her head. She twisted round to smile up at Auntie Belle.

"Hello, Auntie B."

Belle took a hairbrush down from the mantelpiece and started to untangle Marion's thick, damp hair, teasing out the knots. "Such beautiful hair," she said.

Belle was the second-oldest sister. She was less physically toughened than Amelia, softer around the middle; her face was rounded, her upper arms fleshy and a little sagging. But the two women had the same clear brown eyes, the same air of vigor and resourcefulness. Belle was also dressed in a practical uniform of sandals, loose shirt and slacks, her silvering hair cut into a pageboy bob that showed signs of Amelia's more painstaking handiwork with the scissors. Belle did not share her sister's fascination with smashed china. New pots were her thing. She enjoyed the company of the women in the village, where she ran a craft workshop: local women brought their clay pots to be fired in her kiln, and she arranged for the wares to be transported to town and sold to tourists.

There had been three sisters, all raised in this wooden house, all buxom and bright-haired. Only two remained. Marion's mother had been the youngest and prettiest, a brilliant child; but not strong. Despite her vital appearance, Celia had been secretly fragile.

When she was only 19, Amelia and Belle had started to lose their youngest sister. So careless. While they were busy on their energetic projects, Celia had floated away to the city. There she'd studied drama, sung cabaret, had love affairs, produced a child. She'd return to the beach house every now and then – always sparkling, always bringing too many gifts. But the soft sea mists had dimmed Celia's shine. When her mood darkened, she would leave at once; which meant she never stayed for long. Over the years, Celia had visited her sisters less and less.

And in the city, with its late nights and loud days, its electric light and shadow, Celia had started to separate. Her highs had become towering, her black lows abysmal, until there'd been little left in between. Gradually she'd got lost in the troughs and ridges, the heavy waves of her illness. An illness that had probably always been present in her, but that her sisters had not recognized until Celia was far, far out on a dark sea.

Marion had been 11 when her mother died, and although her aunts had never discussed the details with her, she knew that it had been no accident. Celia had been just strong enough to make her own exit.

She was aware of how much she physically resembled her mother; how she too could fly into moods and rages and transports of exuberance, fits of tears or laughter. And she knew how her turbulence provoked her kind aunts, how it summoned tension and anxiety into their eyes. They were vigilant for the signs of distress and madness that they had failed to see in time in Celia. And so Marion tried to be placid and cheerful, to gentle their suspicions. She hated it when they went still and watchful around her.

"Why do you want to go back to the city, sweetheart? The sea air is good for you. Look at the color in your cheeks," said Belle. A quick watchful glance from Amelia, over the mauve rims.

Marion sat still, keeping her head motionless as the brush tugged at her hair, suppressing the strong impulse to leap to her feet and shake out her hair with a shout, to kick and jump about. As a child she'd hated having her hair done, hated the enforced stillness every morning as her mother hacked at the knots with a comb, the tugs painfully communicating Celia's own frustration.

"Leave the child, Belle, for heaven's sake. She'll go if she goes and she'll stay if she stays."

"What's in the city? Greed and grief, that's what. Greed and grief."

Belle had worked out the knots now. The brush made a few last passes through the damp hair, and then Marion could feel her aunt nimbly separating three handfuls, the weight lifting away from her nape as the strands were braided together and secured, the pleasurable tightened sensation at the base of the plait. She was calmed, like a groomed horse.

And sitting here by the fire, watching the rain outside the window, the wet frenzy of the milkwoods, one mad gull spinning high up in the turbulent air, Marion did indeed feel safe – in the warmth of her aunts' affection, in this house that her grandfather had built for his daughters. She wanted to be in here with them, not out in the storm. Perhaps it might be possible to stay for good this time.

Behind her, Amelia sighed with satisfaction. "Voilà!"

Marion turned to see her positioning a piece on the framework of the phantom vase. It hung there, disembodied, bellying out the lost curve.

"Well done, Auntie A! You got a fit." Marion stood and went to her, reaching out to touch the vase.

"Careful," said Amelia, and Marion smiled. After storm and wreck and tidal grinding, now to treat it like crystal. But she was careful.

"You'll never find all the pieces, surely?"

"Of course not. That's not the point. This is not a jigsaw. But we can make it more whole than it was."

"You and your old pots!" Belle snorted, picking out pinches of golden hair from the hairbrush. "Spoils of empire, that's what they are. Flotsam of greed and conquest!"

Amelia directed a private smile at her floating vase and pressed the abutting pieces more snugly together. "But still, very pretty," she murmured.

"Rubbish. Why don't you collect the local pottery, Amelia – now that's beautiful. And useful."

"Stop fighting, you two," said Marion. It was an old argument, and the aunts were enjoying themselves. In this house, nobody raised their voices in earnest.

"Oh, don't go back to the city, darling child," Belle sighed, laying a hand on Marion's smoothed hair. Marion knew that she was thinking of storms and disaster, greed and grief. But her aunt sounded resigned, as one is resigned to history.

That night she dreamed again her dream of Celia: her young beautiful mother, burning, throwing again and again the clear glass vase against the wall of the bedroom. Marion woke with the shattering all around her. It took a moment or two for her ears to clear, her heart to still; to hear only the quiet of the night, with its distant hushing of waves.

Marion used to hide behind the couch or under the bed, barely breathing, waiting for her mother's frenzies to pass. The fits of destruction had been repeated many times, with accelerating rage, until, by the end, almost everything fragile in the house had been destroyed. But in the dream it was always that one episode, that particular glass vase, turning and turning through the air, while around her mother's tall ecstatic figure the room was filled with sparkling splinters and a constant grinding sound of breakage that never seemed to slacken or to cease.

One ordinary evening two weeks before, Marion had taken each of 12 good dinner-plates – plain white china, which she had desired and saved up for and bought precisely because of their blank purity, the only complete set of crockery she'd ever owned – and thrown them one by one at the wall of her flat. For no real reason. A bad day in a bad week. A fight at work, a phone call from an old boyfriend. Not really reasons at all. It had frightened her, had made her feel that she was standing on the edge of a cliff, hurling her possessions into the void. In a way she was still standing there, waiting for the sound of them hitting bottom.

It was this incident that had brought Marion back to her aunts, to the peace of this old house, as consternation had often done in the past. Although never before had she done something so startling to herself, something so alarmingly futile.

But even so, in her heart Marion had not really believed. Her wrist had flicked and the plates had spun from her hand, hair whipping across her cheeks and color flushing the skin; but even as she'd acted out her mother's mad ballet – performed so many times, long ago in another small apartment, when Celia was not much older than Marion was now – she hadn't truly felt the heaviness of madness under her arousal.

And afterwards, standing there with her bare feet – nicked and a little bloody – in the heap of shattered porcelain, she'd known that it had been an experiment. Drawing blood from the perfect skin inherited from her mother, cutting it to find what was inside. She had not entered the fury, had not been lifted away. And with the small wash of relief she'd felt at the ordinariness of her emotions – embarrassment, fright – there'd been a tickle of something else; maybe shame.

None of these things could she tell the aunts. To tell them would be to confirm all their fears; it would force them to make some terrible gesture of recognition. But although she'd said nothing, still they seemed to sense that danger had touched her, that she'd fled to them from some pursuing shadow. This visit, the aunts had been particularly solicitous, watchful, kind.

And so she must continue. She must allow Auntie B to brush out her hair as she had once brushed Celia's; she must go down to the sea and collect for Auntie A the pieces of broken plates and bowls. She must be serene; and so persuade them that Celia's heart had found in her own generous breast a peaceful resting place.

In the morning, when she was packing the car, Amelia and Belle came out to say goodbye. Amelia was carrying a large cardboard box.

"If you have to go, take a little something with you," said Belle.

It would be a clay pot from the village. Belle often gave her presents from the workshop; her flat was full of them.

Driving back along the dirt road, she passed through the village and saw the women walking in twos and threes between the *rondavels* and the pink-plastered hexagonal houses, carrying paraffin tins and plastic drums on their heads. Not porcelain or clay, but functional. They made pottery for tourists, but for fetching their water, they used what worked best.

Back home in the city, Marion opened up the cardboard box and found not a clay pot but Amelia's partially reassembled vase. It was carefully bound up in thin sheets of foam rubber and sticky-tape. She took it gently out of its wrappings and placed it on the dresser.

"Auntie A, it's beautiful," she said on the telephone.

"It's just an old broken thing," said Amelia, sounding pleased. "Of course half of it's still down at the bottom of the ocean."

"But what if you find more pieces to fit?"

"Then you'll have to come and get them, won't you?"

After the phone call, Marion stood before the vase on the dresser for a long time. She had positioned it not centrally, but to one side. Next to it, invisible, was another, vanished vessel: the clear glass vase that used to stand on this same dresser when she was a little girl.

She touched the sides of the vase, the smooth patches of porcelain, the rough absences where the chicken-wire showed through. And she was calmed by the feel of it. These broken pieces would not hurt her: spoils of empire, casualties of storm and wreckage, softened and blunted by time. Lovers on a bridge, a willow tree. And broken as it already was, she in turn could do the vase no further harm. Running her finger over the smoothed-off edges, she poked her fingertips into the gaps, feeling the parts that would always be missing, and the parts that were whole again.

Henrietta Rose-Innes was born in 1971 in Cape Town, South Africa. She is the author of two novels, *Shark's Egg* (2000) and *The Rock Alphabet* (2004). She won the 2008 Caine Prize for African Writing, for which she was shortlisted in 2007, and was also awarded the 2007 Southern African PEN short story award, judged by JM Coetzee. She has also compiled an anthology of South African writing, *Nice Times! A Book of South African Pleasures and Delights* (2006).

LAURI KUBUITSILE BOTSWANA

THE RICH PEOPLE'S SCHOOL

SYLVIA MOVED TO the huge granite boulder, now warm from the early morning sun. It was a ritual when she was here, especially on the cold days. The boulder would catch the sun until it was teatime at school, and when the sun moved completely off the rock, she would move slowly down the dry riverbed making her way back to the corner at the end of the road near the school where she would wait for her Gran.

She would have preferred to stay at home all day, not sitting here at the river. She liked being at home, just her and her Gran. She liked following her around, her Gran carrying the big metal watering can and she the small plastic one, sprinkling the spinach in their tidy plots. Sylvia liked watching the water seep into the thirsty ground. She liked sweeping the yard with the broom made of grass until it lay tidy with engraved swirl patterns across its surface. But Sylvia knew that it would cause trouble if she refused to go to school, so she wasted her morning on her warm river boulder.

A blue-headed lizard climbed very near to the bare leg sticking out from under her neatly ironed uniform. It didn't even know she was there – thinking her leg another part of the stone, it too was searching for warmth. It nodded its head as if in greeting, though only in her mind, because not even a lizard would greet a stone. Sylvia wondered sadly, then who would? Unthinkingly, she rubbed the stone in commiseration and the lizard dashed away in fear.

Lying back, Sylvia gently fell asleep. Her mind took her to her mother, not in distance, not far away in America where she lived with her new family. Her mind carried her to her mother in time. To before school, when she was small and her mother lived with them at her Gran's. They were all happy then.

Then she met the American. He couldn't live in a dry, backward desert, he had said in his big voice that vibrated the walls of their small hut. That was not a life for him. If she loved him, she would go with him. But what about

Sylvia? she had asked. No, a black Sylvia wouldn't do in a family that would be toffee-colored brown. Sylvia could stay with her Gran, she won't mind, it will be better for her.

Then she and her Gran were alone. There was food, for money came every month from America to be collected at the Western Union counter at the post office, jealous eyes watching and nasty tongues talking when Gran and Sylvia left. Sylvia's mother had agreed to leave her behind only if the American agreed to pay for her to go to the rich people's school, the one on the hill where every student grew up to become a doctor or a lawyer. And so he did.

As the car stood running – the American waiting inside, every minute or two shouting "We will be late. We will miss our plane" out the open window – Sylvia's mother stooped down next to Sylvia in the well-swept dirt of the *lolwapa,* even though she wore the expensive white suit the American had bought her. "I will come and see you one day and you will be a big, clever girl. You will go to university and have so many choices and not have to sell your life away like your silly, stupid mother." Sylvia remembered the tears falling from her mother's beautiful eyes, and the long, low moaning sound her Gran made deep in the night while she thought Sylvia lay asleep next to her.

They managed though, Sylvia and her Gran. Sylvia hardly noticed how their sadness hid behind the tasks of living.

Then the time came for Sylvia to go to the rich people's school. On a hot summer morning, she went with her Gran, who carried a thick roll of money in her dress pocket.

When Sylvia saw the school, she thought perhaps she had been taken to another country. Green, grass-covered lawns were being watered from hidden pipes in the ground. Flowerbeds bloomed in every rainbow color. Children laughed and chased each other around brightly painted jungle gyms and swings. Sylvia had never seen a school like this. She only knew the government school near their home with a wide, dusty yard scattered with broken desks. She smiled at her Gran, but her Gran only looked at her with a face Sylvia had never seen before. It was a face of anger and fear at the same time. Sylvia wondered if Gran was afraid of the water shooting from the ground or maybe she was afraid of the children swinging high on the swings. "You must behave now, do you hear?" she said in someone else's voice.

"Yes Ma'am," Sylvia said wondering how her Gran could be frightened and angry when everything looked so lovely.

They walked up the shiny polished red steps of the brick building. A thin white woman sat at the desk. She spoke in English to her Gran and her Gran spoke back looking down at the floor the whole time. She handed the woman the big roll of money and the woman wrote out a paper and handed it to her Gran.

When they went out the door, back to the shiny steps, Sylvia was surprised to see that a small group of children had gathered. They stared at her and her Gran as they walked down the path and out the front gate.

In the morning, Gran woke Sylvia before the sun and washed her in the big zinc bathtub outside. Then she brought out Sylvia's brand new school uniform and shiny black school shoes. "You look smart, Sylvia. Very smart," Gran said, turning her around to see all sides and smiling.

Before reaching the school, Sylvia's Gran stopped. "It's better I leave you here, Sylvia. There's the gate, can you see it?" Sylvia nodded. "You go in that gate and ask for the standard one class. They will take you there, just tell them your name. Be a good girl. I will be right here when you finish." Sylvia looked at her Gran and wondered why she was behaving so oddly. Perhaps she was sad that all day she would be at home alone without Sylvia to keep her company.

That was many weeks ago now. She had found her classroom. Inside was a tall Indian teacher at the front who spoke in English, tilting her head from side to side and smiling, showing her white teeth all of the time. The children in Sylvia's class were small like her, but she knew none of them. Some were black, some were brown and some were white. Sylvia had never seen white children before and spent a lot of the morning sneaking shy looks at them.

When teatime came, Sylvia followed the other children to the tables under the shades near the playground. She opened the tumbler that her Gran had packed in her new school bag. Inside was the left-over *paleche* and spinach from the night before. Her stomach growled when she saw it and she began eating straight away, not noticing that children were gathering around her.

A girl with long braids from the hair salon plaited into her hair said, "Look at what she eats!"

Children stood with their tinned sodas and chips in packets from the shops and laughed. Sylvia, not knowing enough English, understood nothing of what they were saying but became scared as they gathered around her, more and more of them. She stopped eating and looked down at the table hoping that they would leave her alone. Suddenly a boy rushed forward and grabbed her tumbler, the one her Gran had bought new for school, and ran away with it, throwing the *paleche* and spinach on the green lawn along the way. Sylvia tried to catch him but he was big and fast. She shouted, "Stop!" but he didn't. A bell rang and the boy dropped the tumbler and stamped hard on it smiling all of the while. When he ran past Sylvia he said, "Go home Poor Girl!"

Sylvia picked up the pieces of the tumbler and walked out of the school gate. She waited at the end of the road until her Gran arrived. She lied to her Gran, telling her that the teacher said that they mustn't bring food any more to school, that the tumbler would stay there and the teacher would fill it with food instead. "That's very kind of them," Sylvia's Gran said, relieved that all had gone well. Sylvia smiled up at her, agreeing.

That was Sylvia's last day at the rich people's school. Still, every morning her Gran would drop her at the end of the road and pick her up every afternoon at the same place. Sylvia would be full of stories about school and her friends there. At night around the fire where they cooked, her Gran would talk about how one day Sylvia would be clever and rich and they would fly together in an airplane to see Sylvia's mother.

"Your mother did the right thing, Sylvia. You shouldn't think she didn't. We will go and fetch her when you are rich from learning everything at the rich people's school." Her Gran would smile and take Sylvia into her soft jellied arms and hold her tight. Sylvia would be almost happy save for the part that knew lying was wrong and that now maybe because she wasn't going to the rich people's school they would never get her mother back.

Sylvia woke up from her sleepy dream, looked at the sun and realized that she was late. Climbing down from the boulder, she tried hard to walk quickly along the riverbed but the sand kept swallowing her footsteps. By the time she reached the corner where her Gran should have been waiting, she could feel small streams of sweat moving down her back. Where was her Gran? Looking in the direction of the school she could see that it was even later than she had thought; the rich children had all been taken home in their parents' cars. Everything was very quiet.

Sylvia panicked – how would she get home? She didn't know the way well enough through the thin winding lanes in the village. Just as tears began falling down her face, she saw her Gran coming towards her from the direction of the school. When she saw Sylvia, she began to run.

"Where have you been? I thought now they have taken you too and I would be an old woman all alone," she said, grabbing up Sylvia in her arms, holding her tight until Sylvia thought she wouldn't breathe another breath. Then her Gran set her firmly on the ground, holding her out and putting an angry face on hers where it didn't really belong. "Why have you not been going to the rich people's school?"

Sylvia didn't know what to say. She didn't want her Gran to cry when she found out that they might never be able to go and fetch Sylvia's mother in America just because she was frightened of the rich children. "I don't like it there," she said in a soft voice.

Her Gran pulled the big roll of money from her coat pocket and held it out for Sylvia to see. "Never mind. You will go to school near our house. Maybe you'll be a teacher, they are rich too, Sylvia. Do you know that?" Sylvia nodded. "We will not tell your mother. When the school money is enough we will send it back to her and she will come home to us."

She smiled down at Sylvia and Sylvia smiled up at her wise and clever Gran. Then she took Sylvia's small hand in hers and they walked home.

Lauri Kubuitsile is a full-time writer living in Botswana. In practical terms that means she writes anything. Her short stories have been published in *Mslexia, New Contrast, Riptide, Arabesques Review,* and *Drum Magazine* among others. She has two published novellas, *The Fatal Payout* (Macmillan 2005) and *Murder for Profit* (Pentagon 2008). Her children's book, *Mmele and the Magic Bones,* was shortlisted for the African Writers' Prize. She blogs at http://thoughtsfrombotswana.blogspot.com

MY MOTHER, THE CRAZY AFRICAN

I HATE HAVING an accent. I hate it when people ask me to repeat things sometimes and I can hear them laughing inside because I am not American. Now I reply to Father's Igbo with English. I would do it with Mother too, but I don't think she would go for that just yet.

When people ask where I am from, Mother wants me to say Nigeria. The first time I said Philadelphia, she said, "say Nigeria". The second time she slapped the back of my head and asked, in Igbo, "is something wrong with your head?"

By then I had started school and I told her, Americans don't do it that way. You are from where you are born, or where you live, or where you intend to live for a long time. Take Cathy for example. She is from Chicago because she was born there. Her brother is from here, Philadelphia, because he was born in Jefferson Hospital. But their Father, who was born in Atlanta, is now from Philadelphia because he lives here.

Americans don't care about that nonsense of being from your ancestral village, where your forefathers owned land, where you can trace your lineage back hundreds of years. So you trace your lineage back, so what?

I still say I am from Philadelphia when Mother is not there. (I will only say Nigeria when someone says something about my accent and then I always add, but I live in Philadelphia with my family.)

Just like I call myself Lin when Mother isn't there. She likes to go on and on, how Ralindu is a beautiful Igbo name, how it means so much to her too, that name, Choose Life, because of what she went through, because of my brothers who died as babies. And I am sorry, don't get me wrong, but a name like Ralindu and an accent are too much for me right now, especially now that Matt and I are together.

When my friends call, Mother goes, "Lin?" for a second, as though she doesn't know who that is. You would think she hasn't been here three whole years (sometimes I tell people six years) the way she acts.

She still likes to end observations with 'America!' Like at restaurants, "see how much food these people are wasting, America!" Or at the store, "see how much they have marked down the prices from last week, America!"

It's a lot better now though. She no longer crosses herself, shivering, whenever a murder is reported on the news. She no longer peers at Father's written directions as she drives to the grocery store or mall. She still has the directions in Father's precise hand in the glove compartment though. She still clutches the wheels tight, and glances often at the rear-view mirror for police cars. And I have taken to saying, Mother, the American police do not just stop you. You have to do something wrong first, like speed.

I admit, I was awed too when we first came. I looked at the house and I understood why Father did not want to send for us right after he finished his residency, why he chose to work for three years, a regular job as well as moonlighting. I liked to go outside then and just stare at the house, at the elegance of the stone exterior, at the way the lawn wrapped around it like a blanket dyed the color of unripe mangoes. And inside, I liked the curving stairs in the hallway, the gleaming banister, the quaint marble fireplace that made me feel as though I was on the set of a foreign film. I even liked the clump-clump-clump sound the hardwood floors made when I walked in my shoes, unlike the silent cement floors back home.

The sound of the wood floors bothers me now, when Father has some of his colleagues from the hospital over, and I am in the basement. Father doesn't ask Mother to get a little something together for his guests any more, he has people deliver small trays of cheese and fruit. They used to fight about that, Father telling her white people did not care about moi-moi and chin-chin, the things she wanted to make, and Mother telling him, in Igbo, to be proud of who he was and offer it to them first and see if they don't like it. Now, they fight about how Mother behaves at the get-togethers.

"You have to talk to them more," Father says. "Make them feel like they are welcome. Stop speaking to me in Igbo when they are here."

And Mother will screech, "So now I cannot speak my language in my own house? Tell me, do they change their behavior when you go to their house?"

They are not real fights, not like Cathy's parents, who end with shattered glass that Cathy cleans up before school so her little sister won't see. Mother will still wake up early to lay out Father's shirt on his bed, to make his breakfast, to put his lunch in a container. Father could cook when he was alone – he lived alone in America for almost seven years – but now suddenly he can't cook. He can't even cover a pot after himself, no, he can't even help himself to food from a pot. Mother is horrified when he so much as goes close to the stovetop.

"You cooked well, Chika," Father says in Igbo, after every meal. Mother smiles and I know she is plotting what soup to cook next, what new vegetable to try.

All her meals have a Nigerian base, but she likes to experiment and she has learned to improvise for the things that are not in the African store. Baking potatoes for *ede*. Spinach for *ugu*. She even figured out how to make farina cereal so it had the consistency of *fufu*, before Father taught her the way to the African store where there is cassava flour. She no longer refuses to buy frozen pizza and fries, but she still grunts when I eat them, still says that they suck blood, such bad food. Each day she cooks a new soup, which is almost every day, she makes me eat it. She watches as I mold the fufu into reluctant balls and dip them in the chunky soup, she even watches my throat while I swallow, as if to see the balls go down and stay down.

I think she likes it when the people I call our accidental guests come, because they are always over-enthusiastic about her cooking. They are always Nigerians, always new to America. They look up names in the phone book, looking for Nigerians. The Igbo ones tell Father how refreshing it was to see Eze, an Igbo name, after streams of the Yoruba Adebisis and Ademolas. But of course, they add while wolfing down Mother's fried plantains, in America every Nigerian is your brother.

When Mother makes me come out to greet them, I speak English to their Igbo, thinking that they should not be here, that they are here only because of the accident of our being Nigerian. They usually stay only a few days until they figure out what to do, Father is adamant about that. And until they go, I never speak Igbo to them.

Cathy likes to come over to meet them. She is fascinated by them. She talks to them, asks them about their lives in Nigeria. Those people love to talk about victimhood – how they suffered at the hands of soldiers, bosses, husbands, in-laws. Cathy has too much sympathy in my opinion, once she even gave a résumé to her mother, who gave it to someone else who employed the Nigerian. Cathy is cool. She is the only person I can really talk to, but sometimes I think she shouldn't spend so much time with our accidental guests because she starts to sound like Mother, without the scolding tone, when she says things like:

"You should be proud of your accent and your country." I say, "Yes, I'm proud of America." I'm American even if I still only have a green card.

She says it about Matt too. How I shouldn't try too hard to be American for him because if he was real, he'd like me anyway. (This is because I used to make her say words so I would practice and get the right American inflections. I wish Nigeria hadn't been a British colony, it's so hard to lose the way they stress their words on the wrong syllables.) Please. I have seen Matt laugh at the Indian boy with the name that nobody can pronounce. The poor kid's accent is so thick he can't even say his name audibly – at least that's one person I'm better than. Matt doesn't even know my name is Ralindu. He knows my parents are from Africa and thinks Africa is a country, and that's about it. It was the sparkling stud in his left ear that struck me at first. Now it is everything about him, even the way he walks, throwing his legs way in front of his body.

It took a while before he noticed me. Cathy helped, she'd walk boldly up to him and ask him to sit with us at lunch. One day she asked, 'Lin is hot isn't she?' And he said yes. She doesn't like him though. But then, Cathy and I don't like the same things, it's what makes our friendship so real.

Mother used to be cautious about Cathy. She'd say, "*Ngwa*, don't stay too long at their house. Don't eat there either. They might think that we have no food of our own." She really thought Americans have the same stupid hang-ups people back home have. You did not visit people all the time unless they reciprocated, unless it would seem as though you were not gracious. You did not eat at people's homes multiple times if they had not eaten at yours. Please.

She even made me stop going over for a month or so, about two years ago. It was our first summer here. My school had a family cook-out. Father was on call so Mother and I went alone. I wondered if Mother used the dark saucers on her face she calls eyes, couldn't she see that Americans wore shorts and T-shirts in the summer? She wore a stiff dress, blue with white wide lapels. She stood with the other mothers, all chic in shorts and T-shirts, and looked like the clueless woman who overdressed for the barbecue. I avoided her most of the time. There were a number of black mothers there, so any of them could have been my mother.

At dinner that evening, I told her, "Cathy's Mother asked me to call her Miriam." She looked up, a question in her eyes. "Miriam is her first name," I said. Then I plunged in quickly, "I think Cathy should call you Chika." Mother continued to chew a chunk of meat from her soup silently. Then she looked up. Dark eyes blazed across the table, Igbo words burst out. "Do you want me to slap the teeth out of your mouth? Since when have little children called their elders by their first name?" I said sorry and looked down to mold my fufu extra carefully. Looking her in the eyes usually prompted her to follow up on her threats.

I couldn't go to Cathy's for a month after that but Mother let Cathy come over. Cathy would join Mother and me in the kitchen, and sometimes she and Mother would talk for hours without me. Now Cathy doesn't say Hi to Mother, she says Good Afternoon or Good Morning because Mother told her that is how Nigerian children greet adults. Also, she doesn't call Mother Mrs Eze, she calls her Aunty.

She thinks a lot of things about Mother are great. Like the way she walks. Regal. Or the way she speaks. Melodious. (Mother doesn't even make an effort to say things the American way. She still says boot instead of trunk, for God's sake.)

Or Mother hugging me when I got my period. Such a warm thing to do. Her mother simply said oh and they went out and bought pads and panties. When Mother hugged me though, two years ago, pressing me close as though I won a big race, I didn't think it was a warm gesture at all. I wanted to push her away, she smelled sour, like *onugbu* soup.

She said what a blessing it was, how I would bear children some day, how I had to keep my legs closed together so I didn't bring shame on her. I knew she would call Nigeria later and tell my aunts and Mama Nnukwu and then they would talk about the strong children I would bear some day, the good husband I would find.

❖ ❖ ❖

Matt is coming over today, we are writing a paper together. Mother has been walking up and down the house. In Nigeria, girls make friends with girls and boys make friends with boys. With a girl and a boy, it is not just friends, it is something more. I tell Mother it's different in America and she says she knows. She places a plate of fresh-fried *chin-chin* on the dining table, where Matt and I will work. When she goes back upstairs, I take the chin-chin into the kitchen. I can imagine Matt's face as he says, what the hell is that? Mother comes out and puts the chin-chin back. "It is for your guest," she says.

The phone rings and I pray that it will keep her long. The doorbell rings, and there is Matt, earring glittering, holding a folder.

Matt and I study for a while. Mother comes in and when he says hi, she stares at him, pauses then says, "How are you?" She asks if we are almost done, in Igbo, and before I say yes, I pause for a long moment so Matt won't think I understand Igbo so easily. Mother goes upstairs and shuts her door.

"Let's go to your room, and listen to a CD," Matt says, after a while. "My room's a mess," I say, instead of "My mom would never let a boy in my room." "Let's go to the couch then. I'm tired." We sit on the couch and he puts a hand under my T-shirt. I hold his hand. "Just through my shirt."

"Come on," he says. His breathing is as urgent as his voice. I let go and his hand snakes under my shirt, encloses a breast sheathed in a nylon bra. Then, quickly, it weaves its way to my back and unhooks my bra. Matt is good, even I cannot unhook my bra that quickly with one hand. His hand snakes back and encloses the bare breast. I moan, because it feels good and I know that is what I am supposed to do. In the movies, the women's faces always turn rapt right about this point.

He's frenetic now, like he has a malaria fever. He pushes me back, pulls my shirt up so it bunches around my neck, takes my bra off. I feel a sudden coolness on my exposed upper body. Sticky warm moistness on my breast. I once read a book where a man sucked his wife's breast so hard he left nothing for the baby. Matt is sucking like that man.

Then I hear a door open. I grab Matt's head up and pull my shirt on in the space of a second. My bra, startling white against the tan leather furniture, is blinking at me. I shove it behind the sofa just as Mother walks in.

"Isn't it time for your guest to leave?" she asks in Igbo.

I am afraid to look at Matt, I am afraid he will have milk on his lips. "He was just leaving," I say, in English. Mother continues to stand there. I say to Matt, "I guess you better get going." He is standing, picking up papers from the table. "Yeah. Good night."

Mother stands motionless, looking at us both.

"He was talking to you, Mother. He said good night."

She nods, arms folded, staring. Suddenly a burst of Igbo words. Was I crazy to have a boy stay that long? She thought I had good sense! When did we leave the dining table and come to the couch? Why were we sitting so close?

Matt shuffles to the door as she talks. His sneaker laces have come undone and flap as he walks. "See you later," he says at the door.

Mother finds the bra behind the couch almost immediately. She stares at it for a long time before she asks me to go to my room. She comes up a moment later. Her lips are clenched tight.

"Yipu efe gi," she says. Take your clothes off. I watch her, surprised, but I slowly undress. "Everything," she says when she sees that I still have my panties on. "Sit on the bed, spread your legs."

My heart beats wildly in my ears. I settle on the bed, spread-eagled. She comes closer, kneels before me, and I see what she is holding. Ose Nsukka, the hot, twisted peppers that Mama Nnukwu sends dried from Nigeria, in little bottles that originally held curry or thyme. "Mother! No!"

"Do you see this pepper?" she asks. "Do you see it? This is what they do to girls who are promiscuous, this is what they do to girls who do not use the brain in their heads, but the one between their legs."

She brings the pepper so close that I pee right there, and feel the warm wetness on the mattress. But she doesn't put it in.

She is shouting in Igbo. I watch her, the way her charcoal eyes gleam with tears, and I wish I was Cathy. Cathy's mom apologizes after she punishes Cathy. She asks Cathy to go to her room, she grounds Cathy for a few hours or at most, a day.

The next day, Matt says, laughing, "Your mom weirded me out last night. She's a crazy-ass African!"

My lips feel too stiff to laugh. He is looking at some other girl as we talk.

Chimamanda Ngozi Adichie was born in 1977 in Enugu, Nigeria. She studied medicine and pharmacy at the University of Nigeria then moved to the US to study communications and political science at Eastern Connecticut State University. She gained an MA in Creative Writing from Johns Hopkins University, Baltimore, and an MA in African Studies from Yale. After initially writing poetry and one play, she had several short stories published in literary journals, winning various competition prizes. Her first novel, *Purple Hibiscus,* was published in 2003 and won the 2005 Commonwealth Writers Prize. Her second novel, *Half of a Yellow Sun* (2006), set before and during the Biafran War, won the 2007 Orange Broadband Prize for Fiction. 'My Mother, the Crazy African' appeared online in *In Posse Review.* Chimamanda lives between Nigeria and the US, and her collection of stories *The Thing Around Your Neck* will be published in 2009.

ISHWARI'S CHILDREN

ISHWARI WAS THE only river I had ever really seen, and the truest. Some people called her Isri as well. My grandfather explained it to me one day. It was Allah above and this goddess down below. Her names were for her power and her beauty. Dadajan wove fantastic tales around her – her rage, her sorrow, her bounty, her greed inundated the rhythms of his speech and invaded my boyhood imaginings.

We lived in Dhaka, but my Dadajan lived at Noapara, our ancestral village. He was a large man, his girth befitting a man of his worth and station in life. His eyes crinkled when he smiled and sometimes when he wanted to but didn't. His beard was mostly white, with slivers of black proclaiming the youth that still flowed in his veins. He always wore a freshly laundered and starched white skullcap. These were never bought; my grandmother always crocheted them for him.

We would visit Dadajan twice or thrice a year. He, however, visited us frequently. He would arrive with a man in tow carrying coconuts, earthen pots full of live fish and, twice a year, gargantuan sacks filled with rice from his fields. He himself would come bearing stories. Invariably the stories were about Ishwari – the river was swallowing up land like a starving madwoman.

"She's a hungry one," Dadajan would tell me. "She's eating me right out of house and home." The rampaging waves of Ishwari were engulfing huge chunks of land – a lot of which belonged to my grandfather. She was washing away houses and fields; villages disappeared in a matter of days. But Ishwari also gave it back, he told me. "She chews and chews, and spits it right out. No saying where that land'll turn up, though it's better and more wholesome than before."

Still, it was these regurgitations that Dadajan had so much trouble with. The fertile lush lands that emerged from Ishwari's womb were desired by many –

whether they were rightful claimants or not. There were frequent arbitrations required and even visits to the law courts over who owned the newly arisen *chars*. Dadajan would come to consult my father frequently on these matters: as the only son, all of it would most certainly be his one day. I would sit in Dadajan's lap, submerged in sleepy comfort, as they discussed the status of this piece of land or that, hearing about the violence and the persistence of *charuas, char-bandhas*, as these char-people strove to settle the newly surfaced landmasses, learn ing of squatters' rights and other legalese of land disputes.

Whenever we were visiting, I would always accompany Dadajan on his business errands. However, I remember being taken to see a char only once. It was winter then and Ishwari was at her driest. Dadajan was going to see some people on a newly arisen char. We went part of the way on the small *kosha* that Dadajan kept for his personal use. As the slim shape of the kosha slid along the dark riverbed, I longed for the clearer waters of the rainy season. We had two of Dadajan's *kamlas* with us. Abdul Chacha and Alam Chacha were the most trusted of all the men who worked for him. They were brothers and there were other members of their family who worked for ours – had done so for generations. Abdul Chacha, the elder, had worked for my Dadajan ever since he had been capable of bludgeoning sun-hardened clods of earth to ready the fields for planting. He accompanied my grandfather everywhere, a black umbrella and a cloth bag containing necessities for both men hanging from his shoulder. Alam Chacha's responsibility at that time was to lug me (and another black umbrella) around whenever Dadajan took me on his business errands to show me off – the only son of his only son.

Alam Chacha had rowed the single-oar kosha as far as the river had allowed. "We'll have to walk now, *Babu*," Dadajan told me in his rumbly voice. He led the way, striding with his silver-topped walking cane in hand. Abdul Chacha followed, holding the umbrella over him. I was put astride Alam Chacha's shoulders. He had to hold the umbrella up higher than usual to accommodate my head. It must have been quite uncomfortable for him, perhaps even painful – for carrying a six-year-old boy is no joke, but he never complained or even appeared put out. Or perhaps he did and I simply remained unaware of it, secure in the unfeeling obliviousness of the young.

The banks on both sides were splotched here and there with dried *kaash* and grass, like the fine sun-bleached thinning hair of the very old. The verdant riverbanks of Ishwari in full spate had disappeared. As we walked on, the sparse vegetation dwindled as the recognizable riverbanks melded into white sand. The pale winter sun had found the one place where it could relive its former glory and showed no mercy. The sand and the sun dazzled and benumbed my little-boy eyes: the stark whiteness was everywhere, everything around me seemed to glow. It seemed a landscape of an unimagined world, as if I had entered dream-time. Even the sounds of the world appeared to have changed. Gone was the steady thrum of Ishwari; the calm bustle of the household and the village as they went about their day was a distant dream. Instead, all I could hear was the constant rhythmic swishing as the sand shifted beneath our feet and the discordant cry of a hawk as it circled far above us.

This was Ishwari with her water gone, sucked away by winter. The river lay like a tired old lizard sunning its underbelly. I have no idea how either my grandfather or his men knew where we were, or where we were going, for it seemed an endless journey to me as we trudged on and on within that unchanging lucent glare. Safely ensconced on Alam Chacha's shoulders, it seemed as if it was I who was becoming weary with each step.

Then, suddenly, harsh green erupted in front of my eyes. There were trees and houses. As we neared, I saw that, although they looked fairly new, the houses were built similar to our cowsheds. Simple structures of woven mats and bamboo slats held together with twine, they were easy to dismantle and put up again. Yet even our cowsheds were roofed with tin, while these were thatched. There were children playing in front of the shacks. Most of them were dressed in rags of indeterminate color, while a few were naked except for talismans and *tabijes* tied to their waists with the traditional black string. They stopped as they caught sight of us and stared. Abdul Chacha called out, "Hey, where's Kamrun Munshi, do you know?" None of the children moved. "Didn't my words reach your ears?" He bellowed: "Call Kamrun Munshi and tell him that Chowdhury *Shaheb* of Noapara is here." They scattered before him like a flock of sparrows.

We moved into the shade of the few banana trees that bordered the settlement and waited. Alam Chacha lowered me to the ground. A few minutes later a woman appeared, her head and part of her face covered with the *anchal* of her ragged sari. I could see more women gathered a bit away, craning their necks trying to get a glimpse of us and keep their heads covered at the same time. The woman stood in front of Dadajan and touched her hand to her forehead in greeting, "*Salaam Aleikum.*" My grandfather inclined his head graciously in response.

"Well?" It was as if it was Abdul Chacha's curtness, not a sudden breeze that ruffled the sand at her feet. She said something in an inaudible voice. "Speak up, woman," ordered Abdul Chacha. "Where is Kamrun Munshi?"

She raised her face slightly and repeated "He's not here." She paused and added, "He's gone to the market. This time of day, the men…"

"So who are you then?" It surprised me that Abdul Chacha seemed to be speaking to her as he was; why was he so angry at this woman?

"I'm his wife," came the low reply.

"Wife! Oh, you're his woman. You charuas..."

"Abdul," the calm voice of Dadajan interjected. "There is no need to be like that." Abdul Chacha immediately bowed his head and took his place behind Dadajan. "So you are Kamrun's wife? Well, I am Akram Chowdhury from Noapara. We have come a long way. And I have my grandson with me. Do you think we could sit in the shade somewhere and have a drink of water? It is unfortunate that your husband is away. I had business with him." The covered head bowed and turned away murmuring an indistinct invitation. We followed her to her yard. The other women trailed behind us, their chatter a gentle susurration like the swirl of river waters.

When we reached her yard, Kamrun Munshi's wife set out a wooden *jolchouki* for Dadajan to sit on. The low stool looked old and weatherworn, but the intricate carving still bore witness to the loving craft that had gone into its making. She said something to some of the other women, who slipped away immediately. They stood there, the rest of them, just behind Kamrun Munshi's wife, as we inspected the ramshackle shed of her home, the neat yard with its corner covered with pats of dried cow dung, chewed-up pith of sugarcane and a heap of unidentifiable rags to be used for fuel or perhaps to be sold. A washing line was drawn taut from the house to a banana tree, on which hung a red and green striped sari as tattered as the one she was wearing. A few scraggly-looking chickens were clucking about aimlessly.

"You seem to have settled in quite nicely," Dadajan said with a proprietary air as he sat on the jolchouki. He pointed his cane to the chickens, "Do they lay well? Do you have a cock for breeding?" There was a coarseness in Dadajan's voice and the way he spoke, as unfamiliar to me as the shimmering terrain we had just traversed. As he spoke, the women who had left returned – one of them carried a small wooden piri and the others came with eatables. She placed the piri near Dadajan's feet and motioned for me to sit on it. Two tin mugs were placed near his feet for us as well as a few batashas and coconut narus in a battered tin bowl. To offer just water to a visitor was unthinkable, even to these people.

Kamrun Munshi's wife came and stood near me. She motioned to me with her hand and said in her soft voice, "Eat, Babu." Her anchal had fallen away and I could see her face clearly for the first time. She had the kind of spurious prettiness of the countrywoman that faded with age and work. I chose a creamy brown batasha and sucked on it, the crumbly sweetness melting in my mouth.

Dadajan picked up a mug and took a sip. "This is very good. Go on Babu, try it." I drank from the other mug. Sugar water. Dadajan smacked his lips and asked, "Where is Kamrun Munshi? Leaving his young wife all alone in this place. Where are the other men?" The children appeared suddenly – their ghost-faces peeked out from behind the women, peered out from the corner of the house. They watched us as silently as their mothers.

"The men-folk are not home this time of day. It is so in the villages too."

"Why has Munshi gone to the marketplace?"

"We had some eggs and some vegetables. Also some fish from Ishwari. He will sell them and bring rice."'

"Eggs, vegetables. I see you've begun planting." Dadajan said as he looked at the patches of darker earth to the west. "Watermelon, tomatoes, cauliflower. That is good, it will hold the soil down. So you have quite settled in. How many of you are there?"

The woman stood in front of us with her eyes lowered and dug at the earth with her toe. "In our house?" she asked.

"No, no," Dadajan waved his cane impatiently. "All of you, here. How many?"

"Oh, a few households," she replied vaguely. Dadajan looked at Alam Chacha and inclined his head slightly. Alam Chacha slipped quietly away through the yard into the settlement. There was a sly chittering of insects all around us. Dadajan smiled. "Listen, *beti*, you people have just come here. I know it will be very difficult; mainlanders often have no understanding of the hardships of the charua life. But I am a man who lives under Allah's eye. I have to see to it that all within my power live lives that are useful and fair, and that justice is done to them."

Kamrun Munshi's wife looked at the ground as she said softly but distinctly, "We work. It is very hard, but we work as Allah allows us."

Dadajan nodded. "Yes, yes, that is as it should be. But there are many kinds of people in this world of Allah's. There will be men who will say that this land is not ready to be settled yet, that you must not live here yet. The chars that arise, there are many disputes as to who owns them." He stroked his beard, "Me, I am a simple man. I leave it to the laws of Allah and the laws of the land to tell me what is mine and what I should have. But others, you see, they are not always so scrupulous. That is what I wanted to talk to Kamrun Munshi about."

There was a silence as Dadajan paused. Kamrun Munshi's wife looked away to the half-hidden children. They were losing their unaccustomed diffidence and were edging closer to us. "There are those who think nothing of burning up a few houses, uprooting fruit-bearing trees, bullying and intimidating innocent people," Dadajan resumed. "They tell themselves that the things that they destroy belong, after all, only to charuas. I do not say that this is right, merely that they think like this. Yet it is a sin to see hardworking people like you get hurt this way."

Dadajan paused again. He picked up a naru from the bowl in front of him and nibbled on the flat, brown-colored disc. "You must tell whoever comes that you live here for me," he said abruptly. "Then they will no longer bother you."

Kamrun Munshi's wife raised her face suddenly and looked directly at Dadajan for the first time. "But no one has bothered us."

"They might. They will." Dadajan popped the whole naru in his mouth and munched noisily. "Make no mistake – they will come."

He took a sip of water and picked up a batasha. As he was about to take a bite, the woman said: "We have lived on chars before. Our men know what to do."

Dadajan smiled. "Of course they do. But what I say will make your life easier. Tell Kamrun Munshi to come and talk to me. Then he can talk to the others." There was another pause as, instead of putting it into his mouth, Dadajan crumbled the half-moon of the batasha in his hand and let the pieces drop away to the ground.

"The fish you talk about, the fish that he has gone to sell, Ishwari's fish is not just for everyone. Most of the river and the fish *ghers* in this region, I own the leases." Dadajan shook his forefinger at her playfully. "Where is he catching them from?"

The woman pursed her lips as if the words that had already escaped her mouth had been too much.

"I will be going to see the administrative officer. As a local man I feel it is my responsibility to watch over these new lands. I must tell him that he is not to worry, that I have let good people, good charuas settle here. I must tell him how many houses, and people and animals are here, it is important that he know these things." He pointed his cane at the chickens as they ambled mindlessly nearer. "You have chicks too, I see. You breed them to sell?" The woman hesitated for a moment, then nodded.

Just as Dadajan asked "How many do you get a month?", Alam Chacha walked back with a rooster held tightly under one arm. He came and stood behind me.

"*Boro Amma* will want to cook *morag-polao* with this for the Young Master," he said. My grandmother always cooked this dish for my father when we came visiting. Usually she had two or three roosters all plumped up awaiting our arrival. Perhaps she had forgotten this time.

Dadajan smiled indulgently and stroked his beard. "My son, my only son, has brought his family to visit his old parents. He grew up here, and so my men all feel like brothers to him. They are always careful to look after him properly when he is here." He spread out his hands, palm upwards, "They love him like a brother and like to give him all they can." He turned to Alam Chacha, "Why don't you tie its legs up? You'll find it easier to carry."

The woman had been looking steadily and unblinkingly at the rooster while Dadajan spoke. Suddenly she spoke in a very clear voice. "Of course. Your only son, of course, he must have this. There is no need to pay us for it. You must take it as a gift, from us poor charuas." She became silent again as if this speech had wearied her, and she had said all that needed to be said for the measure of that day.

"We must leave now. Tell Kamrun Munshi to come and see me," said Dadajan and strode towards the path by the banana grove, swishing his cane in the air with a casual disregard. The delicate silver filigree on the handle winked in the sun with a knowing air. Suddenly it slipped from his hand and whacked the face of a little boy who was standing close to the path watching us leave. "Ahha. Poor thing, is he hurt too much?" The half-naked child gave a soft whimper and tottered towards the women who stood silent. None of them moved to gather him in, none of them even looked at him. "Is he one of yours?" Dadajan asked Kamrun Mumshi's wife. "Abdul, give a ten-taka note to the child. Poor thing. Hey *picchi*, buy some chocolates okay? Come Babu," he called me, "we must go."

The woman did not answer, nor did she move to take the money from Abdul Chacha. Dadajan walked away. Abdul Chacha waited a few moments then tossed the note to the ground and followed him. Alam Chacha had already picked me up and sat me on his shoulders for the return journey.

We were well on our way before I asked why none of the women had picked the child up – wasn't his mother there? "Charuas are like that," Dadajan told me. "They move around so much. The very soil that they settle on, that itself is temporary, no saying whether it will remain the same or even be there in a month's time. So they become different from us. They hold this life Allah has so graciously given us lightly, as of no consequence. And so they do not have proper family feeling, not even for children."

The rooster squawked once, then subsided to a guttural cackling as it hung head downwards from Abdul Chacha's left shoulder. "They are like that. Still, I try to do what is within my power for them. In the eyes of Allah, we are all one, all equal," I remember Dadajan saying as the boat slid smoothly into the water.

If the journey there had seemed long and arduous, the return trek seemed as endless as the weary waters of Ishwari.

It seems to me that it was merely the shimmer of sun and sand that burned that visit so permanently into my mind. The char that I had seen is as dead as Dadajan now and it is only my act of remembrance that gives life to that charua woman. The clarity of those images dulls the other childhood memories that I so desperately long to relive. I remember listening to the steady splash of the oar for a while. And I remember Dadajan stroking his beard with a quiet satisfaction and saying, "We are all Ishwari's children."

Shabnam Nadiya is a writer, poet, editor and translator based in Bangladesh. The isolation individuals face because of boundaries of class, gender, race, age and religion are central to her writing. Her work has appeared in a number of international anthologies and periodicals.

RAVI MANGLA UNITED STATES

AIR MAIL

"IT'S LIKE A messy bedroom." Mr Peters said to open his lecture on Chapter 14 – 'Developing Nations and Emerging Markets'. Chapter 9 – 'The Colonization of Africa' – began similarly as he used the metaphor of picking teams in gym class to explain the Berlin Conference. The Crusades were like a game of king of the hill, the American Revolution was a heated argument with your parents, and the Berlin Wall was the picket fence between you and the neighbors with the satellite dish and hot tub and trampoline. He complacently thought of himself as the 'cool teacher' and upheld this title by relating to his fifth-grade class and their generalized interests, since he himself was not so far removed from the plights of childhood. As he spoke colorfully and comically about immigrants in cartoons and the adopted children of high-profile celebrities, he wheedled nods of acknowledgement from even the sleepiest and most doleful of students.

Tommy left class no less confused than when he entered, conjuring misshapen visions of wooded forests and spear-wielding tribesmen extracted from snippets of television. He imagined a civilization unearthing fire for the first time and attempting to sculpt a wheel out of stone but settling on an octagon.

The bus dropped him at the mouth of his neighborhood. He walked home past lawns mown to a fine crewcut and under the arcs of sprinklers. He saw the Nguyens' house. His mother hadn't cared much for the Nguyen family ever since their cat ate all the geraniums in her garden and then they blamed her when the cat got sick.

"What are developing nations like?" He asked his parents over dinner.

"Developing nations?" his father said with an eyebrow raised.

"I think he means Third World countries, honey," his mother said.

"How should I know? I've never been."

"The Merrimans went to the Far East last spring. I remember Mrs Merriman saying it didn't smell very nice because there isn't a good sewage system in place," his mother said.

"Makes sense. Why would they want to go there when you've got the best cities in the world right here – Chicago, New York, Los Angeles," his father said, counting off his fingers, as a spray of mashed potatoes fled his mouth, "Miami, Dallas, Atlanta... Philadelphia... Boston. Boston is one hell of a city. Every great city is right here, I don't get why you'd waste all that money for bad sewage."

There was a short chapter on the Gulf War in their textbook. Anirudh's teacher Mr Sidhu used the word 'decadent' to describe Western culture. Anirudh didn't know what it meant but there was something undeniably lush and grand sounding about the word. He liked the bold juxtaposition of the syllables and muttered the word softly to himself as he walked home down the dusty road with his books under his arm. "Dec-a-dent." Some of his schoolmates on bicycles pedaled past him, teasing him affably about having to walk home. A woman hung colorful silks from the balcony of her home, resplendent in the fierce sunlight. Anirudh thought about the West. He had seen Europeans and some Americans in the town before – there was an Australian who lived at the end of the road, but still the West seemed like an uncharted frontier; distant and unfathomable.

Anirudh's father was a civil servant and their house was modest. Over *daal* and *paratha* he asked his father about America and the West.

"What is America like?"

"How would I know? I've never been."

"Maybe I'll go one day."

"You? Go to America?" He laughed. Anirudh admired his father. He, however, did not admire his sense of humor quite as much, which was often at his own – or his mother's – expense.

"You know the Chaturvedi family visited last year for their niece's wedding. They said the cars are large and everyone eats outside of the house." His mother said.

Outside of the house? Anirudh tried to envision this world of large cars and outdoor food. It wasn't like the exploding warehouses and shootouts from the American movies he had seen or the wide roads and lavish edifices in his textbook. It seemed so strange. The image he sketched in his mind, assimilating all these elements, looked no more believable than a comic strip.

The following morning, Mr Peters announced the class project for the second semester. They would compose letters to children of the same age in a developing nation. Some of the students groaned. Then again, they groaned at the implication of any sort of work. Mr Peters groaned, out of the habit of mimicking the temperaments of his class.

Tommy composed his letter perfunctorily. Without so little as a heading, salutation, or valediction (which they were taught earlier in the year) he scribbled:

My name is Tommy. I'm 12. I like playing baseball and basketball. What is India like?

Would whoever received it even be able to understand it? Could they read or write? Surely, they wouldn't know what baseball or basketball was. Would he receive a letter back?

A week later, Mr Sidhu brandished a large envelope in front of his class. The project had been a surprise. He passed out the letters to his students. Anirudh unfolded his: *My name is Tommy. I'm 12. I like playing baseball and basketball. What is India like?*

It was very short. He shrugged and began crafting his response.

On the way home, Anirudh was overwhelmed with thoughts of grandeur. He saw the broad, shining windows of Western skyscrapers towering over the throngs of city dwellers in silk ties and dark suits as he passed the grimy fronts of the spice and sweet shops, the mercer and seamstress. He heard the drumming of hard-soled shoes on the sidewalk, the rustle of clothes, the chorus of professional voices talking into their mobile phones, the horns of cars and the noise of buses braking abruptly. And then there was the sound of his own feet on the narrow dirt road, forlorn amid a sprawling blanket of silence. He envisioned the gold-handled door of boundless possibility alongside the hewn wooden door of his own potential, the paint rubbed out and hinges rusted. There was a world beyond his own, a garden outside of the cocoon he yearned to break free of, to find his wings, to traverse the open sky, to breathe in the sweet flowered air. He felt at once a sense of wonder and adventure followed by a deep-seated longing as he saw himself in the grimy window of the jewelers and was reminded of who he was again – Anirudh, the son of a modest civil servant, destined to follow in the footsteps of his father. "Travel is a silly thing," his father maintained. "You go out to see the world and then what? What have you got?"

Mr Peters flourished the envelope in front of his class. He passed it around so each of the students could see the tiles of gold stamps and strange writing and the red ink imprint spelling out the word "AIR MAIL". Some students forwarded it brusquely to the next, while others gawked at the alien markings.

Tommy unfolded the letter that was handed to him:

Hello Tommy,

My name is Anirudh. I like games and movies and being with friends. I play cricket sometimes. My teacher Mr Sidhu said cricket is similar to your baseball. India is good. I go to school and go to the store sometimes to buy sweets and gum with my money. What is America like? What food do you eat?

It lives! It breathes! He was no creature from another planet. It was as if a boy no different than himself had just been birthed into existence. He composed his reply with a vigor that was absent from his earlier effort. He showered Anirudh with a long string of questions.

Hey Anirudh,

America is great. I like hanging out with my friends and going to movies too. My favorite foods are pizza, sesame chicken and spaghetti. What do you use to pay for things? What's your school like? Do you have TV? What movies do you watch? Do you wear a towel on your head? Do you have a car? What kind of sweets and gum? What holidays do you celebrate? What religion are you? Do you have any brothers or sisters?

Though he found some of the questions odd, Anirudh was happy to answer each one. The rupee was their form of currency. He was Hindu and not Sikh. It was typically the Sikhs who wore turbans. He explained the holidays of Holi and Diwali. He watched mostly Bollywood films but had seen American ones as well. He also liked pizza and ate it when he went to Chandigarh to visit his cousins.

Tommy explained the restaurant culture and fast food phenomenon. He described New York City, Hollywood and Disney World. Tommy was fascinated by the celebration of Holi. The concept of a day dedicated to running amuck in the streets and throwing paint at one another amazed him. His family celebrated major holidays by going to church – he much preferred the idea of throwing paint.

Tommy had begun preparing his letters before class. He was giddy when a new one arrived. He grew impatient, counting the days between correspondences. It was an enthusiasm school had never afforded him. While the other children in the class gradually lost interest, Tommy wrote page after page. Their letters grew longer and more personal. Mr Sidhu and Mr Peters continued to mail out the boys' letters after the project had finished. At the end of the school year, without the slightest hesitation, they exchanged street names, towns, states and postal codes and began writing from home; each standing in the doorway of their future, at the dawn of adolescence, looking out onto the vast world before them.

Ravi Mangla lives in Fairport, New York. His short fiction and poetry is accessible online at *Hobart, Pindeldyboz, elimae, McSweeney's Internet Tendency* and the *Boston Literary Magazine*. His story 'Popemobile' in *Dogzplot* was nominated for inclusion in the 2009 Best of the Web anthology.

GROWING MY HAIR AGAIN

I AM CROUCHING beside the bed, my palms flat on the deep red rug that swallows my sobs. The rug is warm. It is a mother's hand. My posture is – I hope – appropriate to the occasion. My mother-in-law is watching me, her eyes hawk-like even through her own tears. She sniffs and says, "You're not crying loud enough. Anyone would think you never loved him. *Bee akwa*!"

She never approved of me. I had an excess of everything. Education. Beauty. Relatives. Hair. Sure to bring any man down. At the thought of my hair, my palms go cold. By this time tomorrow, it will all be gone. I shall be taken to the backyard by a group of widows, probably all of them strangers. One of them, the oldest, will lather my hair with a new tablet of soap (which will be thrown away once it's been used on me), and then shave it all off with a razor blade. I shall be bathed in cold water. Strange women splashing water on me. Cleansing me to make my husband's passage easy on him: a ritual to make the break between us final so that he is not stuck halfway between this world and the next shouting himself hoarse calling for his wife to be at his side when he rejoins his ancestors.

"You should cry louder. You sound like you're mourning a family pet. You are a widow, *nwanyi a*! Cry as if you lost a husband! *Bee akw*a. Cry!"

In one word, she distils my life: widow. Even though Okpala has been dead for a while – three months to be precise – I am only officially now becoming a widow. Three months were needed to organize a befitting burial. To have the invitation cards printed. The cow ordered. The dancers reserved. Three months in which Okpala's body stayed in the only mortuary with a generator in Enugu and I gained a moratorium on widowhood. But all that is about to change. Tonight, I shall be given the badge of honor: a head so cleanshaven that sun rays will bounce off it. I wonder if she is observing me as I lift one palm and run it across my hair, the whole length of the thick mane of shiny black hair that grazes my shoulders. I suspect that Okpala's mother has always been jealous of it, what with her downy hair like the feathers on the underside of a chicken and a receding hairline that gets worse by the day. Still, I must not be too hard on the woman. She did not invent the tradition of shaving widows' hair, did she?

"Is your hair more important than my son?" Her voice is hoarse.

Every time she came to visit Okpala and me in Enugu, she complained of the amount of time I spent grooming my hair.

"Nneka, the way you look after this your hair, one would think it was your entrance to heaven."

She complained so much that Okpala asked me not to go to the salon while she visited. "When she goes, you can continue." I listened. Okpala was not one to be disobeyed.

I spent the last three months visiting salons on an almost daily basis. Changing hairstyles every day. Experimenting with different styles. I was a perfect client: I surrendered my head to the hairdressers and said, "All yours. Do with it as you wish." I had *shuku* done: an intricate basket of braids. I had it plaited with broad black thread and standing up like nails protruding from my scalp. I had it permed and bobbed like a beret. All the time painfully aware that soon my choices would be limited. In the last three weeks, I tried to grow dreads and despaired when my hair refused to knot, resorting to thin braids that took seven hours to put in. My mother-in-law watched my changing hairstyles, her lips a spout of disapproval that got longer and longer. "Anyone would think you did not love him." I ignored her. I had them taken out yesterday. I poured palm kernel oil on it and wrapped it up in a scarf. And today, I tugged and combed until it was a shiny mass of blackness. I touch it again. I hear the old woman hiss.

I know that if she could, she would have turned me out of the house. And not just this humongous villa in Osumenyi with red and maroon carpeting in every room – Okpala had no sense of decoration – but the duplex in Enugu as well. Prime property that. A sprawling large house that my mother-in-law had brought a barefoot prophet to bless the day we moved in. *Daba daba da, Jehovah El Shaddai, Jehovah Yahweh, Bless this house of your humble servant, Okpala. Keep him safe from the evil eye. Surround his house with spiritual military forces. Yaba Dabba Dab.* I had walked out mid-prayer – the man's toes distressed me and that angered Okpala.

Okpala's anger was always a wild hurricane. It cleared everything in its path: family pictures, tables, chairs. Nothing was spared.

This morning, my mother-in-law caught me in the kitchen. Bored and hungry and sick of sitting on the bedroom floor to be besieged by crying relatives, I had gone to raid the pantry. Nothing in it appealed to me. I opened the fridge and found the transparent bowl with my Christmas cake raisins soaking in brandy. I started soaking them a few days before Okpala died. Christmas is only a month-and-a-half away now. The raisins called me and I answered. I pulled out the bowl, dug my hands in and grabbed a handful. I threw them in my mouth and chewed quickly, the raisins exploding furiously, releasing the brandy trapped inside. I was like a madwoman. I grabbed some more, a trail of brown liquid seeping through my clenched fist and snaking down my hand. I was on my third helping when she walked in.

"So, this is where you are? The widow's food not enough for you?"

I wished I could talk back but years of habit are difficult to break.

"In some places, the only food a widow is allowed to eat for a year is yam and palm oil. And yet you think you're too good for *nni nwanyi ajadu*."

I licked my lips, wiped my mouth with the back of my hand and tried not to think of the food that I have been served since yesterday. Tasteless grub: no salt, no pepper. Just plain white rice and even plainer tomato stew. For a widow must not be seen to enjoy food; all her meals for the one-year mourning period must be made without any salt or pepper. And I know I am lucky; it is a lot better than yam and unspiced palm oil. Plus, I get to eat with a spoon. In some villages, my mother-in-law drummed into me, a mourning widow only eats with two long sticks. Whatever food she drops belongs to the spirits; it's her husband's share.

"My son should never have married you. You're a witch, *amosu ka-ibu*. You cannot even cry for him."

I tasted raisin and brandy on my tongue. I ignored her. She has called me worse. 'Murderer.' I killed her son. I was the one who sent the four teenage armed robbers to his boutique on that Friday night while he was stocktaking. The police told us he was shot at close range, in his heart and in his head. He had probably refused to hand over the cash and tried to fight them; his table was overturned. I did not tell them that Okpala did not need to fight to overturn tables. All he needed was enough anger.

I married Okpala straight out of university with a brand new degree in sociology. He was a trader with a boutique on Ogui Road. I had gone there to look for a graduation dress; he was reputed to have the best at affordable prices. I saw something I liked, a short-sleeved dress the color of a fresh bruise on light skin. It was the most gorgeous thing I had ever seen but the price tag put it beyond me. Okpala convinced me to try it on, his hands tapping on the table behind which he was sitting. He insisted on giving it to me as a present if I invited him to my graduation party. Five weeks later, he had paid my bride price.

My mother liked him. She said he had busy hands: hands like his which could never keep still were the sort of hands that kept the devil at bay. The sort of hands that spun money. "Nneka, he's a good man. You're lucky to have snatched him, *eziokwu*."

At the wedding, Okpala's hands flailed and waved as he danced. At the high table, reserved for the groom and bride, he played with the spoons and the forks set out for the fried rice and the dried meat, tap tap tapping on the table like a restless child. My mother, resplendent in her white lace wrapper and blouse – paid for by Okpala – leaned over to me and whispered, "Busy hands. If you marry a lazy man, your suffering will be worse than Job's. *I ga-atakali Job n'afufu*."

Even when we had our first dance, his hands could not keep still. They went around my neck, around my waist, around my buttocks. My mother danced close to me and winked. "This man loves you very much," she whispered and danced away, waist shaking, her behind wobbling to the boom bam bang of Oliver de Coque and the Expo 76 Ogene Super Sounds.

The wedding tired me. The smiling and the eating and the dancing. A success, everyone said and therefore nobody left until really late. The DJ kept playing music and Okpala and I kept being asked to dance. Okpala loved dancing. It was his passion and so he did not need much encouragement. "*Bia gba egwu nwoke m*," and Okpala would be there, dragging me with him, my multilayered wedding dress getting heavier by the minute.

"No, Okpala. I'm tired. No more dancing. *Mba*," I tried to protest but his hand manacled my wrist and I had to get up, all the while smiling because it was my wedding day and because he was whispering furiously: Smile, smile, *muo amu*.

When we finally left and checked into the Royal Suite of the Presidential Hotel he had booked, all I wanted to do was sleep, wedding dress and all. Okpala would have none of it. "My wedding night and you want to sleep?" All the while his hands moved, tapping on the long thin mirror beside the bed, on the huge brown table opposite the bed. And when I said, "Okpala, darling, I am really tired. Whatever you have in mind can wait until I've had some rest," his busy hand connected with my face. I saw flashes of lightning as Okpala pummeled me. And when he dragged me naked to bed, all I could see was this huge darkness that had started to consume me.

"I hope that at least, when the guests start coming, you'll show a lot more emotion than now." She sounds guttural, like a masquerade. I almost feel sorry for her. I think of my son. It cannot be easy to lose a child.

Tomorrow, the first guests will begin to arrive. Okpala was a rich man, so his funeral should reflect that: five days of receiving mourners. First, my townspeople, Okpala's in-laws. They will come, as is customary, with a dance group and some drinks. The following day is for Okpala's siblings' in-laws. After that his mother's people. Then members of the different associations he belonged to. Then the general public. They will all come with money, wads hidden in envelopes for me, but I shall see none of the money. His brothers will take it and give me what they think I need. But I don't care. I have enough money in my bank account, and the boutique is doing well.

In the out-kitchen behind the house, huge pots, *osite*, are being set up for cooking. Cassava. Rice. Meat. Four different varieties of soup. Truckloads of beer and soft drinks have been arriving for the past two days. There is a huge stock of palm wine. Cartons of wine. The St Stephen's Gospel Band has been hired to provide the music. Okpala's brother insisted on inscribing drinking glasses and beer mugs with Okpala's name and date of death, souvenirs to hand out to people. He also had key rings made with Okpala's picture. But he said the key rings were not for everyone. They would be given only to members of the traders' association to which Okpala belonged. Frankly, I find it all a bit vulgar, this recent trend to memorialize the dead in key rings and plastic trays and wall clocks. But what can I do? I have got no say in the matter. I am only his widow.

"Tomorrow, you'd better not show me up. You'd better cry well."

I know what I am expected to do. To scream and hurl angry words at death. *Onwu ooo, death, why have you taken my Lion? Why have you taken my man? Onwu, you are wicked. I joka.* To cry, my voice above everybody else's, the loyal wife's. To beg, when he is being put in the ground, to be allowed to go with him. *Chi m bia welu ndu m ooo, my God, take my own life too.* I shall struggle with Okpala's burly brothers who will try to stop me from crawling into his grave, pleading to be buried with my husband, the best man in the world, my son's father. They will tell me to think about my son. He needs a mother. He is still a child and has just lost his father; he does not need to lose his mother too. Think about him, they'll say. *Jide obi gi aka. Hold your heart in your hands firmly, so that it does not slip and splinter.*

I think about my son. Four years old. The reason Okpala's people have not kicked me out yet. Will not kick me out. I am the mother to Okpala's heir. If I had had a girl, his witch of a mother would have had me on the streets by now and then what? Who would marry a widow with a young daughter? But I have a son, so I get to keep the boutique. Afamefuna is my trump card. Too young to understand death, he is playing in his room, crashing toy cars and asking Enuma, the househelp, if his daddy was back from his trip. Afamefuna has been asking that question since the night Okpala died and I told him his daddy had gone away and saw a light come on in his eyes.

"Five years of marriage, and all you could manage was one child. One. Good thing it was a boy. I warned Okpala that college destroys their wombs with all that knowledge. Too much knowledge is not good for a woman. It destroys their wombs. What does she need all that education for, eh? He should have married another woman. One that would have given him many more sons."

When Afamefuna was one-and-a-half years, I became pregnant again. I had, by then, become adept at avoiding Okpala's busy hands. Making sure his food was served on time. His clothes clean and ironed. The house tidied and welcoming. But in my eighth week of pregnancy, I slipped. I burnt his supper: *egusi* soup with snails he had ordered especially from Onitsha. The snails, charred, clung to the bottom of the pot, curled up like ears. Okpala liked egusi with snail and, as I realized within a week of living with him, it was akin to a mortal sin to serve it up less than perfect; the punishment smarted even after forgiveness had been granted. So, that evening, when I smelt the soup burning, I knew what was in stock for me. I tried to recuperate it, to scoop up the snails and with some water douse the burnt taste. Nothing worked and The Hand descended on me while Afamefuna watched from behind his bedroom door. Okpala upturned the bowl of soup, my burnt offering, on my head and the soup ran like tears down my cheeks and soiled the white blouse I had on in readiness for the Legion of Mary meeting at St. Christopher's. Of course, I could not go any more. The pepper in the egusi stung my eyes and the smell of burnt soup found its way into my nostrils and nestled there cozily. When I went to the toilet and released clots of blood, I knew that Okpala had martyred my baby, sent it back to its source before I even had the chance to cradle it in my arms. I knew I never wanted to give him another child, male or female.

The week Okpala was away, seeing to new supplies in Lagos, I went to the Riverside Private Hospital and had my tubes tied. The night he came back and called me to his bed, I touched the tiny scar that only I could see and felt it throbbing warm under my hand and I smiled. When he released his manhood inside me and spoke to his seeds, ordering them to give him a son – Okpala wanted another son desperately, to raise his status among his peers – I wanted to giggle out loud.

I lift my head and turn towards my mother-in-law. She is sitting on my bed. I look beyond her and see my new life stretch ahead of me: a multi-colored wrapper infused with the scent of fresh possibilities. No Okpala. My future secure in the fact that I have his son. An independent woman with my own boutique. I shall regrow my hair. Nurture it and delight in its growth. Maybe in a year or two, another relationship. I am in no hurry, though. I shall savor my freedom first. My eyes meet those of my mother-in-law and I feel it coming. I do not even want to stop it: a laughter that comes from deep inside my belly and takes over my entire body.

Chika Unigwe was born in Enugu, Nigeria, and now lives in Turnhout, Belgium, with her husband and four children. Her novel *On Black Sisters' Street* will be published in July 2009 by Jonathan Cape in the UK and Random House in the US. A version of it was published in Dutch in 2007 by Meulenhoff/Manteau as *Fata Morgana* and will appear in Italian in November 2008 (Nerri Pozza). She was shortlisted for the 2004 Caine Prize and has won the Commonwealth Short Story Award.

DIPITA KWA CAMEROON

HONOR OF A WOMAN

I KNELT ON our bed – the one I shared with my sister Muto – and peeped through a crack in the termite-infested plank window. My mother was still sitting on the veranda, waiting for Muto's return. Muto and Mama never stopped fighting. There was some repulsive force between the two of them that pulled them apart – if not together for a fight.

I couldn't understand what made my sister stay out this late almost every night – although she was 18, three years older than me. It was past 11; I could tell from the stillness that hung like a sackcloth over the village of Mukunda.

I shrugged and went back under my sheets, covered my ears from the mosquitoes, and thought about Papa. He died when I was 10; and Mama went away, leaving us with Auntie Katty, my father's elder sister. Auntie Katty was anywhere between 50 and 60 years old. For four years she took care of us from the meager income she got from selling *miondo*. I was happy because the frequent quarrels and fights between Muto and Mama ceased. I relived those beautiful evenings when Mama was away and we used to sit around Auntie, cracking *egusi* under the bright moonlight, with a cold wind whistling through the leaves of trees in the surrounding bush. We would listen reverently to what she told us was the Honor of a Woman. Muto hardly ever went out then. She too seemed to love those evenings. Then last year Mama came back and took us away to live in a rented two-roomed plank place while our father's house, situated on the outskirts of the village, was shrouded with grass and almost collapsing from lack of use.

"Where have you been?" I heard my mother demand. "Why are you coming back at this hour?"

I quietly crept back to the window.

I saw Muto try to push past Mama only to be violently pulled back by her forearm. She almost toppled over. I held my breath and waited for the worst.

"I'm talking to you," Mama shouted. "Stand here and tell me which devil you have been chasing around Mukunda all night while girls of your age are all in bed!"

Muto pulled her arm free. "What do you want from me?" she snapped.

I recognized that vicious glare in her eyes that often announced her readiness to claw like an angry cat.

Mama sighed. She looked as though cold water had just been poured on her flaming heart. I also realized that she was probably getting old. If it had been five years ago when she was 41, Mama would have welcomed Muto with a questioning slap. Now instead, I heard her saying in a subdued voice: "My daughter, roving the neighborhood from one room and off-license to another like an evil spirit, will yield you nothing but dishonor and destruction... Look, this world is fast becoming the proverbial calabash of diseases..."

"It's my life!" Muto shouted. "Let me live it the way I want. Maybe I should ask you this: when it was your turn to change men the way you changed your underwear, which resulted in your giving birth to two bastards, whose advice did you heed? And if you hadn't killed someone's husband in your bed, would you have run back here to bore me with your hypocrisy?"

It was true that Ewolo had died on Mama's bed in her rented apartment in Kumba last year, precipitating her return to Mukunda to avoid his widow's wrath. By reminding Mama of this, Muto had stepped on a dry branch.

I heard the slap fall hard and loud on her face, sending her staggering backwards for balance. Like the cat tattooed on her thigh, Muto recoiled quickly. Before Mama knew, she was all over her, punching and clawing. It all happened so fast. The next moment Muto's neck was caught in Mama's right armpit. In the struggle to free her head from Mama's raining blows, Muto clawed the more and her fingers soon found the top of Mama's blouse. She ripped it open. Her mouth immediately found one of Mama's breasts and her teeth sank into the nipple.

Mama and I screamed in unison. I ran out in my worn nightie. Mama was holding her breast with blood trickling down her fingers.

The neighborhood was now fully awake.

I thought I would faint as I saw Muto race into the dark night, spitting and wiping her mouth with the back of her hand.

The atmosphere calmed down after the wound was dressed and Mama had been given some drugs by the nurse who lived down the road opposite the school compound. But she couldn't stop mouthing curses.

"Bad luck will follow you all the miserable days of your life!"

"Take those words back!" the nurse rebuked her.

"I won't! Muto will never see peace as long as she lives if I am the one who gave birth to her," she kept shrieking as she lay on her bed. "Wherever she goes, it will hang on her head like a hive of wasps." She went on ranting right into her sleep.

Three days after the fight, Auntie Katty was sitting on a low stool and leaning forward on her walking staff, shaking her head in an all-knowing fashion. She said she had come to inquire about Mama's health, and to see if Muto had returned home. Mama was now feeling better. The wound had been stitched. But Muto had not been seen. Her clothes and Mama's traveling bag had disappeared the night of the fight.

"Come here, Penda, and sit down," Auntie said to me, shifting to create space for me on the stool. "I want you to listen, and listen well."

She then turned to face my mother.

"People say I speak too much. And I won't stop speaking. I have been quiet for so long that I am afraid that if I die today without emptying my mind, I too may not see peace in the other world. After all, who has ever developed rotten teeth from giving advice? My mouth is even too full at my age." She bit into a piece of kola nut and crunched.

"Endale, you are the cause of all your misfortunes," she went on slowly. "You thought youthfulness was like a cowry that never faded. I will tell you again that you lived a dirty life that you never thought could rub off on your daughter. When your own mother complained and begged you to slow down, you beat her and dragged her about like a dog with a deadly disease. You told her that a cripple like her couldn't give birth to a beautiful girl like you. You left the house and abandoned her to die in misery. And the poor woman actually grieved to her death…"

"Stop it, Katty, please!" my mother cried.

"I won't stop!"

"I wish Muto had killed me!" Mama muttered, covering her face with a pillow that was already wet with sweat and tears.

"Muto can't kill you because you didn't kill your mother. She is merely repaying the debt you owe. And this is how the circle will go on and on; you owing your mother, Muto owing you, her daughter owing her, her granddaughter owing her daughter, and so on.

"Like others before you, you are caught in that vicious circle of woe – an endless chain of curses." She paused to reflect. "Your mother died and was buried in your absence. You gave my brother the worst days of a man's life. If Muto thinks today that she is a bastard, she has every right. If after all those years of marriage to my brother you could still stand in public and tell him he wasn't man enough to make a woman pregnant, I wonder what you want your daughters to feel. Thank God I was there for them. Now you are afraid Muto is taking after you. Who do you blame?" She paused to take another bite of the kola nut.

"However, I think you can help yourself break this spell. That is why I came. As soon as you are strong again, go to your mother's grave and plead with her. Tell her – tell God – you are sorry."

After she left, my mother wept.

Every morning she would peep into our room to see if Muto had secretly returned. And I would see the disappointment and gloom in her eyes when she saw that I was there alone. Soon I began to feel that she didn't care about me. She spent her time worrying about Muto, who had caused her so much pain. When I complained to Auntie, she reminded me of the story of the prodigal son and advised me to cheer up.

"You are still a young woman," she said. "Soon you will know the mother's love for her children – even the one that is a thief."

From then I tried to understand what my mother was going through. Though I couldn't really feel it, I tried my best to make her happy. This was very hard indeed.

And it became worse when Malodi Steven was bitten to death by a green mamba that had been caught in his trap. Malodi was the man who paid our rent. Though he was married, he had been hanging around my mother since the week she returned to Mukunda and took us from Auntie. I hated him for cheating on his wife. But he was the only one who succeeded in making Mama really laugh during those miserable two months after Muto's disappearance. His death plunged Mama into the darkest gloom that I had ever known her to be in. This was the third man she had lost within five years. She went for days without food and hardly spoke to anyone. I thought of running away to live with Auntie, but I didn't want to increase my mother's pain, so I stayed.

Then one Saturday morning, six weeks after Malodi's death, she told me she had decided that Auntie should accompany us to my grandmother's grave. She needed to be cleansed.

❖ ❖ ❖

The house was like I had expected; buried with climbers and filled with the stench of death.

Death!

Yes, that was what I instantly felt. I looked around while Auntie and Mama cleared the grass from the graves in readiness for the cleansing ceremony. I was in the corridor, opposite what had once been the children's room, when I heard the groan. At first I thought it was my mother. But outside, I could hear Mama chanting: "Turn away your face from my sins, strengthen me..." Then I heard the groan a second time, clear but very feeble. It was coming from our room. One thought crossed my mind: there was a ghost in there.

But it was no ghost. It was the ragged figure of my sister, who must have been brought here, lethally sick and abandoned, by a lover who hadn't the courage to confront our family. There were moldy pieces of bread around the urine-soaked clothes on which she lay – probably her only food during whatever number of days she had been here, and bus tickets to and from several towns along the coast. She must have had some serious trauma during those three months to render her now unable to walk or talk.

The next day we packed back to my father's house – our real home – to nurse our sorrows.

Two days after our return, Mama and I were sitting on the bed beside Muto. I saw my mother wrestle in futility with the sobbing lump in her throat as she watched her source of pride now looking like a masquerade with sunken eyes on a fleshless skull.

I saw Muto's lips twitch in an effort to speak.

Mama held her hand. Somehow she imagined what Muto might have wanted to say. The tears now ran freely down our cheeks.

"There is nothing to forgive, Shushu," Mama said hoarsely, calling Muto by the pet name Papa used in those days when he came back home in the evening happily tipsy and wanted Muto to serve his food. To our father, Muto was Shushu and I was Coucou.

As though reliving those times too, I heard Muto call me Coucou. She held the tips of my fingers with her cold and shivering hand and attempted a feeble squeeze.

"Do you think we shall be happy again, sitting beside the fire and roasting maize and plums while it rains outside?" she whispered faintly.

I wouldn't cry, I told myself, even though my heart was on the verge of splitting in half with grief. I had to be strong in order to give her some of the strength she needed most.

"You are not dead, Shushu," I said. "Yes, you will be fine again. Mama and I shall take you to the hospital tomorrow."

"I know I don't have money," Mama chipped in, still holding Muto's other hand. "But your sister and I will take care of you. Auntie promised to pay the bills. You will be your beautiful self again and we shall start a small farm behind the house."

"And in the evening," I added, "we shall go visiting Auntie and help her tie *miondo* and crack *egusi*."

It was like we were living a common dream.

Muto sighed, fastened her grip on my fingers and looked out of the open window.

"Mama," she whispered, and raised her hand to point. "Can you see the stars dimming and the moon hiding behind a thick blanket of clouds?" she asked, with a distant look on her face.

"Yes, Shushu," Mama replied. "We have wandered away from each other for too long. The elements are this night burying our long years of unhappiness – the wasted honor of our womanhood. But in a short while, the stars will shine out again and the moon will turn her face towards our home to restore what we have lost – the joy of children in their loving mother's bosom."

Far away an owl hooted what my mind registered as a confirmation of Mama's pronouncement.

Dipita Kwa is a writer from Cameroon. His works of fiction have appeared in online magazines and his first book, *Times and Seasons,* was published by Cook Communication in February 2008.

VANESSA GEBBIE WALES

THE KETTLE ON THE BOAT

IT IS MORNING. Papa is loading some bags onto our little boat. I ask him where we are going. He says we are going to the other side of the lake.

"Why are we going to the other side of the lake, Papa?" I ask again. Papa doesn't answer me.

"Why are we going, Papa?"

"Little girls ask too many questions," he says.

Mama is taking down the curtains. There are two cracks in the window. I ask again.

"Mama? Why are we going to the other side of the lake?" Mama hides her face in the curtains.

Something inside me knows something.

❖ ❖ ❖

I am Qissúnguaq. It is an Inuit name. It means 'little piece of wood'. I am six years old. I live with my Papa, my Mama and my baby sister. On one side of our house is the sea, on the other side is the lake. This lake is so big I cannot see across. In winter the water in the lake freezes as thick as thick. Then the sea freezes. Some men cut blocks of ice and make icehouses.

Once, they cut a block with a fish inside it. The fish looked at me with big eyes. Its mouth was open.

Papa traps animals, shoots them and skins them. In winter the snow is red with blood. In summer he goes out in his boat and catches fish. He guts the fish black red and the birds scream. He hangs the empty fish on wooden gallows in front of our house. They hang there for two weeks. I like to go and visit them, watch their eyes shrivel up, dry and fall out. I keep the birds away.

When the eyes fall out the fish are ready. Mama cuts them down, dries them and packs them in salt, so we have fish to eat when the ice comes back. For a long time there have not been enough fish.

Once, Papa went out to help catch pilot whales. The whales were smooth, shiny and black. They made the water boil with froth. Papa trapped the whales and the water in the bay was as red as the snow. I remember it. There are no whales in the bay now.

Sometimes Papa shoots big geese with his gun. I pull off their feathers and the down flies round the kitchen and tickles my nose, then Mama cooks some meat, dries some on the gallows. The geese have not arrived this year. Papa waited and waited. He had his gun ready behind the door. Now it is too late. They will not come now.

Sometimes there is not enough soup to fill the pan on the stove.

❖ ❖ ❖

I am on our small boat with Papa, Mama and my baby sister. They don't often take little girls out in boats. It is cold, I am bundled up. My cheeks are frozen. The motor is going put-put-put.

There is a kettle on the boat. It is our kettle from home, the one that goes "hushhhh" when it boils. It is balanced on a cardboard box. I wonder if it has water in. Mama is rubbing her fur boot softly up and down the kettle.

I am glad it is on our boat. That kettle is magic. It fills the room with a big cloud, a warm cloud, and the window gets covered in giant's breath. Mama wipes the glass with her fingers and shows me how to make shapes. When Papa comes back from emptying his traps, the cloud escapes and goes outside. It looks like fingers in the air. They mix with his breath then disappear.

Papa is sitting beside me, one hand on the tiller, the other holding my sleeve very tight. I will not fall in, there are not many waves. It is hard to see my Mama's face because she has a hood up. She is opposite me, turned sideways so she is facing Papa, not facing me. She has the kettle near her legs, and my baby sister is on her back in a caribou papoose. I can just see my sister's head. Her eyes are black beads. Black holes in a hood.

It is a long time since I've been out in the boat. It lives in a tin shed next to our house; even in the summer it lives in the tin shed. Papa pulls it up on wooden poles on the ground for it to roll better. I help him rub the weed off it. The weed is green, and the boat is red.

We are going somewhere. It is a special day. This should be fun, but it does not feel like fun in my belly. I want to ask Mama now where we are going. But Papa is cross, so I don't. Mama is busy with my sister, busy keeping the bags and boxes straight against the rocking of the boat. The curtains are in a bag.

The boat rocks on the lake and I hold on. Papa's hand is tight on my sleeve. He lights a cigarette, a dry old cigarette from a tin under the table. Because it is cold, I can make smoke in the air too, and I blow a white cloud when Papa does. I hope it will make him smile. I have not seen him with a cigarette before. Not in his own mouth. I saw a cigarette when they gave one to the man from over the lake.

We do not have much to give to visitors. We do not often have visitors. We are just me, my Papa, Mama and my sister, some fish in salt and some meat. That's all there is.

The kettle boiled for the visitors. The man and woman from over the lake. The man with the cigarette and the woman with a shawl tied under her chin and no smile. She held my arm and felt it. She said I was strong. When the kettle boiled I could not see them for the cloud.

Mama has a big belly under her coat. She says it is a stone in her belly. When she says that I laugh.

I see something. I look up and see a big bird in the sky. I pull Papa. I say, "Look Papa! It is a goose!"

It is. It *is* a goose, a big fat goose and it flies round so close I can hear wings pushing the air away. It lands on the lake a little way away from the boat. Mama looks at Papa. He looks at the goose.

I say, "Papa? Shall I get the gun and you can shoot the goose for us?" but Papa does not answer. He is watching the sky, and he is sitting up straight. In a while he sits back, and says, "There is only one goose."

I am sleepy with the rocking of the boat. I rest against Papa and doze. When I wake up, my Mama has the kettle on her lap. I know there is no water in it then. The stone in her belly is pushing the kettle off her knee, but she is holding it there with a mitten. She is holding it to her with one hand on its handle, the other stroking it round.

Now I can see the shore a long way away, and I can see three houses, they are wood. There are no people.

I look at the shore because Mama is looking at the shore. Then I look back at Mama. She is holding her kettle on her knee, holding it tight with her mittens. She has hunched over it. My sister on her back is wriggling, and Mama shrugs her shoulder to move my sister so she is not bent in the papoose. My Mama is holding the kettle like it might break, holding it gently but steady. She is holding it, hunched over, and her lips are moving.

I cannot hear what she is saying. My ears lean forward to listen but all I hear is the slap slap of the lake against the boat, the put-put of the engine, and the whistle of my Papa's breathing.

Something inside me knows something again.

"Mama? Is the kettle to go away?"

Mama does not answer me. She looks up, a fast look. Even though I am small I can feel this… it is a special day, the kettle has to go away. Mama is sad.

I look back at the shore. I look at the shore and the houses, no bigger than my little fingernail when I hold up my hands and squint through my fingers at the sun. So I do that. I cover my face with my hands and look at the houses through my fingers. They move around, they are brown birds that will fly up into the gray sky, wheel about and scream.

As the houses get bigger, they rock up and down like they are boats. There are two people there now. I do not think for me at that moment. I think for Mama.

The boat comes to the jetty, Papa throws a rope to the man. It is the man from across the lake.

We go up the ladder. Papa and I, we go up the ladder. There is weed on the lower steps. It slips my feet and he holds my hand. He has a bag round his shoulders. At the top I look back into the boat. I wait for Mama, but she does not come. She is not looking at me. She is holding the kettle, looking back over the water.

There is the woman from across the lake. I look up at Papa. I cannot see him properly even though he is close and I can smell his Papa smell. He gives my hand to the woman. I have mittens on, but her hand is hard, cold. Papa gives the bag to the man.

I say, "Papa…?"

"These people will look after you," he says.

I stand and let the woman hold my hand. I watch my Papa going back down the ladder.

Then I see a shape in the sky! Behind Papa there is another goose in the sky and I shout to him.

But it is not a goose. It is only another brown bird.

I think I shout, "Mama?" Then I know I didn't because no noise came out. I only shouted in my head. Mama heard it though.

Papa is starting the motor, pulling on the string, one, two, three. Our little boat is naughty. It only ever starts after five pulls on the string.

Mama nearly stands up. She holds onto the side of the boat and she has the kettle in her other hand. My baby sister and the stone in Mama's belly are so heavy. They bend her over and I think she will break, I can see her trying to stand up straight. And I hear the motor start to go put-put.

My head says "Mama?" again, and the boat moves away from the jetty. Mama holds on and lifts her head up. I think she is looking at me but I can't see properly. There is too much water.

Then Mama swings her arm and throws the kettle into the lake. Papa catches hold of her and she sits down again. The boat rocks a little.

The kettle bobs on the lake like a round gray bird with a big long beak. It rocks on the water when the boat begins to go away. I don't watch the boat. I watch the kettle rocking on the waves. The kettle-boat-bird. It is coming closer to me, slowly, and I think if I can hold tight to the ladder and go back down, maybe I can get it.

I hold the woman's hand and wish hard for the kettle to come to me. I wish that the man will help me on the ladder and not let my feet slip on the weed. I wish that I can go somewhere where the kettle will send giant's breath round my head so no one can see me.

But my wishes are heavy wishes. They fill the kettle-boat-bird up too much and it tips forward and drinks the lake through its beak. It sinks.

I watch where the kettle has gone. There is a mark on the water and the brown birds are screaming. I look up and follow the boat. It is very small. It is not going the way we have come, it is going a different way. When I look back to the mark, it has gone. When I look back to the boat, it has gone too.

The brown birds here have big beaks. They are screaming over the water. I know, if Papa makes another gallows, and if they hang fish to dry, these brown birds might steal the fish's eyes.

If I am not there to help, how will Mama know when the fish are ready?

Vanessa Gebbie is from Wales. She is a writer, editor and creative writing tutor. Her work has been widely published and has won many awards (Bridport, Fish International, Per Contra and The Daily Telegraph among others). Her debut collection *Words from a Glass Bubble* (Salt Publishing 2008) was nominated for the Frank O'Connor Prize. A second collection is forthcoming in 2009.

SEQUOIA NAGAMATSU UNITED STATES

MELANCHOLY NIGHTS IN A TOKYO CYBER CAFÉ

IN THE EVENING, Akira walks down the busy streets of Tokyo's Ueno district to the neon-lit back-alley markets of Ameyokocho and browses the myriad souvenirs and discounted leather jackets. Around nine, nine-thirty, the crowds begin to disperse, which in Japan doesn't really look like dispersing at all but more of a reshuffling of people: tourists consult dog-eared guide books for their next destination while vendors close up shop, locking their stalls or booths and putting merchandise into the backs of vans or on carts attached to their bicycles. There are certain vendors who Akira suspects are homeless like he is, the ones who stay later because they have nowhere to go. Sometimes he catches himself wanting to talk to them, share stories, but he knows that such things are unlikely to happen. They want to hold on to the moments where people acknowledge their existence just as much as Akira wants to pretend to be just another young, hip Japanese man going shopping like everyone else.

Most nights begin like this for Akira, who is a 29-year-old *furita* or young, working homeless person. Before he was reduced to two duffle bags that he carries with him everywhere, before he constantly counted the yen in his pockets – which all have holes that need to be taped or stitched shut – Akira was an office worker at a small printing company that eventually went out of business. His father had died in a gas factory accident years ago and, not wanting to burden or worry his already ailing mother, he has never told her the truth about his life.

The weekdays are always much the same, filled with odd jobs cleaning parks and sweeping floors. But Saturday and Sunday nights are different because

Yoshiko, a particular street vendor, a woman that Akira knows quite intimately but has never spoken to in person, shows up to sell Japanese calligraphy prints and silk-screened t-shirts.

Akira begins his weekend nights at Takahashi's Internet Point, a cyber café complete with personal cubicles, shower facilities and a small kitchenette, which he has called home for the past several months. Reservations are typically not allowed at the café but the owner, Mr Kenji Takahashi, has taken sympathy on Akira. He says that Akira reminds him of himself when he was that age.

After showering and eating rice balls with tuna fish stuffed inside, a meal that Akira has grown accustomed to eating with great regularity, he makes his way to the Ameyokocho Street Market, a bustling maze of alleyways filled with the smell of fresh fish, exotic fruits and knock-off Louis Vuitton handbags. He always takes the same route, past the cherry trees lining the marsh-like banks of Shinobazu Pond in Ueno Park, through the crowds of the bullet train station and to Asakusa Street, where the same African hip-hop dancers practice their moves every day for passers-by and Americans with tip money.

Akira always easily spots the woman at the calligraphy stall. He buys a small toy or pen from a neighboring vendor after pretending to browse so he has an excuse to loiter. She is beautiful, he thinks, but tired and worn, with strands of gray hair circling the two buns she wears her hair in. She never seems to stop working, always rearranging items and rearranging them back to the way they were and never failing to welcome prospective customers with a gentle, "Irrashaimase!" It always seems she's in deep thought, thinking about something troubling that makes her eyes seem to wince and tear even from afar where Akria watches over her.

Several months ago, during one of his moments of inconsolable melancholy, Akira came across an article in the *Mainichi News* about a group of people that found life too unbearable and had met on a website designed to bring people together who did not want to end their life alone. The group was found hanging from trees by hikers in the Aokigahara Jukai forest near Mt Fuji.

Immediately, Akira became obsessed with the idea. He imagined himself in the forest, looking up at the shadows of bodies that seemed to descend like reaching fingertips, calling him to join them. He read the article over and over again and found a similar website. He read postings with headings like "I have the pills", "Let's do it tonight" and "There is no other way out". Akira could not help but feel a strange energy coming over him as he read about people who had experienced the same things he had or worse and wanted to end their suffering or shame. He entered chatrooms and began talking to people, telling strangers how it felt to be forgotten, how it seemed that no one cared. And then, almost evading Akira's attention, a private chat window popped up on the corner of the screen.

"Onaji Kama no Meshi o Kutta." Akira repeated the words in his mind: "We have eaten from the same rice pot." Her name was Yoshiko and already, before Akira could respond, he could see the ellipses in the chat window telling him that she was writing more. He cracked his knuckles and dragged the chat window to the center of the screen and began to type.

Akira established a routine with Yoshiko from the beginning, chatting every night after she returned home and tucked in her daughter. Akira explained that he used to see this time of his life as a *koshikake*, a stepping stone to something better, but that every day had gotten harder and harder until he felt that any effort to improve his circumstances would be futile.

"I want to work," Akira typed. "I am not lazy. I hate how people think that because you don't have a home you're lazy. I need to work so I can find a home but then they tell you that you need a home to get work. What kind of system is that?"

"*Ashimoto o miru*, they are exploiting your weakness," Yoshiko responded. "People like to forget about the sadness of the city. People choose to be blind to it. It makes their hearts cold."

Yoshiko tells Akira about her situation, that she is always alone because her husband is a slave to a company who has stationed him on the other side of the country. She has to manage alone with their daughter, who suffers from autism, while also selling calligraphy prints to make extra money for food. She knows no one in the city, having grown up far away in Nagasaki, and doesn't have the luxury of making friends. Although the details of their situations are different, Akira finds comfort in Yoshiko and can understand why she said they came from the same place when she first contacted him.

He can see the ellipses in the chat window appearing and disappearing, telling him the exact moments when Yoshiko is stopping to think. These anxious silences are what Akira looks forward to most when he talks to Yoshiko. They make him feel as if they are together, as if the ellipses appearing and disappearing are like the movements of her chest when she breathes.

Many times the idea of meeting in person comes up but Akira always backs away. It didn't take long for him to figure out where Yoshiko worked in the city based on their chats but a part of him is still ashamed that he is homeless. For now, he is content with what the two of them have – a little support and understanding when they both need it and nothing more.

Meanwhile, tiny trinkets and an assortment of pens build up on the computer desk in Akira's cubicle at the cyber café. They are lined up and arranged neatly, each one a reminder of another day that Akira could not walk a few feet further and cease being invisible.

"I feel as if I'm on a sled on a very big hill in winter but with no one to push me," he tells Mr Takahashi one evening. "I'm not so sure that I even have the sled any more."

Mr Takahashi nods and places his hand on Akira's shoulder, not really knowing what to say except for what he always says: "Things will get better if you believe it. Good fortune comes to those with patience and good hearts."

Akira thinks about his father's death, his mother who is now alone and why, if good fortune comes to those with good hearts, he ended up in his current situation at all. "Life is a kind of tortuous progress," Mr Takahashi always says. "Good things will come but sometimes suffering is needed to realize it." Akira is not so sure.

Leaving Ameyokocho, Akira makes his way back to the cyber café. Most days, he walks quickly and without pause, weaving between the crowds on the sidewalk like a jockey. But on this night something catches his attention.

On a bulletin board on the wall of one of the train station bridges, he notices a simple flyer partially hidden by the clutter around it: "Printing Press Operator Needed for Part-Time Project – Payment to be discussed." There is no email, no phone number, only an address and a handwritten map instructing interested parties to go there during daytime hours and to dress all in white. Akira tears the flyer from the bulletin board, folds it neatly and sticks it into his back pocket.

The paper gently grazing him with each step through the thin fabric of his pants, Akira imagines what the earnings might be, how he might be able to manage to save enough to move out of the cyber café and most of all how he would meet Yoshiko in person for the first time, perhaps treating her and her daughter to a trip to the Ueno Zoo, snow cones in hand as they walked pass exhibits, buying them anything that their hearts desired at the gift shop at the end of the day. He smiles and bites his lip to stop himself from grinning on city streets for no apparent reason. After all, the flyer could have been up there for months, the position filled long ago. But unable to stop thinking about the possibilities, Akira takes out the flyer from his back pocket and begins following the map. Soon, he finds himself standing in front of a dilapidated five-story building on a small sidestreet, doing something he has not done since childhood – hoping for and dreaming about the seemingly impossible.

The next morning, in the same spot he had occupied the night before, Akira gazes at the building, now a little less sure about the prospect given the broken windows and graffiti he had failed to see in the darkness. He is dressed all in white as instructed in the flyer and holds a crumpled copy of his CV in his hands. He thinks about Yoshiko, who did not sign on last night. Akira knows that at these times, she can barely get out of bed to the computer, that she sometimes locks herself in her room as her ten-year-old daughter screams all night, not capable of telling her mother what she wants or fears. He knows the details of these things because Yoshiko has told him, but Akira already understands that she is drowning. He felt the same way when his father died and the night he met Yoshiko online, when the thought of death seemed to be the only source of possible relief.

There are no lights on inside the building, which is entirely made of wood and seems reminiscent of days long past, overshadowed by the skyscrapers just down the street. Akira walks to the front door and pushes the buzzer.

After standing outside for several minutes, Akira is about to leave when he hears somebody fiddling with several locks. An elderly man pops his head out and stares at Akira suspiciously, or perhaps in fear, and utters not a sound except for the guttural noises when he clears his throat. The silence grows awkward and Akira is beginning to think that maybe he is at the wrong building but then suddenly the old man opens the door and makes a gesture for Akira to enter. The old man is slight, the top of his balding head barely reaching Akira's shoulders. He introduces himself as Seiji Kobayashi and quickly turns away, leading Akira down a dusty hallway lined with trash and pieces of wood propped up against the walls. Nearly everything is painted white. There is a strange feeling inside, that whatever world Akira has come from, he will be leaving soon as they travel deeper into the building, down into the basement.

Akira cannot see anything as he takes his last step off the stairs and it isn't until Seiji pulls on the cord of a single light-bulb dangling in the middle of the room that he is able to explore what he has walked into: a nearly empty room painted all in white and occupied only by a cast-iron printing press that must be at least one hundred years old, sitting at the center of the room. Akira tries to hide his surprise, though his eyes betray him whenever he gazes upon the antique before him. Seiji walks toward the printing press, picks up a letter on a page-setting tray and begins to tap it against a metal corner of the press, a heavy clinking sound pervading the room like old pipes creaking in winter.

"I understand that this is not what you were expecting," Seiji says, staring off into space, looking a little like he is having a conversation with God, in his white robe.

Akira takes a step back. "Well, to be honest, no."

"Have you worked on printing presses like these before?"

"Well..." Akira begins to recall a childhood memory: making New Year cards with his mother using rubber stamps. "Some similar experience, a long time ago."

Seiji's gaze shifts to Akira, his eyes glazed from the light above him. "What are your thoughts on electromagnetic pollution?" he asks quite seriously.

Akira stares at him. His lips part but nothing except his breath comes out.

"The fact is," Seiji goes on, "Aum Shinrikyu and other doomsday groups, as you might call them, got it wrong. The sarin gas attacks in '95 were a tragedy. But that doesn't mean the purpose of these groups was wrong. Panawave made its share of mistakes as well. Our leader said the world as we know it would end years ago but it didn't. But that doesn't mean that it won't."

Seiji stops.

Akira watches him place a page-setter on a metal plate on the press. He seems to use all of his available strength to pull down on a lever while his left foot pumps on a large paddle on the ground. A part of Akira feels intimidated and frightened by Seiji, who continues to work at the press. He begins talking about the natural order of the planet, how the electromagnetic waves of modern technology and communication have upset this balance and will be our undoing. He says that he wants to save people. He takes a stack of papers from the press and hands them to Akira.

"Now you see how it's done. You might as well distribute these around the city after you leave."

Akira looks down at what appears to be a newsletter. *"Fuku sui bon ni kaerazu"* – "Spilled water does not return to the tray" – the headline reads. Seiji hands him a set of keys and tells him that he may work when he wishes and that he can only afford to spare 3,000 yen a week but will allow him to sleep in the building if it is needed. "After all," he goes on, "there is nothing to steal unless you plan on strapping the printing press to your back." Akira leads the way back upstairs, suddenly halting in front of a picture hanging on the wall that he did not notice coming in. "My wife and daughter," Seiji explains, staring deeply into the photo, "taken two weeks before the sarin attack on the Metro. My daughter survived but she has – forgotten me since that day."

That night, after Akira has spent the day passing out newsletters, placing copies in news-stands and on bulletin boards, he anxiously awaits for Yoshiko to sign on, so he can tell her about his day. He is not sure when or how he fell in love with her – their relationship was distant in so many ways, yet at the same time more intimate than what many couples feel for each other. Akira forces himself to forget that it was the thought of ending it all – and not just the painful moments but the beautiful ones as well – that brought them together in the first place. He wonders what proportion of happy moments to sad ones are necessary for a person to sincerely want to keep living and hopes that he and Yoshiko can both get there together.

Akira takes out a copy of the Panawave newsletter that he has kept for himself to pass the time. He is surprised to find himself agreeing with much of what he reads. Perhaps not the end of the world parts or the mysterious tenth planet that would supposedly cause the magnetic poles to shift, resulting in global catastrophe, but the underlying spirit of it all. He sees the responsibility we must take for the planet, our home, ensuring a future for the next generation, how we must care for those animals that we have led astray with our sonar and electro-magnetic waves – like the whales and dolphins that beach themselves, slowly dying under the watchful eyes of curious and concerned bystanders. Akira empathizes with the pain that Seiji must carry with him and begins to realize that when he said that he wanted to save people, he really meant his daughter. "It is the only way I can protect her. It is the only way I can still be her father," Seiji had said earlier that day, barely above a whisper.

A melodic chime rings, letting Akira know that Yoshiko is now online. He pulls up his chair close to the keyboard and begins to type, asking how she is, about her daughter. Akira anxiously waits for her to respond so he can type more and tell her the good news about the new job, the possibility of being able to move out of the cyber café in six months, and how he wants to take her and her daughter to the zoo one day. But there is no response. For a brief moment, Akira sees the ellipses on the screen, telling him that she is typing something, but they soon disappear without a word sent. He begins to type, "You can talk to me..." but the sound of a door creaking shut, followed by the disappearance of Yoshiko's name, tells Akira that she is no longer online.

Back at the printing press the next day, Akira works furiously, shifting gears only to bundle stacks of newsletters with pieces of twine. The faster he works, the sooner the time will pass until he can return to his cubicle at the cyber café to check on Yoshiko. Seiji has given him new pages to print. He has told Akira that, compared to other things he will print for him, these pages will be among the most important. Instead of something far-reaching like global warming, planetary destruction or the altered migration patterns of marine life, these pages deal with something on a much smaller scale – family and community.

"People have forgotten how to care for each other, for themselves. We can't expect them to care about the world if they don't care about what's in front of them every day," Seiji said to Akira when he handed him the new plates. Throughout the day, Seiji leaves Akira for extended amounts of time, coming back to check on his progress and to talk, both of them revealing a little more about themselves through awkward silences and opinions.

"People don't understand us," Seiji says, staring at the picture of his family, hanging on the barren wall. "Most people don't want to understand. My daughter says that I killed her mother. She says she has no father."

Akira is unsure of what to say and continues working, nodding to let Seiji know he is still listening.

"Where were you during the sarin attacks?" Seiji asks.

"I was at home with my family. We saw it on the news."

"I was at a toy store buying a present for my daughter. When I left to go to the Metro, the entrance was blocked. I didn't know why." Seiji places a hand over Akira's, stopping him from working for a moment. "We all share the blame for Aum Shinrikyo's crimes. It's easy to be lost in fear and sadness. It brings people together but often for the wrong reasons. It blinds them."

Akira nods and looks into Seiji's worn eyes, seeing an emptiness that is all too familiar. "I know," he says.

When it is time for Akira to leave, he finds he is no longer afraid of Seiji or the building, and takes with him a few words that Seiji says before he leaves. "We're all far more alike than we'd like to believe and it is this that we must strive to remember."

The next few days are much the same for Akira, working at odd jobs in between time with Seiji at the printing press and racing back to the cyber café at night to check if Yoshiko is waiting to talk to him. He does not allow himself to sleep, for he might miss her if she signs on. It is only during the early-morning hours when his body allows itself to rest. In this time, he imagines Yoshiko's tiny silhouette lying in bed beside her daughter, the movement of their shadows quick and uneven as if they were both crying, gradually slowing down until their forms are quiet and motionless.

When the next weekend arrives, Akira goes to the Ameyokocho market as he always does to be with Yoshiko. But his steps are slow now, heavy – not like the urbanites around him, impervious and indifferent to the world. He walks with a new-found awareness of the faces that he passes, the stories behind each of them and as he does, he imagines Yoshiko at the market, rearranging her calligraphy prints and t-shirts. He can almost see her waving to him, letting him know that she's all right and that she knows who he is at the same time. But as Akira approaches the entrance to the street market, he can already see that Yoshiko isn't there.

Akira doesn't have to keep walking but he continues anyway and buys a small toy from a neighboring vendor. He gazes over at the empty spot where he can almost see Yoshiko smiling back at him. He walks toward the place where he imagines her and just stands there for a moment, closing his eyes and then leaves.

At the cyber café, Mr Takahashi is reading a newspaper at one of the bistro tables, sipping on some tea. He greets Akira and asks him to join him and share the dinner that his wife has made. Akira wants to go back to his cubicle but he is hungry and this meal would mean another few hundred yen saved. He sits as Mr Takahashi sets the table, bringing back bowls of rice and a plastic container full of salmon and eel slices.

"*O-genki desuka*? Are you okay?" Mr Takahashi asks as he sits down, with concern in his furrowed eyebrows.

Akira nods, cracking a half-smile.

"You look sad, like you've been crying."

"I'm fine, really. It's just the cold weather today." Mr Takahashi nods, knowing that it is more, but decides to leave Akira alone. He hands Akira a piece of the newspaper and the two of them eat silently and without pause.

Akira thanks Mr Takahashi for the meal and retires to his cubicle. On the computer screen, he can see that somebody has left a message for him – Yoshiko. "*Ishin Denshin* – There is a silent understanding between us," the message reads. Akira repeats the words out loud, imagining Yoshiko's voice behind them. He does not sleep all night and only leaves the cubicle when going to the bathroom becomes an emergency.

In the early morning, Akira realizes, more out of exhaustion than logic, that he needs to stop and goes out into the lobby for the paper and a cup of coffee. And there, on the front page, he sees their faces – Yoshiko and her daughter, gazing back at him. Akira closes his eyes, convincing himself that he is seeing things but their faces remain whenever he opens them. There is a strange, burning sensation spreading throughout Akira's body and it seems as if nothing can extinguish it.

He returns to his cubicle and checks the news online, hoping that if there is no mention of it there, it could be a mistake. But as Akira scrolls down the page, he comes to a photograph of two body bags being rolled out of an apartment building – one smaller than the other. Akira stares at the photo; his eyelids, unable to close, begin to burn and tear. He touches the screen and holds his arm like that until it becomes weak and uncomfortable and he can hold it no longer.

In the months following the death of Yoshiko and her daughter, Seiji confesses to Akira his abandoned plans to take his own life, journals strewn with grief over his wife, the guilt that he felt and that his lost daughter had projected on to him.

"When I walk in the crowded streets in this city, the isolation pulls at me like strings unraveling my heart. It saddens me that only tragedy can bring these people together. The bonds, no matter how blind, are erased so easily like chalk on a blackboard, leaving only a trace of what was once there. I cannot bear this."

Akira keeps the photos of Yoshiko and her daughter from the newspaper close to him always. He might have wallowed in his sadness, in some unfounded guilt, but he does not. Instead, Akira continues to walk to Ameyokocho as he always did when Yoshiko was in his life. He walks past the cherry trees, through the train station and down to Asakusa Street where the same African hip-hop dancers practice their moves. He looks upon the faces of the people around him, vastly different in their own ways, but each having a story not unlike the other, connecting them together in our most human and fragile moments.

Sequoia Nagamatsu is an American – originally from San Francisco and educated in Iowa. He currently lives in Niigata City, Japan, where he teaches English and is working on a story collection and novel. His plays have been performed in San Francisco and his stories recently appeared in *Elimae* and *Underground Voices*.

JUDE DIBIA NIGERIA

AMONG STRANGERS

"SHAME ON YOU!"

That was what she said, spitting on the dry ground at the same time. I only found out the meaning of her words days later, after I had forced my cousin to translate it for me. This was after I had had trouble sleeping because I could not erase the bitter look in her eyes from my mind or the sad pitying look that followed it.

"Shame on you!" She said so in Igbo.

They say that language unites a people. That was the common saying. That was why wherever you may find yourself in the world, no matter how remote the place is, when you find someone who speaks your tongue, you are immediately brothers or sisters. You are one because your language unites you. My language instead alienates me from my people. It has made me an outcast, a stranger to my kinsmen. It was long coming and somehow I knew.

I remember when I was about five or six years old, Mother was sitting on the veranda with two of her sisters and they were laughing, with tears streaming from their eyes as they enjoyed their girly gossip. They were as animated with their gestures as they always were when they spoke in their language – Igala. I was always fascinated by their gatherings because I was acutely aware that I was an only child and also because they were so different from me. I was a male child. I wore my short knickers and singlet most of the time and was forever enthralled by Mother's flowing skirts and traditional blouses and the wrappers – *lapas* – which she wore sometimes. Many times I would stick my small head under her skirt to stare up at the darkness. I remember being shocked once when I had crawled under her legs just after she had taken a shower and to my horror when I looked up I saw she had only a tuft of hair there and no penis like I did. I remember that also because she had screamed loudly, dragged me from beneath her and slapped me silly until I cried for hours. But this particular day when I was about five or six, I remembered picking out some words of what Mother and her sisters had been saying and practicing them over and over again that afternoon. The next time they were gathered together in their small *laughing-weeping* group I surprised them all when I suddenly announced shyly:

"Oma Onekele..."

A grave silence followed after that. Three pairs of eyes stared hard at me. Three mouths dropped open in surprise almost all at once. Three pairs of eyes all looked back at one another and suddenly burst out laughing again with inevitable tears of joy in their eyes.

"What did you say?" Mother asked.

I looked around me in discomfort. They were all staring at me with muted interest and awe. I suddenly felt so small and insignificant in their presence. Three pairs of eyes gawked at me. Six arms folded in interest and my stomach sank in fear.

"Oma Onekele," I said again bravely.

"What does that mean?" Aunty Mercy asked deliberately.

Again I felt three pairs of eyes staring hard at me.

"It means *boy*!" I answered cautiously.

Three mouths dropped open in surprise almost all at once. Their eyes met each other and suddenly burst out laughing again.

"You mean you understand all we talk about?" Mother asked shrewdly.

I nodded even though I only understood a little of what they said, but I was too intimidated to say so.

"Oma Onekele," Aunty Gold cooed. *"Don't tell your father o!"*

Their eyes held me in burning incarceration almost as if daring me to refuse. I acquiesced and they looked away to continue with what they were discussing. This time they switched to Hausa and I was forgotten.

I remembered that day so well because of what Aunty Gold said. Don't tell your father o! You see, my father was an Igbo man married to an Igala woman. My father spoke only English when he was at home with us because he believed strongly that his child should be well educated and must learn to speak English the Queen's way. No vernacular was permitted at home whatsoever. I have heard him speak Igbo many times with his friends, relations and even with Mother. My mother, even though Igala, was brought up in Kano with her sisters and thus could speak Hausa and over the years she had learnt how to speak Igbo and Yoruba to boot. She was a well-rounded Nigerian in my mind. But still I was never allowed to speak vernacular at home. I always wondered whether this rule was an attempt by my father to ensure that I did not take up my mother's tongue instead of his. Why else would Aunty Gold make me promise not to let my father know some time that I understood what they said?

I guess a part of me had always been curious about how my father came to marry my mother, a non-Igbo. From what I knew of my father then, he was a very proud man, some say a unique trait of the Igbo, but I believe each tribe has its own sense of self-importance. My father had been a young, handsome and very driven man in his days, so Mother told me when I was still quite little and her eyes still shone lovingly when she spoke of him. A lot of people who knew him then at the University College of Ibadan described him as the most promising young economist major in the Social Science Faculty. He was bright and he was proud and he believed he was better than the whites. He mastered the English language and even dazzled his lecturers with the scope of his vocabulary. His friends mocked him jokingly, referring to him as, "*Onye Ocha, Nna di Oji*" (White man, whose father is black).

Mother met Father in those days. They fell in love and language united them. Inter-tribal unions were very rare then, Mother used to say, but she had found a good man and language was not going to keep them apart. Those days, she spoke Igbo like an *Ada Obi* – an Igbo chief's first daughter. Not many men could resist her charms then, she often boasted, not the least Father.

Years later, when I was a little older and Father had taken to coming home very late and very drunk, I shed many silent tears when I watched my mother worry about this '*Ononojo*' – Stranger – whom we no longer recognized. She still had group sessions with her sisters, but this time there was no laughter present in their gatherings, instead many, many tears. I cried silently too. Because, by this time, I no longer understood her language nor did I understand the language of my father. I didn't know then, but I was lost.

Not long after Father changed, after Mother and her sisters called him *Ononojo* and after I had shed many silent tears, Grandma Nne came to live with us for a short while. She was very old and was suffering from a liver problem and, as Father was her eldest son, it was decided that she would move in with us. Old she may have been, but she still had her wits about her. And that old hatred for my mother, who was never her choice and who sacrilegiously was not Igbo.

Grandma Nne spoke only Igbo and all of a sudden my home was filled with the strange language. I was still not permitted to speak vernacular or broken English at home, yet I had to think up a way to communicate with Grandma Nne, who regarded me with the same evil eye she cast on my mother most times.

No one could really accuse me of lack of trying to speak the languages of my parents. I tried. I tried every night before I fell asleep and in the morning when I woke up, but the words and meanings eluded me. Sometimes I would feel the words coming to me, baiting me ever so seductively, but as soon as I opened my mouth to say something the words withdrew themselves back to their secret place in the corner of my mind – not quite hidden, just barely there, enough to tease and taunt me. Enough to make me give up trying eventually.

It was a harrowing experience the first time I witnessed my parents fighting. It rained that night. I remember it so clearly, because I was frightened by the claps of thunder outside and the cruel darkness the house was thrown into after the lights tripped off. I got out of bed and made my way toward my parents' room. I stopped by their door. It was opened slightly enough for me to make out Mother standing with her hands on her hips, tears in her eyes as she shouted at Father. Father glared back at her and warned her to shut up. They both were speaking in English. I understood every word they exchanged; every abuse they hurled at each other. I watched Father hit Mother and the force of his blow pushed her face the other way and, as Mother crouched in pain, her eyes caught mine. I stood frozen to the spot. I watched Mother approach me. When she got to the door, I thought she would reach out to me for comfort but instead she slammed the door shut in my face. Shutting me out.

Grandma Nne's moving in was the straw that finally broke the camel's back. Her fights with my mother were legendary. They ranged from the mundane to the totally bizarre. You see, there was that episode when she explicitly told Mother that she could not eat meat due to her weak teeth and that Mother should not bother putting any in her meals; as soon as Mother carried out her instructions, she ran crying to Father with her meatless meal, complaining to him that his wife wanted to starve her in her son's house. Mundane! There was also that time she accused my mother of being a witch who was sucking her blood at night. Bizarre! Yes, their fights were legendary but Grandma Nne's coming played its part in destroying our family. As Father's excesses grew, she encouraged him night after night. On the night Mother packed her bags and left with me in tow, she had overheard them talking of Father's other wife in the village, Father's true Igbo wife. He had another family that we knew nothing about. It seemed nothing then could save this family.

Mother had confronted them, but I knew nothing of what they all said. Grandma spoke rapidly in Igbo and so did Father. And Mother, in her tears, responded in Igbo – even though she was not one of their own. Many times they all pointed at me and I just sat still, listening to all the strange words being hurled about and feeling so out of place and helpless. I didn't share their language with them. It was the language that bound them together; the same language that severed me from them. Even at that age, I worried that there was no place for me in their world or this world.

We left that night, Mother and I. I remember we stayed with Aunt Mercy for a little while and when her husband began to fidget we moved in with Aunt Gold until Mother found somewhere small for us to move into. It was tough afterwards, but we survived from year to year.

In those passing years, I could not shake off that old instruction about not speaking any form of vernacular and thus I grew up to be an adult who could speak no local language. I tried listening to Mother and her sisters when they met, but it was no longer there, my ability to pick out their words and learn their meanings. It was as if one had erected a huge *iroko* tree to shield the sun from shining through. That was how it felt when I heard a local language; it was as if something was blocking me from deciphering its meaning.

So, that hot August afternoon as I stood in my father's compound in his village, waiting to see his dead body and pay my last respects, I felt like an alien among his kinsfolk. They spoke to me in their language, waiting for me to respond, but all I could do was offer an appeasing smile while I shook my head. I knew my discomfort was visible in my eyes and they all saw it. I was a full-grown man now and Mother had told me to go for his burial – he was after all my father. I agreed and came, knowing that I was the one who had finally become a stranger. I was now the 'Ononojo'.

"Shame on you!" My stepmother said bitterly as she spat in front of me.

She said so in a language I had disassociated myself from. These days, it never occurs to me to think of myself as an Igbo man. In my subconscious I am a black man, an African man and finally a Nigerian man. For a long time now, there has not been room for any language to claim a part of my identity.

Looking at her brought back a flood of memories, most of them not so pleasant. She was after all the other woman, the Igbo woman who made it possible for my mother to raise me alone. She spoke of shame in a tone that exonerated her from any, yet she was the one who had the most to be ashamed of. Not once had my father made any attempt to find me after Mother and I left all those years past. I remember I wrote him some letters and one in particular when I had finally gotten admission into Kings College. I thought he would be proud of me, but I heard nothing from him. I gave up then.

I feel no shame. Maybe some regrets, but no shame whatsoever. When the red cloud of dust rose as the vehicle taking me away from the village sped off, I was somewhat glad that the link that tied me to my father and his people like an umbilical cord was finally severed by my father's death and burial. Now, they would always be strangers to me and I to them.

Jude Dibia is a Nigerian novelist. His writing explores issues around love, family, exile and gay relationships and he was the winner of the 2007 Ken Saro-Wiwa Prize. Dibia's second novel, *Unbridled,* has been published in Nigeria and South Africa and shortlisted for Nigeria's most prestigious literary prize.

KONSTANTINOS TZIKAS GREECE

A BOY AND HIS KITE

IT WAS ON Clean Monday, the day kites are traditionally flown here in Greece, that the truth was unveiled to me. I was 11 back then, the day of my epiphany. I was watching the kites scattered all over the bluish canvas; I watched from my bedroom window, since we never flew kites ourselves. The kites jerked and twitched spasmodically, like harlequin spermatozoa striving to find their way to the majestic ovum of the sun. I watched the miraculous impregnation of the azure uterus, wondering what child might actually come out of a union between a kite and the sun. I imagined the kites frantically sprinting towards that coveted, fertile sphere of warmth; the one that rose highest would be the lucky one to fertilize the Shiny Round Lady. Their offspring would combine the best features of its parents: something breathtakingly beautiful, lethally dazzling, invariably airborne, with a predilection to suicide by hurling itself onto telegraph posts.

Even before that Clean Monday, that fateful *Kathara Deftera,* I was fully aware that I was different, perhaps not even human. I bore no similarity to any other person I knew. To me, people were blatantly and unremarkably crude, as glued to the ground as could be. But I was different: one with the breeze, dainty and graceful like no other being in my immediate environment. It must be said that neither of my parents looked entirely human. However, their zoomorphic qualities were hardly admirable: clammy, with their red mugs, their countenances of idiocy. They could have been swine desperately trying to pass for human.

At first, I thought I was a bird. I had no other dreams but of flying. Soaring above deserts like a vulture or hovering over the towering behemoths of a futuristic metropolis, in the guise of a mutated pigeon with red eyes and dark feathers. Fluttering every evening, to the extent that I often woke up exhausted, as if I had been sleepwalking… only I was actually *dreamflying.*

Over the years, I kept looking at the birds and observing them, seeing them as my brothers and sisters, my true relatives. I would observe their beaks and wings and touch my own face, struggling to find any conspicuous similarities. I believed that my skeletons and internal organs must have been birdlike, and I anxiously awaited the day that I would be transformed into a giant swallow.

And then, on the 11th Clean Monday of my life, on the day we celebrated the beginning of the abstinence period, the cleansing period, when meat and dairy would not be consumed until Easter, I was cleansed and reborn in an altogether different fashion. I did not abstain from eggs and steaks, I abstained from human nature itself, finally coming to the realization that I am neither a man nor a bird, but a *kite*.

There was no other explanation. I felt such intimacy watching those variegated speckles on the sky's blue-veined complexion that I must have been related to them. I was a kite, yes. A living, breathing, talking kite, no doubt, but a kite all the same. One who had lost its way and had ended up stranded in sublunary misery, exiled from the freedom of the skies.

I longed to reunite with my kind. And since it was Clean Monday, what better way to merge with my pack again, now that they were visible, proudly sporting their feathers – before they emigrated to other climes or returned to Kiteland?

Shreds of cloth, string, ribbons; I used them all to adorn myself, to be a kite in appearance as well as in spirit. I glued them all on me and inspected myself in the mirror; I was as colorful as one could be. I was ready.

I stood at my window, puffed some air and jumped.

I felt myself momentarily leveled, swept by the air currents, glimpsing across at my fellow kites.

Then, of course, I crashed down, in the front yard. My mother came out of the front door, shrieking. Not wearing her glasses at the time, she thought all the colorful stuff surrounding my little body was blood and intestines and other matter oozing out of me.

I had 115 stitches. And, as I lay on the ground, the kites in the sky above were a vast concourse of high-flyers blackening the sun.

❖ ❖ ❖

I'm 57 now. I've long given up any notions that I may be a kite. Or at least, I've tried. After my botched attempt to fly, my parents took me to a therapist who seemed particularly keen on examining my unconventional case. I kept telling him about my dreams; I even imitated the movements of a kite. I had become a bit of joke by this time. I was so indignant at the stark idiocy of the man analyzing me that I kept blurting out all sorts of gibberish. I told him how kites communicated with each other; I even squawked a few phrases in

Kitean; I talked about the formal customs of proper kites at table; their social hierarchy; and the legend of the Great Blue Kite, the bravest kite of all, who flew high, higher than any other kite ever ventured to go and was so beautiful that the Sun decided not to burn him and spared his life.

I used to provoke my therapist with all sorts of wisecracks; I was determined to drive him to madness. One day, I walked in his office, all wrapped up in string, announcing that I was ready to be repatriated; to fly back to my motherland, a mountainous community somewhere in the Andes where all kites lived together in peace and love, breathing the cool air of that altitude. On another occasion, I walked in hand-in-hand with a lovely purple kite, which I promptly introduced as my future wife.

Great days they were, back then. The imbecile therapist was ludicrous. And my little show kept on until my late teens, when I finally grew out of it.

But since then, my life has been colorless and earthbound. I started working in an office. No, slaving, actually. And, as time went by, I completely forgot my kite roots. I was an excaudate kite, devoid of color and joy, bleached and featherless.

Until today.

Today, something changed.

❖ ❖ ❖

It's Clean Monday today. Every Clean Monday in the last five years, I have driven all the way up to Lavrio, an industrial zone filled with broody, dusty hills and semi-abandoned factories. This place soothes me, detached and lonely as it is. I just stand here, gazing at the multitude of kites looming on the horizon. I can't help but identify with this depressive area.

There's a kid here today. He's about 17. He wears a denim jacket, faded blue jeans, a yellow shirt and a pair of sunglasses. He doesn't seem to notice me or simply does not care. He is trying to fly his kite.

It is a large kite, bright green and yellow, made of the cheapest fabric. It's cute. But it's torn. It's tattered. It's adorned with at least four or five sizable holes. It cannot fly. It will never fly. It's like a bird with broken wings.

Still, the boy perseveres. He keeps moving back and forth, trying to push the kite upwards, waving it like an obnoxious banner, hurling it with all his strength in a last-ditch attempt to lift it up and keep it there, hoping that the air currents will be generous enough to comply… as if the kite wasn't torn up… as if the boy wasn't clumsily mixed up in his own string.

Something moves me in this picture. Granted, the boy reminds me of myself and the kite exudes a certain decadent beauty but there's something more: the passion. The boy's desperate efforts to achieve the impossible. It's obvious he will never get it up; still he tries… in vain he tries… for hours. I watch from a distance, hypnotized by his repetitive movements and the atonal drone in the air. He must have tried getting the kite up 14 or 15 times already. I take my Polaroid out and start taking pictures of the boy. He moves frantically around, almost ecstatic, a Bacchus in Levi's, and the colors mix up, the colors of his clothes and the colors of the kite, they become one, a vibrant psychedelic blur amidst the heat of the noon.

Finally, the boy gives up. He raises his hands in the air one last time, as if bowing to the forces of nature, a strange pagan gesture, thanking the air even though it wasn't a favorable day. He then carries the kite slowly, ceremoniously, and tosses it into the only dustbin here. It's like a funeral ceremony. He is mourning the fallen of the battle, the perished warrior. He stands in front of the dustbin for a while. Finally, he leaves.

Half an hour later, I go to the dustbin. I pull out the entombed kite, dust it off and examine it. It's like a mirror to me.

❖ ❖ ❖

It's evening, and I'm back home. I've brought the kite with me. In the bedroom, I lay all the pictures on the floor. I carefully examine how the boy moved and jerked and struggled… I place them in chronological order: from the first attempt after I had my camera out, to the ultimate resignation. I peruse them.

I spend the night sleeping with the kite, gently folding the wood and the metal and the ripped plastic.

I wake up. I have an excellent idea: fly the kite. I have some fat rope in the kitchen, second drawer to the left. I strap the kite on my back. I stand at the ledge of the window, excited, a new Icarus. I take a deep breath. I jump…

I fly. I'm exhilarated. A big smile plastered on my face.

Oh my. I reach the sun. A big orange bubblegum. I can already feel the revitalizing rays on my dry skin.

… I wake up.

That dream was great.

Why not give it a try?

I go searching for that fat rope in the kitchen, second drawer to the left.

Konstantinos Tzikas was born in Athens, Greece, where he also resides. He is a journalist and has also worked as a teacher of English and translator. He has just finished his first play, a one-act drama on the repercussions of isolation.

PETINA GAPPAH ZIMBABWE

BEFORE TONDE, AFTER TONDE

DHEDHI SLAMMED THE door behind him so hard that my new red coat that Mhamhi bought at Matalan fell on the floor on top of Shingi's parka. Against the black of Shingi's jacket and the dark color of the carpet, my coat looked like bright blood on a very dark road. Shingi didn't take the jacket with him when he left and Dhedhi didn't see it. He would have thrown it out with all of Shingi's other things, if he had seen it, but like Dot on *EastEnders* always says, sometimes you don't see the things that are right in front of you.

Rozzer from next door barked when the door banged. Through the walls, I heard Mo shouting to him to keep quiet. I peeked out of my door when I heard the door bang and saw the jackets on the floor in the hall. I also saw Mhamhi doing what she always does when Dhedhi shouts and bangs doors behind him. She sat on the stairs with her mouth falling down at the corners. Dhedhi's anger remained in the house even after he had left. It formed a cloud that settled in the spaces in the cracks and seeped up past the staircase and Mhamhi's falling face to the bedrooms and the bathroom.

They were fighting about Shingi again. "You have to see him," Mhamhi said. "We have to find him. Things can't go on like this. He is our son, our only son now."

"I have no son," Dhedhi said.

"We must submit to God's will," said Mhamhi. "If we put our faith in God and trust him to find a way, he will bring Shingi ..."

"I do not know anyone called Shingirai."

He used Shingi's full name, and he shouted at Mhamhi in Shona, two things he does when he is very angry. My Shona is not that good any more. I mean, I still *speak it* and everything, but I don't always remember the right words to say to my grandmother when my mother makes me talk to her on the phone. I do remember afterwards, but the words don't come easily when I am actually talking to her. And I can hardly follow my grandmother sometimes when she uses totems and proverbs and stuff like that. But we have only been here two years, since I was nine, and I am not so *daft* that I could forget a whole *language* just like that.

When I am not at school, where it is English all the time, Mhamhi talks to me mainly to complain about Dhedhi. Dhedhi hardly talks, he just shouts and gives orders. It is really hard to keep up a language when all you hear are complaints and commands, complaints and commands, the same stuff over and over again. It's not like back home where everyone says all sorts of different things in Shona. I should say back in Zim, really, I suppose, because London is our home now.

❖ ❖ ❖

Mhamhi sat for about ten minutes before I heard the stairs creak and she came up to my room. Her face was all puffed up.

"Did you hear your father?" she said.

I tried to pretend that she had not spoken at all and kept my eyes on my PlayStation. I pushed the buttons on the analogue controller to see if I could get Trinity to kick two of the Matrix agents at the same time. Shingi could make Neo and Morpheus kick ten agents, and when I remembered this, I missed him so much that I forgot that I had sworn never to talk to him again. I managed to kick two of the agents, and it might have been three but I found it hard to concentrate because Mhamhi said again, "Did you hear your father?"

"Uh huh," I said.

"What manner is that of talking to your mother?"

"I mean, yes Mhamhi, I heard him."

"You see the way he talks to me, like I don't exist. I pray to God that when you get married, your husband will not treat you in this way."

And she went on and on about how she is the one who works to put the food on the table, and is it her fault that he cannot get a job and I tried to switch off my mind but it is hard to do that when your mother is sitting in your room and telling you what an awful and unfeeling person is your father. What is worse is that she never explains why they shout at each other all the time and, worst of all, why Shingi just up and left like that without saying goodbye. Then she said we had to pray for Dhedhi and for Shingi, and made me switch off my PlayStation so that we prayed together.

❖ ❖ ❖

He is angry all the time now, Dhedhi, and he shouts over every little thing. Like that time when I asked him if I could change my name and he asked what was wrong with it.

"No one else is called Patience," I explained, "it's a word and not a name."

"Patience is a perfectly good name," he said. "That was your aunt's name."

"Yes, but no one here is called Patience. I mean, Dhedhi, this is not like Zim, where people are called funny things like that boy Genius who won the hundred meters race that time, or Memory in Miss Mashava's class or ..."

"Zim Zim *kuita sei*? What do you know about your country? Is this a way that a girl of your age talks to her father? Why does your mother not teach you some manners?"

He really lost it then, he shouted and said I was not to question his authority, and if Patience was a good enough name for his sister, it should be good enough for me.

I said "Sorry Dhedhi" and we watched *EastEnders*. Dawn kissed Ian and they were rubbing their arms all over each other and I was so afraid that Jane would catch them and just when it was getting really exciting, Dhedhi told me to do my homework in my room.

"But Dhedhi, I *have* done it. I want to watch *East...*"

"Go to your room this minute."

When Mhamhi said, "Why not just let her...", he interrupted her and told her to get out of the room as well.

"Kamani," he said. "Both of you, out, get out, get out *now*."

Mhamhi and I went up the staircase and she pushed me into her room. We sat on the bed and she held me and cried and all I could think of was whether Jane had caught Ian and Dawn, and what she would say if she found out that Ian had given Dawn a credit card because Dawn had agreed to pretend to be Ian's wife even though Jane was his girlfriend. I sat there wondering what would happen next and trying to listen to the sound of the television, but Mhamhi was crying and I could hear loud cheering which meant football and so I wrote and rewrote the story in my mind and tried to block out Mhamhi's voice saying "Look, look, see what your father is doing."

❖ ❖ ❖

He didn't always shout, Dhedhi – he used to laugh a lot. He whistled a lot too, whistles that were not any tune in particular but that were just a sound that was always there, like our maid SisiAnnie singing Chimbetu songs in the kitchen, or Mhamhi laughing with her friend Auntie Sue from next door. But that was ages ago, back in Zim, before we came to England, before Tonde died.

I wrote a story last term for school about the thing that I miss most about

Zim. I thought for a long time about what I missed. I suppose I could have written about Tonde or about our dog Spider, but they are not *things.* I miss things like the sun always being there, or having a garden to run around in. I miss Blakistone, my old school, and answering questions in class without worrying if Kylie and her friends are going to make fun of me and laugh at me afterwards for knowing the right answers. I miss walking home with my friend Mandy, and going around the greenways and walking without our shoes on. Most of all though, I miss our swimming pool, and that's what I wrote about.

Miss Norman said I was creative and had a good imagination. But I could tell she thought it was just a made-up story. Kylie even said there are no pools in Africa; people there live in huts in the jungle like on *Survivor.* She doesn't know *anything* though because our house was really nice and everything. It was not a very big swimming pool. Like I explained in the story, I could swim five lengths when I was in Grade Two and I was only seven then. Tonde could swim 10 lengths and one time he even did 20 but he had to sit and throw up because he swallowed so much water. Mhamhi found him coughing by the side of the pool and yelled at him because he had asthma and he was not supposed to do anything that might cause an attack. But he died anyway.

And we moved to England.

❖ ❖ ❖

They talked about it even before Tonde died – moving to England I mean. But Dhedhi wanted to stay. "We will not run from our problems," he said. "These bastards will not be around forever, and if we leave, that is just what they want. Things cannot possibly get worse."

Things did get worse though; everything started to change, not quickly like what happens on *EastEnders* but slowly, in little bits. The pool was the first thing that changed, it got all yucky and green because Dhedhi said there wasn't enough money for the chemicals. SisiAnnie had to cook outside all the time because there was never electricity.

Mhamhi yelled into the phone all the time at the electricity people. "One hundred and thirty-five power cuts in the last four months," she said. "And your bills get higher and higher. This is intolerable. Don't make stupid excuses. Hello, hello, hello."

We stopped eating all sorts of nice things because Mhamhi said everything was expensive. We couldn't even go to Sweets from Heaven or to Scoop for ice cream. I didn't mind too much because the ice cream started to taste all funny.

The Scoop people said that was because the power cuts meant that the ice cream wasn't always fresh and it melted a lot and they didn't always have enough milk, they said, because the new farmers had killed all the cows and eaten them. In the end it didn't matter because the Scoop people closed the shop and another one opened that made all these toys that had all these funny signs on them and that was because they were made in China. Tonde got a remote-controlled car from there for his birthday. It went around the room once and got stuck under the sofa, and wouldn't move even when Dhedhi changed the batteries.

Other things changed too, lots of things like having to carry lots of the new money called bearer checks just to buy bread. You had to be careful with it because it was almost like a newspaper, it tore that easily. And we couldn't have Cartoon Network or Nickelodeon any more on DSTV because Mhamhi said we didn't have foreign currency.

The biggest thing that changed, though, was that Tonde died.

❖ ❖ ❖

We don't have a maid in England. SisiAnnie stayed behind so there is no one to look after me when Mhami is at work. Shingi used to look after me, but since he went away, I look after myself. But she is breaking the law because the law here says adults are not supposed to leave kids alone, or else they are jailed.

"We did not come to England to end up in jail," Mhamhi said. "So make sure that you do as I say."

She said that I have to look after myself after school.

"None of us can count on Dhedhi," she said.

He is never here in the afternoon, anyway, and when he is, it is like he is not here at all. He doesn't have a job even though he went to university and everything and had a really good job as a manager with this company that makes beer and stuff like that back in Zim. But it was okay, we have food and clothes and everything because Mhamhi has a job as a pharmacist at one of the Boots in Oxford Street. But after Dhedhi failed to find a job, there wasn't enough money for us and everyone they had to help in Zim, Mhamhi said, and so she took another job, looking after old people five nights a week. It was really weird at first, not having her around at night because she came home after I was in bed. It was even weirder having Dhedhi cook for us, and he laughed when Shingi and I complained about his funny meals.

He went to loads of interviews, Dhedhi, all over London he went, and one time, he even went to Birmingham. He tried a job in a factory but that lasted only one week. Weeks and weeks and weeks, then months and months and then a whole year passed and still he didn't have a job. Then Mhamhi said he should try registering with her agency because there was always work there, and that was the first time he shouted, really shouted I mean. "I did not come to England to wipe white people's bottoms," he said. Only he was much ruder than that, he said *matuzvi evarungu* which is a really bad way of saying white people's shit and it is such a bad thing to say that you are not supposed even to *think it*.

Then one day, just like that, he just stopped looking for a job and began to spend all his days typing really fast on the internet. When he is not on the internet, he watches boring Sky Sports. I *hate* football more than I hate *anything else* in the world. One time, Shingi and I looked at the computer to see what he spends all his time doing. We tried his and Mhamhi's and Shingi's and my name for the password, but that didn't work. "Try Tonde," I said, and Shingi tried it and it didn't work.

Then he typed Tonderai and it worked.

We found that Dhedhi spent most of his time at a forum where people from Zim wrote really awful things to each other about politics and stuff like that. The forum said 'Welcome, Zanuimhata'. That's the name that Dhedhi used on the forum. He spent all his time shouting at all the politicians in Zim and at everyone on the forum calling them morons and idiots.

"We are stuck here, estranged from our homeland, fucking economic refugees because a moron who shits like you or me won't give up power," he wrote. "And *mhata* like Mukoma, Pakuru and Senior defend him, even as the country dies because your shallow minds are wrapped in liberation bullshit." The people called Mukoma and Senior then shouted at Dhedhi and said he was the *mhata*, and he shouted back and on and on it went and it felt weird to read all these things written about my father who was pretending to be someone else.

❖ ❖ ❖

I walk home fast after school, without talking to anyone, like my teacher Miss Norman told us. That's because the streets are full of pedophiles who like to have sex with kids and then kill them. They don't look evil or anything like the Nazis in my Indiana Jones game, they drive around in their white vans looking just like anyone else and that's why we are not allowed to talk to strangers. I found it weird at first to ignore adults all the time because in Zim you are supposed to greet older people and be polite to them even if you don't know them.

So anyway, I walk home on my own without talking to anyone, and I let myself in. Sometimes Mhamhi leaves food for me to heat in the microwave. But one time after Shingi left and Dhedhi had thrown away all his things, I came home and there was nothing to eat in the kitchen and he was drinking beer and being Zanuimhata on the internet.

"You should learn to cook," he said without looking up when I said there was no food. "My sisters could all cook at your age."

In the kitchen, I switched on the gas stove to make scrambled eggs. It wouldn't light up, and I remember Mhamhi saying that sometimes she had to switch on all four plates at once just to get one lit. I did that and turned the knobs up really high and then clicked on the gas switch and the flames were ever so big and my braids were on fire and melted and burned my face and neck and I screamed. Dhedhi put out the fire and the only good thing about being burnt was that he put his arms around me just like he used to even for no reason, and he picked me up and helped me put on my coat. And I cried and cried even though it was not that bad because I wanted him to continue holding my hand and he did, all the way to the hospital.

"Superficial burns," the doctor said, "You know better than to play with fire." I opened my mouth to tell him what really happened but I closed it again.

❖ ❖ ❖

Then I woke up one night to hear Dhedhi and Mhamhi and Shingi yelling at each other. Shingi banged the door behind him and never came back. I waited and waited and he never called to explain or even just to say hi. Dhedhi put all of Shingi's things in bin bags and threw them out when Mhamhi was at work. He became really strict and everything with all sorts of new rules for me. "I do not want you to wear trousers," he said.

"But it's part of my uniform," I said.

"Wear the skirt," he said, and to Mhamhi. "Make sure the hem is below the knees and cut her hair. No child of mine is going to look and dress like a whore."

Mhamhi said, "She is only 11."

"All the more reason for her to start learning values."

Mhamhi only said I should pray for Dhedhi and said nothing more, not even how cold it was with just a skirt and tights. I prayed ever so hard but Dhedhi didn't change his mind and everyone laughed at me because I was the only one in a skirt when it was freezing. Kylie laughed and said I looked like Gus from *EastEnders* with my hair cut off. And I thought it was so unfair because whores are people who have sex with lots of boys and I hate boys almost as much as I hate football.

❖ ❖ ❖

Mhamhi got all weird after Shingi left.

She didn't talk about him at all, except when she pleaded and argued with Dhedhi. She started to go to this other church called the Temple of God's Deliverance, UK. She made me wear frilly dresses and sit while people sang and danced and prayed aloud all at the same time. Something about the faces reminded me of the man with the dirty dreadlocks who stands near the lions at Trafalgar and who always says "Lord take me back to Jameeeca, please take me back to Jameeeca, Lord take me back to Jameeeca", and it's the only thing he says and Shingi said he is a mad, sad bastard.

Some of the ladies dance up and down the middle passage where there are no chairs, and then they fall to the ground and start shaking. I used to worry because all the ladies wear skirts and I didn't even want to *imagine* if their knickers started to show – that would be too *awful* – but there are two ladies called Sister Jocelyn and Sister Mattie who rise up from their seats to straighten the skirts of the fallen women so that nothing shows. They don't need to do that for the men, of course, because they wear trousers, and anyway, it is only women who tumble over and fall with the Holy Spirit.

❖ ❖ ❖

On *EastEnders,* it is always the littlest things that change the way the big things turn out, like Jane remembering that she didn't switch the lights off in the café which means she goes back and doesn't see Ian together with Dawn, or Pauline not having enough change for her underground ticket which means she has to go to ask at the newsagent and she misses the train, and that's how Joe catches up with her and they get married; well, that's how Tonde died.

His asthma medicine ran out and none of the pharmacies had the stuff to fill up his inhaler. Mhamhi and Dhedhi looked everywhere. But there was none anywhere so Mhamhi asked Auntie Sue from next door to get the medicine when she went to South Africa. But then her flight was canceled because there was no fuel for the plane. She went in the end, but she came back two days later than she should have and on the day before she returned with Tonde's medicine, he had an attack at school. Mrs Mawere, his teacher, called the ambulance, but they said there wasn't one because there was no fuel. Mrs Mawere drove him to the hospital herself. He died in her car before they got there.

That's what happened with Tonde, little things that didn't go right.

Mhamhi clutched Tonde's inhaler and she would not let it go. She even carried it with her to the funeral. Tonde's coffin was *really* small, I didn't know that they made coffins that are the right size for kids. I suppose someone must measure them because his was just right and it fitted him and everything. Dhedhi got very drunk at the funeral. Shingi says he saw him crying but I never did. He kept saying *achamudya president mwana wangu, achamudya chete,* and I didn't know what he meant when he said the President should eat Tonde.

"This is what happens when life becomes cheap," Uncle Steve said to him, but I didn't know what that meant either because Mhamhi always said life was getting really expensive.

❖ ❖ ❖

It's like everything is divided up in halves, there's the half before Tonde died, and the half after Tonde, only it doesn't feel like a half but almost like that's how things always were and it's like Tonde had never been. Seven months after Tonde died, Mhamhi and Dhedhi sold the house and car and everything. Auntie Sue took our dog Spider and two weeks after that, we moved to England.

No one wants to talk about Tonde, not even Shingi. He is 17 and I am 11 and the gap between us is even bigger without Tonde in between. Only my grandmother talked about him sometimes. She introduced me to people in Zim as *'hanzvadzi yeuyu mushakabvu'* which means 'the sister of the dead one', and I wish she would just say his name, Tonde, like they do on *EastEnders* when people die. Den is still Den, and Mark is still Mark. No one pretends they don't have a name any more. No one calls them just *the dead ones.*

I close my eyes sometimes and I try to remember his face. All the pictures of him are in a drawer in Mhamhi's bedroom that she keeps locked. It has all her secret stuff like her contraception pills that she thinks I don't know about. Tonde is locked up in that secret drawer.

I am trying hard not to, but I am forgetting his face.

❖ ❖ ❖

On the night of the day on which Dhedhi banged the door so hard that he made Shingi's and my coat fall in a heap of red and black to the floor, Mhamhi didn't go to work because she was feeling sick. There was a ring at the door and I opened it and there was Shingi. I screamed so hard that I felt my ears sing, and I clung to him and wouldn't let him go.

"Whoa," he said, "where's the fire?"

He lifted me up and I put my face next to his. He smelled like Dhedhi smelled when he had been drinking. Mhamhi came down to see what the noise was for, and when she put her arms around him, it was both of us that she hugged. I was so pleased to see him that I forgot that I was angry that he went like that, without saying goodbye.

"I can make Trinity kick two agents at once," I said. "Let's have a game now."

"Sorry, Peshi *shaz*, I can't right now," he said.

"You shouldn't have come," Mhamhi said. "Your father is still so angry."

"I came to tell you that I am moving up north."

"Where up north? Who will you stay with?"

We never heard the answer because at that moment the door opened and Dhedhi walked into the room. He looked at us like he didn't see us. He walked straight over to the computer.

"*Manheru* Dhedhi," Shingi said.

"I don't greet animals," Dhedhi said.

"Animals, Dhedhi, animals? But you can do better than that, surely. Pigs and dogs, isn't that the phrase you are looking for? Isn't that what your President calls us, pigs and dogs?"

"Leave this house this minute," Dhedhi said. "I will not have a sodomite under my roof."

"*Your* roof? What, have things changed that much since you kicked me out? Because here I was thinking that Mhamhi is the only one who is working. Or is it only your roof because *mune machende* and she does not have them too, your dick and your balls?"

"Shingi."

My mother started to cry with her hand over her mouth. My heart was beating so fast I thought that everybody could hear it. I was too shocked to say anything because Shingi was saying all these words that you were not even supposed to *think*.

"But hang on, I have balls too," Shingi said. "But that does not make me a man, now does it, not to you anyway, right, Dhedhi? I am not a man, but tell me are you a man? Are you a man?"

"Patience," Dhedhi said without looking at me, "go to your room this minute."

I knew better than to argue and I fled without even looking at Shingi. But I didn't go to my room. I sat looking down at them from the top of the staircase. They were so busy looking at each other that no one noticed me there. When

Dhedhi spoke again his voice was low. "I will not tolerate a sodomite under my roof."

"This is England Dhedhi, England," Shingi said. "I can suck dick and no one cares. I can take it up the ass and no one cares. I can even get married if I want to. No. One. Cares." He started to hum that tune that they play on *EastEnders* when people are getting married like Kat that time to Alfie. He did a twirl around the living room that he did not complete because my father struck out at him with his fist and hit him. Shingi laughed and Dhedhi punched him again in the face. It was not one bit like Indiana Jones punching the evil Nazis or even Dennis hitting Phil Mitchell on *EastEnders* because it was real and it was my father doing it to my brother. It was real and Shingi's face was full of blood. I did not know that people could laugh and cry at the same time.

Dhedhi said "Sodomite, sodomite," every time he hit and kicked him. "Fight like a man if you think you are man," he said.

He raised Shingi and hit him again and this time Shingi fell hard and hit his head against the staircase. Mhamhi cried and shook him and said "Shingi, Shingi, Shingi" over and over and still he did not get up. When Dhedhi walked out of the house, he did not slam the door behind him. It closed softly without a sound and my red coat and Shingi's parka remained on their hooks on the door.

Petina Gappah is a Zimbabwean writer and lawyer living in Geneva. Her story collection, *An Elegy For Easterly*, will be published by Faber and Faber in April 2009 in the United Kingdom, and in June 2009 in the United States. It will also appear in more than six other languages. Her first novel, *The Book of Memory*, will be published in 2010.

KEN N KAMOCHE KENYA

RETRENCHED

MAINA READ THE letter quickly. The words didn't make sense. No one believed it would ever happen to him, as only those who had no godfathers to protect them would be laid off.

He would receive 40,000 shillings severance pay. The dismissal letter urged him to set up in business and wished him well in his new career. The retrenchment was unavoidable, and the City Council regretted the decision. His throat went dry. New career? What career exactly did the city fathers have in mind for him? What was he going to tell his wife?

"This is the way life is," his supervisor said. "Today it's you. Tomorrow it could be me. It's called belt-tightening. We have to tighten the belts so we can barely breathe."

A heavy and somber silence hung on the usually noisy Fees and Rates Section. Those who had not been handed the poisoned chalice focused their gaze on the invoices and payment vouchers on their desks, afraid to look at the faces of their less fortunate brethren. But if they enjoyed any consolation, it was short-lived. Their pain was a blend of uncertainty and fear, the pain of not knowing who would be next.

Maina took his pay-off and traveled back to his village near the small, provincial town of Nyahururu, where his wife lived with their two sons, Mbuthia and Karanja. That was it for Nairobi. The city that took him in when he so desperately needed a job had now cut him off, cast him into the wilderness, like a bare bone thrown to the dogs.

Rose was astonished to see him, but like the good wife she was, she didn't pester him with unnecessary questions. She behaved just as he had coached her, to show deference and wait for him to supply whatever information he deemed necessary for her to have. She hadn't been expecting him back for another two months.

The children were still at school when he got home. She offered him a mug of porridge and inquired into his health. They made small talk for half an hour and then she excused herself. She had to go to the market to buy groceries for the evening meal. When the children returned home later that afternoon, they played with their father delightedly, oblivious of the pain he so effortlessly hid from them. Whenever a smile or kind word was called for, he offered it perfunctorily, swallowing hard every now and then, as though to stop himself spewing out the bitterness that simmered in the pit of his belly.

In the days that followed, Rose sensed that her husband wasn't going back to Nairobi. He never spoke about his work. In fact he hardly spoke to her at all. She waited patiently for him to open his heart to her and tell her what was ailing him. But he couldn't bring himself to tell her he had lost his job. What would she think of him? Would she still obey him, and think of him as the husband and provider? Would she respect him as the man of the house?

He took to getting up at the crack of dawn and walking away from the house even without having had breakfast. Perhaps if she sees me leaving she'll think I'm still working. Perhaps she'll think I've been transferred to the local Town Hall. For days he didn't even see the children, because he left before they awoke and returned late in the night, long after they had gone to bed.

For the two boys, it was just like before when Daddy was away in the big city they had always dreamed of visiting. The city with the bright lights that shone from metal trees and buildings that hugged the blue skies above, or so it seemed to them in the pictures Father brought back.

The noisy juke-boxed bars at the market square provided a welcome sanctuary, and Maina quickly developed a reputation as the local tycoon. He soon became a permanent fixture at the Happy Inn. His drinking hours started early, usually at lunch time, when he would get together with a band of unemployed villagers to eat a kilo or two of sumptuous goat ribs and knock back bottle after bottle of water-cooled Tusker.

It didn't take long for the local idlers and bar regulars to discover that Maina had set up camp permanently in the village where he was born, and more importantly, he had brought back to the poverty-stricken village sufficient evidence of the city's largesse. They treated him like royalty. And he responded with a cultivated alacrity, beaming with pleasure as the locals greeted him with extravagant honorific titles that got more imaginative as the beers loosened the tongues.

Maina particularly liked being called *Mutongoria* – The Leader. With a glint in his eyes, he led them from one night of frenzied, drunken amusement to another, his magnanimity well-oiled by the severance pay.

With his heavy pockets and smart suits, he was irresistible to the barmaids. He particularly liked Wanja, she of the haughty looks, high cheekbones and stiletto boots. He offered to pay the rent for her room above the bar where they spent many evenings together.

One Sunday morning, while nursing a debilitating hangover, he saw his wife wiping tears from her eyes. He peered at her through the heavy fogs of the hangover, then shut his eyes, willing her to go away. But she remained there, next to him, stubbornly glued to their single bed. She sat without stirring, thinking he was asleep, and wept in silence.

The anger in him made him tense up, then shiver, as if he had a fever. He sensed that her action was the sign he had been hoping to avoid all along. The confirmation that she had given up on him. *So, now she thinks I'm totally useless! She's given up on me and thinks I'm not man enough to hold down a job and support my family*! The words took shape in his mind but refused to roll down his heavy tongue, disobeying the drunken spirit that was beating a cacophonous rhythm in his head and trying desperately to drum the words out of his mouth. He turned on his side, hoping the throbbing in his head would subside. But it only got worse.

He knew the time had come for him to talk to Rose. Sitting there next to him was her way of demanding an explanation. He understood that all right. *She's a good wife; knows when not to talk. I'm lucky to have a woman who doesn't talk back, unlike that damned Wanja at the Happy Inn.* Maina would have nodded in appreciation were it not for his headache. He turned to face his wife. *What am I supposed to tell her now? Admit I was fired, laid off! That I have no income? That I'm just a lousy adulterous alcoholic? Never*!

"You're awake?" he growled.

Rose turned in alarm to face him. She quickly dabbed at her eyes, then looked away. She had no idea what to say to him. She had heard rumors. She looked for the words like someone struggling to speak a foreign language they haven't used for years.

All she could think was how forgetful he had become. He had lived so long in the big city that he appeared to have forgotten how thin the walls of their little houses in the village were. For Rose, the little village was just like the wicker basket she used to carry vegetables to the market. Anyone who cared to glance in her direction could see whether she was carrying carrots, tomatoes or cabbages. She muffled the sobs and refused to face him, even as he grabbed her hand and drew her towards him.

"What's the matter with you, woman?"

She remained silent.

He had never seen her like that before. Without warning, he picked up a pillow and threw it against the wall. Fearing he was going to beat her up, Rose clasped her head in both hands and wailed mournfully. *Wui-wui-wui-ehh*! The sorrowful moans cut through the morning air and right through Maina's heart. He tried to reach out and hold her hand to calm her but she brushed him away, then threw herself in a dejected heap on the earthen floor. She banged on the floor with her hands and continued wailing.

At that moment the boys burst into the room with such terrified looks on their faces that Maina could not bear to look at them. He rolled over and faced the wooden wall, which only glared back at him as if daring him to a fight, if he was man enough. He slammed his eyes shut and pulled the blanket over his head, to shut out the cries of the little boys who were trying desperately to calm their mother. Unable to bear the sorrowful tones of their mourning, he jumped out of bed and ordered them to leave the room.

"Out! Out of here!" he thundered. "Go and do your crying outside! You wanted to talk, eh? Now we're talking! Just get out of here!"

Rose got up on her feet and bent down to protect the boys, whose frightened screams could be heard right across the village. Maina shoved them out of the open door and promptly jumped back into bed. The breath was coming out of his nostrils in quick, explosive gusts, like a raging bull about to charge.

The boys had never seen their father in that state before. Their mother led them out of the house and they walked the half-mile to their church. The service passed like a blur for Rose. She saw the pastor's lips move as if he was chewing on some inaudible words that only the blessed few could hear. She cast furtive glances across the congregation and was convinced she was the evil one, the only one who could not share the glory of the word of God. *What have I done to deserve this? Is this why Maina has abandoned me*?

She begged God to give her the strength to talk to Maina, to ask him to forgive her whatever she had done. The two of them had to stay together. The children needed them that way, together. Like a family. Just like before, when he was away in the city.

She tried talking to her husband. But her words bounced off the wall of silence he constructed around himself like the echoes on the new school building. The days dragged along, one after the other, like the market women walking in single file carrying their sacks of vegetables on their bent backs.

The burden of his relationship with Wanja and his waywardness weighed down on Maina like a yoke. It bore down on his body, while his feet ploughed the ground beneath him, digging a trench into which he knew he would eventually fall.

"You must talk to me, my husband. I know it is not true what they're saying. Please tell me it is not true." Rose peered into his eyes but saw nothing there. Only a lifelessness that she could not recognize in the eyes that once laughed with her and shone like a torch.

Maina looked away. It was better for her not to know. The words to describe his secret life with Wanja remained like a lump in his throat. The confession she was asking for refused to contaminate the sacredness of their bedroom. It nibbled at his heart and ate into his head. He stared stubbornly at the wooden wall.

For several days, Maina became the ghostly shadow that wandered about the narrow winding village roads, afraid to venture anywhere near the bars where the role of Mutongoria no longer beckoned to a man with a heart full of shame. Every day saw him wander farther and farther away into the dark forest that teemed with buzzing gnats and mosquitoes and made his heart flutter and swell with the wild anticipation of unseen dangers.

He looked with longing into the deep crevices on the sides of the hills and wished they would devour him as they devoured the porcupines and cobras that dwelt deep within them. He saw the heavy branches of the *mugumo* trees and knew they would carry his feeble frame with no difficulty. No one would find him there, hanging 20 feet above the ground. He would be safe. He would be rid of the memories of his return to the village, the memories which hung around his neck, preparing it for the coarse fibers of a strong sisal rope.

The more Rose tried to open him up, the tighter he clamped himself shut, seeking a quiet place in the depths of a shell she never knew he possessed.

"If there's something I've done, please forgive me." She sobbed and buried her face in her trembling hands.

She shook his shoulder late one Sunday morning to wake him from a drunken stupor. He sprung out of bed and grabbed her shoulders in a vice-like grip.

"Leave me alone!' he bellowed. "You can't help me. I'm not worthy... just... just leave me. Go, go away!"

The forcefulness of his anger rocked her and for a moment she thought her shoulderblades would shatter. At that moment, the house erupted with the cries of the boys in a rejoinder to their father's harsh words. And Rose knew her shoulders would never shatter. As the boys' wails reverberated in her ears, she trembled violently and an unfamiliar strength began to percolate through her arms and hands. Her hands reached out and grabbed Maina's arms, pushing him away from her gently and with an effortlessness borne of years of raising sacks of vegetables on to her back.

Maina wobbled as the life seemed to drain away from him. His glassy eyes glared at his wife and then looked down to his feet. Rose helped him sit on the edge of the bed and dried the tears that trickled down his face. She put an arm on his chin and tried to raise it. His eyes remained closed.

"What is this pain that came to afflict us?" moaned Rose. "Sleep, my husband. Get some sleep. We'll talk when we return from church. We'll talk, and pray together. Everything will be as it was before."

She covered him with a blanket, the way she tucked the boys in. He obeyed, and Rose was pleased. He was just like their little boys.

An hour later, Maina sat up in bed and threw the window open. He lit a cigarette and let his head slide back slowly onto the pillow. He watched the end of the cigarette burn and knew he was watching his own life smolder away. The smoke wafting up to the ceiling told him that his very soul was flying away from him, never to return. *What about my new career*!

In his confused mind, he conjured up blurred images of himself running a shop at the market center, chatting excitedly with the customers as he wrapped up their loaves of bread, kilos of sugar and cans of cooking oil, listening to the jingle of coins as he opened the cash-register, ready to reap where he had sown. He felt the new crisp 500-shilling notes and saw himself holding them up to the light to determine if they were counterfeit, just like the shopkeepers did. He smiled to himself. *They're genuine, and I'll be rich. I'll be the local tycoon from now on. This time, for real.*

He closed his eyes and inhaled deeply, imagining he was smoking a cigar. *Yes, one of these fine days… I'll no longer be like these poor villagers who smoke roll-up cigarettes. I'm moving on to cigars. Because I'll be the leader*! He jumped out of his reverie and sat on the edge of the bed.

"But I AM the leader!" he gasped. "That's what they call me, back at the Happy Inn! Mutongoria! Why am I not smoking a cigar right now?"

He glared around the room, like a man emerging from a nightmare, trying to figure out where he was. He got on his feet and walked with unsteady steps in circles. Round and round. His mind urged him to look for something but he had no idea what. He turned on the radio. The regular Sunday morning service was on air. The pastor was saying: "If your hand causes you to sin, cut it off!"

Maina froze and glared at his hands.

He saw the cigarette in his hand and angrily threw it to the earthen floor. He stepped on it with his bare foot and didn't feel any pain as he continued squashing it into the ground until it was as flat as a piece of paper, the breath hissing angrily through his mouth and nose.

Hands trembling, he reached under the bed and pulled out the metal box in which he had brought back his belongings from the single room he rented in Nairobi. It was locked. He couldn't remember where he had placed the keys. He searched for them everywhere, turning the room inside out. He pulled out drawers from the wardrobe and threw their contents out, scattering them around the floor. In a matter of minutes, all their clothes were strewn about the room. But the keys were nowhere to be found. He tore at the blanket and searched under the mattress. There was nothing there.

He rushed out of the bedroom and into the kitchen, frothing at the mouth, hands shaking uncontrollably. He found a knife and ran back into the bedroom. Rose wanted to talk. Perhaps this was his chance. He would prove to her he could take care of his family. He had the money. But the shadow of Wanja still hovered about him, mocking him. He tried to pick the lock with the sharp edge of the knife but gave up in frustration after a few minutes.

He decided to go out and buy a screwdriver. He reached for his trousers which were hanging on a nail on the wall. Before he could put them on he heard a jingle and a grin spread across his face as he reached into the pocket and extracted a bunch of keys. Struggling to remain calm, he unlocked the box and picked up the small traveling bag in which he kept his severance pay. There were three notes in the bag. Three 500-shilling notes. His hands trembled as he searched in the box for the rest of the money. It has to be here somewhere! Forty thousand! Where could it have gone?

The pastor on the radio continued reading from the Bible: "And if anyone causes one of these little ones who believe in me to sin, it would be better for him to be thrown into the sea with a large millstone tied around his neck."

Maina pictured himself sitting at the Happy Inn, surrounded by a crowd of fellow drinkers and hangers-on. Drinking and laughing merrily late into the night, Wanja perched on his lap, rubbing his back and whispering in his ear. He saw the career he struggled to define dwindle away. And he knew there were never going to be any chatty customers offering him their hard-earned cash.

"That Wanja woman!" he screamed. "She's behind this. She and those good-for-nothing scavengers." Fearing his head would explode, he grabbed hold of it with both hands and leaned forward, sobbing and breathing noisily.

What am I going to do now? What is there to tell Rose? Who will pay the boys' school fees, and buy them food and clothes?

It had taken him exactly three months to squander the start-up capital for the undefined career the City Council had prescribed for him.

The pastor droned on: "If your hand causes you to sin, cut it off!"

"I blame no one! I did it! I betrayed my family! I betrayed my dear wife, ohhh… Rose!" His tortured voice echoed back at him, as if mocking him for his transgressions.

He picked up the knife and approached the radio. His eyes burned with a mixture of fear and rage. If the pastor had been in that room, he would surely have slaughtered him. He pulled his vest over his head and let it drop slowly on the bed. Then he peeled off his briefs and let them drop to the floor. He stood there naked, glaring around him, and crouching as though afraid of an unseen enemy.

"It is better for you to enter life maimed than with two hands to go into hell, where the fire never goes out."

The pastor's stentorian voice rocked the room and made Maina tremble with fright. He dropped to the ground like one of Rose's sacks of cabbages. Then he forced himself to sit on the hard, cold earthen floor on the very spot where he had tried to dig the cigarette into the ground with his bare foot. His eyes filled with tears. He clutched the knife tightly in his hand.

"And if your foot causes you to sin, cut it off. It is better for you to enter life crippled than to have two feet and be thrown into hell."

He looked again in the direction of the radio but couldn't see it. The tears now flowed freely down his face, blinding him. He started to moan, and his body shook uncontrollably as he cried like a baby. Blurred images flew across his face. He heard voices in his head. People were saying: what kind of a man is this, who leaves a loving wife, keeps a bar woman, squanders his money and cannot support his family? He saw Rose's face lean down to sneer at him. Then he saw her wander away and sit on the lap of the new Mutongoria in the Happy Inn.

"I know it will happen!" he screamed with frenzy. "She will go. She will leave! I cannot face her any more! I cannot pretend to love her. I cannot claim to be a man any more! What kind of a man am I?"

"And if your eye causes you to sin, pluck it out."

He lashed out and hit the radio, sending it crashing to the floor and under the bed. But the pastor refused to be silenced.

Maina lost himself in the wails that reverberated across the room, the wails that sounded as though they were coming from a hundred professional funeral mourners.

"They plucked me out like a sinning body part! Oh… ooh… what was that word again? Retrenched! Aiaih! They cut me out, and now I am no more… cut out… no longer a man. I cannot face Rose… oh-wui-eh! Forgive me Rosie, Rosie…"

He felt no pain as the knife sliced through his manhood. And then everything went very quiet.

All he could hear was the voice of the pastor mocking him from under the bed:

"It is better for you to enter the kingdom of God with one eye than to have two eyes and be thrown into hell."

But he ignored it, as a tranquility washed over him, soaking his mind with images of the smiling face of Rose. And even as he tightened his grip to stem the flow of blood, he knew she would understand. Not a foot, nor an eye. Only blood. She would understand. The pain would cleanse him.

Ken N Kamoche was born in Kenya and currently resides in Britain. *A Fragile Hope,* his debut collection, made the Frank O'Connor Long list (2007), and in 2008 was shortlisted for the Commonwealth First Book Award. One of the stories in the collection, 'A glimpse of life', won second prize in the Olaudah Equiano Prize for African Fiction in 2007.

THE VOLUNTEER

SHARING DOESN'T WORK. The kids surge forward like a shoal of piranhas when she begins her countdown.

"Fifty-nine, fifty-eight, fifty-seven...." Carrie calls out, as the second hand of the cheap clock on the wall skips its way through each child's one-minute turn.

Her throat is raw from yelling "Wait" – or the word she thinks may mean that, though when she hears her voice, she's not sure if she's using the one meaning "to wait" or "to swim". She hasn't been in India long, and spends most of her time among her husband's English-speaking, IT-savvy, foreign-returned friends.

Here in the Shelter Home for rescued children, the textbook Hindi she's learning is a frail thing. The children yell in robust dialect and she's battered by noise.

Rakesh, the tallest boy, steps in. When Carrie gets to zero, he grabs the toy that looks like a rubber sea urchin on a tether and holds it high above the tangle of waving hands. He teases, looking this way and that, then gives it to Guddu, who can't even yo-yo it the way it's meant to be done, as the kids close in on him.

"Get in line," she yells, and drags a giggling small boy to what would be the end of the queue, if there were one. Ramu glares at her with his unfathomable eyes as she pushes him in between the wriggling bodies that twist beneath her hands.

This is ridiculous. She can't do this.

Last week there'd been a dozen kids. She'd brought them a plastic basketball and a hoop that hung over the door. Those who weren't playing had heckled; it had been loud, but fun. Today the hoop is history, 18 children fill the four rooms, and some kind of critical mass has been reached.

The new ones are not disruptive on their own. Ruby, for instance. She's 10, maybe 12, found sleeping in a train. She says her parents got off somewhere and never got on again – which the counselor, a bright young girl who comes on Mondays, has said is a lie. She thinks Ruby's been sexually abused, maybe trafficked.

The girl hangs around the edges of the maelstrom, watching. She keeps straightening the red kerchief over her freshly shaved head and wiping her palms on her sagging frock. She's not making a sound.

I can't do this, Carrie thinks. They need professional help; this is a job for dedicated people, not me.

She looks around for the woman in charge, the one they all call 'Didi', elder sister, though she's old enough to be grandmother to some of them. Didi is busy over by the sink, making sure that the last child to finish the cocoa and cookies Carrie brought is properly washing and putting away his glass.

Didi has no family of her own left, for some dark reason she's never revealed to Carrie, and so she took this job. Didi keeps things in order. She doles out the food and counts socks and keeps after the kids to bathe. She was the one who had all their heads shaved, because of the lice.

"Didi-ji, can you please help me?" Carrie calls out, in excessively polite distress, but now the woman is taking the youngest boy out to wash because he's pissed his pants again.

"Stop it!" Carrie yells, in English, as hands grab for the toy again, "Get away!"

But they go on shouting and straining around her until Rakesh takes back the toy and gives it to another of his buddies.

What a mess. She's amazed at herself for thinking she could make any difference here, when the whole operation is so shaky. One woman, managing 18 kids. Volunteers dropping in and out. Some guy running around trying to find their parents, trying to get them into school, dealing with police...

And her. What does she know about children? She isn't sure she wants any. She and Shankar are still in the experimental stage, they don't even know where they want to live. Right now he wants to work with the outfit that brought him back to his hometown. He says he wants to be part of "The Indian Millennium" – and the next one will be that. Where does she fit in, without so much as a work permit? He says there's a lot of red tape. He needs to look into it.

Shankar thinks she could be as happy as his sister, who has two kids and so many friends that her cellphone is welded between shoulder and ear. She runs a boutique and wants Carrie to come and sit with her among the silk and sequins, but Carrie has nothing to say to the well-dressed women who talk of georgette and crêpe, of which restaurant is best for lunch, of nursery schools and hairdressers and temperamental servants. Carrie thinks that, if she's going to live in the Third World, she should at least be doing something for the common good, some kind of service.

And so she'd donated her Thursday afternoons to being here, though now she wishes she were back in the house in the neighborhood where sounds are muffled in leaves and masses of bougainvillea blooms. She wouldn't have to go any farther away than that to find quiet.

"*Pani*!" someone yells, "water's coming out."

The children dissolve in a squirming puddle as they fight over the dripping remains. The light inside had floated in some viscous fluid that is leaking over all those small, grasping hands.

"It's dead," Carrie announces, since she's temporarily forgotten the word for "finished". As she confiscates shreds of the flimsy plastic that feels so much like skin, she wonders why she'd thought it could last. In the store, the red light that glowed at the end of each throw had lured her inner child; the gross feel of the thing had appealed. She doesn't want to have to think of consequences all the time, of imminent disasters like this.

Ramu glowers at her as she wrests the last bit from him. He never got a turn, and his resentment is not hidden.

"A woman brought him to us," Carrie had been told. "But she wasn't his mother. Someone gave the boy to her. He may have been kidnapped... Sounds like he was passed from hand to hand for a few years."

Carrie imagined a string of dusty villages when she heard that, places she'd only seen from the road. A child wrapped in a blanket, staring up at strangers with those unreadable eyes as they hurry him from place to place, in the dark.

What could anyone do for him?

"Wash hands everybody," Carrie says, sticking to the things she knows they need to do. "Wash that stuff off your hands, then we'll draw."

Water shoots out the side of the defective tap. Their clothes get damp; their hands drip dry.

The kids spread a blanket on the cement floor. It bunches up on the sides. In this part of town, buildings are pressed thin by other buildings, rooms are compressed to corridors. Didi unlocks the cupboard and passes out drawing books; she dumps two piles of worn crayons, front and back. Sharp voices ricochet off the walls.

Carrie sits and is shocked. The cold goes straight through blanket, sari, petticoat and Neva Quilt long johns.

"Where were we?" she asks, blowing on numb fingers.

"J!" several voices shout.

Last week she'd asked them what they wanted to draw on the blank pages in the back of their messy, used coloring books. From the English Aunty, they said, they wanted the English alphabet. They chant "A for Apple, B for Ball..." like a mantra that changes them for a moment into smart kids in spotless white socks and pressed uniforms from élite schools.

"J for....?" she asks.

"Jug," one of the bigger boys calls, maybe Rakesh. He'd been to school, some, before he ran away from a home he refuses to talk about. He says "Good morning" to her when she comes at three o'clock.

She draws a lopsided pitcher, like the Mexican jug her mother used for lemonade. She wonders if they've ever seen such a thing.

"Jackal," comes another voice and she makes her signature hieroglyph dog with a longer nose. They tell her to make the tail bushy. They must have seen jackals.

She sketches for the younger ones and they scribble color over her halting lines; the older ones copy and embellish. It keeps them busy. Aside from a minor skirmish over the one crayon that's the color of jackal fur, all is quiet.

And cold. There's a smell caught in the cold, an acrid tang off their shabby sweatshirts that feel clammy, slightly oily, to touch. The scents of crayons and paper and damp feet hang immobilized in the air.

"See, Aunty, see," one after another, they wave their pictures in her face.

She tells each one how good each picture is. In each she finds some separate virtue: "So colorful!" "So tidy!" "See the green face – isn't that funny?" as she runs a hand over the chilly stubble on their heads.

It's easy to praise. The end is near. She feels freedom coming. Now all she has to do is tell her stories and she can go.

She thinks, as she passes out the last compliments, that she will call the Director the minute she gets home and tell him she can't come any more. She'll say she needs to focus on learning Hindi first. He's a busy man. Four times out of five she's called him, he's been out of town, conferencing with fellow activists or searching for funds. He'll soon forget she'd ever been there. The kids aren't all that used to her; they'll forget, and she'll go off and find other noble tasks – raise funds for saving bustards or Gangetic dolphins, maybe. She'd be good at that. She has people skills.

Or she could go back to Seattle.

Didi is fussing, trying to put things away. Ramu is still curled over his work, not looking up as Didi scolds.

"Let him finish," Carrie says. "He can listen while he draws."

She tells her stories, a folk tale about a king whose bed whispers riddles beneath him, and a fable with talking animals. When she talks like a muttering bed leg or a greedy donkey they stay still, even when the words are lost in her twang or disappear in the forest of faulty grammar. She acts a complete fool, hamming, rushing toward home and recovery. After every day she's come here, there have always been those blissful first four days at home, in which she didn't have to think. Only on the fourth night did she start waking up, staring into the dark, wondering what food to take, what stories to tell. She's been fighting her nature, this is clear. She should have left the job to those who are comfortable with it.

"Goodbye, Aunty!" the children chorus as she stands and shakes out her clothes. A couple of the quieter ones touch her feet for blessings. She never knows what to do with the feeling of soft fingers on her toes. It makes her think they must have had homes, once. There must have been parents to teach such extreme manners.

Or is it Didi's doing? She's just the type to teach them this because she thinks it's what they need in their world – humility, lots of it.

A small girl hugs Carrie's knees and almost trips her. Rakesh pumps her arm in a hearty handshake, grinning, trying to be British.

So much energy is pushing her out the door that Carrie begins to feel good about going. The kids will some day spill out the gate with all that energy. Like water through a burst dam, they'll find some level.

Didi is pulling at Ramu's sketchbook, wanting to put it away. He's resisting, and so Carrie steps between them to say: "Let me see."

On a single page he's made his drawings, tiny, complete. His kite flies among silver clouds. His lamp has a coiled cord plugged into a wall socket, perfectly drawn. His mouse sits beside a hole, his jackal by a bush, his jug on a table.

"This is beautiful!" she cries. "Look, everybody!"

No one turns toward the book she holds high; they're too busy pushing for space, cleaning up, horsing around.

She kneels beside Ramu and puts an arm around shoulders that feel like a coil of wire. But suddenly she can feel him lean, just a little, away from the cacophony, toward her.

She must say something, and finds the first words that come out are: "I know what I'll bring next week."

He doesn't look up, but neither does he pull away.

"I'll bring paints and brushes and we'll make real pictures!"

What am I saying, she wonders. They'll make a mess. Didi will kill me. I haven't painted since eighth grade.

He stays there, under her arm. His eyes move from the floor to her feet. She can feel his stiff body waiting for something more, more than touch, more than she can give, but she cannot move.

Lucinda Nelson Dhavan first came to India on a Fulbright Grant, and has been living there ever since. After several years on the staff of a local newspaper, she has returned to writing fiction. Her stories have appeared in *Gargoyle*, *Sweet Fancy Moses*, and online in, amongst others, *Carve* and *The Paumanok Review*. She is working on a novel.

ADETOKUNBO GBENGA ABIOLA NIGERIA

THE ALBINO

WHEN BANTY YELLOW entered the shed, he found that the box guitar was not in the usual corner. Did I keep it outside? he thought. Did I keep it the bush at the back of the shed? He dashed out of the shed and came to the yard. Holding his hand to shield his eyes from the rays of the November sun, he moved to the bush at the back of the shack and looked through it. The guitar was not there. He came back into the shed and went to the corner again. A heap of clothes, a mound of clay, a coil of wires, and a pile of sand sat scattered on the ground. It was here in the morning, he thought. Here at this corner. Here by the clothes. Here near the mound of clay. Scratching his leg with one hand, he bent down and used the other to rummage through the heap of trousers, shirts and pants. After a long moment of doing this, he sank to the ground and sighed. The guitar is missing, he thought. His best friend was gone.

"Banty!" someone shouted from outside. "Let's start going for rehearsals."

Banty didn't answer. Seconds later, the door of the shed was pushed open, and a young man in his twenties entered; a frown adorned his face. "What's happening?" he asked. "Why are you sitting on the floor like that?"

"The guitar has been stolen," Banty said, his voice dull. "Solo is out of town. Majek Jeggs will never give me a guitar. He hates albinos."

Silence fell between both men. Banty shook his head, sighed, and stared at the ground. It must be one of the neighbors who took it, he thought. A neighbor who saw an albino as trash; a stinking trash; a twelve-storey pile of trash with a magnificent stink, a stink polluting the streets and lanes of Benin City, a stink with an enormous sign at the roof that read: "This is trash". Banty rose to his feet, turned so his face didn't directly face the sun, and leaned against the side of the shed.

His companion came to meet him.

"We'll still go to Hotel Philomena for rehearsals and the show," he said.

"We'll rent a guitar."

"No, Thomas!" Banty said. "I'm not going. I can't play without a guitar, and nobody in Benin City would rent a guitar to an albino."

"We must try," Thomas said.

Banty turned from him in anger and marched through a backyard to the building in which his room was located. As he moved towards it, he was filled with despair about the treatment of albinos. Would he never escape this treatment, he asked himself, this treatment for which there was no cure? Would there always be no cure, no cure for this treatment which was the cause of his sickness? This thought in his mind, he walked through the doorway and went to his room. Without taking off his shirt, he lay on his bed and stared at the ceiling. Normally, when he was in his room, he felt sheltered from the stress of the outside world. Not this time. His songs were sighs of sadness, his thoughts were a jumble of bitter experiences, his images were a kaleidoscope of ragged pictures, and he shook his head from side to side and then looked around him. The walls of the room stood over him in their stark bleakness, the cobwebs mocked at him from the wall, and the ceiling spread out a canvas of soot and smoke-stained asbestos over him. Feeling that the pain in his heart was about to explode, he turned, lay face down on the bed, his white hand clutching at the bed sheet. As he moaned and sighed, he heard footsteps on the corridor, and the door of the room was pushed open. Thomas stood in the doorway.

"We must go to Kimayo's Studios," Thomas said. "Kimayo is your friend, he'll allow us to rent his guitar."

"No," Banty said. "It's all over. The witches have won."

"Pull yourself together," Thomas said, going to meet him. "This is the big one for us. Our opportunity. Once the recording companies hear you sing at the show, with me backing you up, we'll get a contract. Our troubles are over. It's goodbye to poverty."

Thomas's words struck a chord in Banty's soul, and he raised himself up, got out of the bed, and sat at its edge. There was an intent look in his eyes.

"Why is it so difficult for me?" he asked. "Why is the whole world against albinos? Why?"

"The world does not know it's the heart that matters," Thomas said, "not the color of the skin."

Banty ruminated on Thomas's reply for a long moment then stood up. He pulled off his short-sleeved shirt and got a long-sleeved one from the top of the chair. He put it on, careful that the sleeves covered his hand up to the wrist. This will shield my hands from the sun, he thought. He grabbed a wide-brimmed hat from the ground, slapped it against his head, and put on a pair of sunglasses. The hat was to prevent the sun from beating on his head and the sunglasses to shield his eyes from the rays from the sky.

"Let's go," he said.

A group of boys, like an army of cut-throats, stood in front of a one-storey building at the street corner. Banty recognized Felix Amadasun, a man with frog-like eyes and a scarred face, among the men. Banty knew that Felix was always in police cells for violence and petty stealing. He derived a huge delight in taunting Banty any time he passed on the street. Don't let him taunt me now, Banty prayed. Now, when I don't want to become a slave to anger, my friend of many years that always leads me to trouble and failure. Don't let him taunt me so I don't become a prisoner of violence. But as he and Thomas passed, Felix coughed.

"Unfortunate European," he said to Banty. "Where are you going?"

His heart beating wildly, Banty strolled on, not saying anything. He heard a finger being snapped behind him, a whistle that sounded above the sound of the afternoon, and footsteps shuffling and moving in his direction. He and Thomas were surrounded.

"Are you deaf?" Felix asked Banty. "I asked you a question."

Thomas was angry.

"You have no right to do this," he said

Before Banty could stop him, one of the boys grabbed him by the shoulder, removed his hat, ran down the street, turned a corner, and disappeared

"My cap!" Banty shouted, about to race after him, but another one of the thugs seized him; while Felix held a knife against his cheek, removed his glasses, and pushed him to the ground.

"Next time I ask you a question, answer me," he snarled, "or I'll kill you."

Banty climbed to his feet; he wanted to rush at him as he held out the knife, but Thomas grabbed his hand.

"No," he said. "Do you want to get murdered?"

"Let him come," Felix said. "I'll murder him. I'll throw his carcass on the street. Nobody will do anything to me."

Banty allowed Thomas to hold him. He didn't want to get murdered. Besides, there was a crisis with the guitar. He didn't want something added to it to completely rule him out of the show. But walking down the street, the sun's rays on his bare face and yellow hair, he felt a stream of anger rise up in his heart.

By the time he and Thomas reached Kimayo's studio, Banty's eyes were red from the blast of the sun's rays, and they blinked and squinted like those of a cat. He missed his hat and sunglasses, but he couldn't replace them because he was down to his last money. He hoped Kimayo would lend him a guitar to end this march through streets of hell. But when he and Thomas pushed the studio door open and got into the dim-lit room, they found that Kimayo was not around. A lamp that stood at the corner of the room sent out a strong yellow light towards the door, and Banty squirmed, turned his back to it, forcing down the urge to scratch at his itching eyes. But he faced a full-length mirror, which reflected the light of the lamp straight to his face, and he looked away and muttered under his breath. Suddenly, the door at the back of the studio was pushed open, and a man came in. Banty noted that he wore a blue shirt over jeans and frowned when he saw Banty.

"What do you want?" he barked.

"Kimayo," Thomas said.

"He is not around," the man said, staring at Banty.

"We want to hire a guitar for a show this evening," Banty said.

The man's eyes narrowed.

"We don't hire guitars to albinos," the man said.

"But that's not true," Thomas countered. "Kimayo gives him his guitar during shows. Why are you saying he doesn't rent them out to albinos?"

"Kimayo is not around," the man said. "I'm his manager. And I say I don't hire guitars out to albinos."

Banty felt Thomas' hand around his hand.

"Let's go," he said. "Let's leave here."

As Thomas turned to go, the man beckoned to him.

"You better take my advice before it's too late," he said. "My father once told me that the friend to an albino will give birth to an albino. If you don't want to give birth to an albino, avoid your friend."

"You can go to hell!" Thomas told him, and he and Banty went out of the room.

At the porch of the studio, Banty stopped walking. He felt as if his face were on fire, and he couldn't see anything at a distance of more than five meters from where he stood. Ahead of him, the light poured from the sun, a furnace with an inexhaustible amount of fuel; the flame from the orb seemed to increase with every second, the fire from the core blazing with ever-greater intensity. The street before him was blurred; the passers-by were images that melted into nothingness immediately they were seen; and the awareness of cars only came after they had passed. In Banty's eyes, the houses were lines and circles that stood in his vision, and the images of red and green and yellow colors that swam in his vision made him stretch out his hand like a confused man. I can't walk through the sun, he thought. I can't walk through the street. And he drew Thomas' attention to a bench at the corner of the porch and shambled to sit on it. Understanding his condition, Thomas went to sit beside him. As they sat, Banty reflected on the scene that had taken place inside the studio, shook his head, and swore under his breath. The wave of anger that had crawled in his heart after the encounter with Felix began to stir once again, but he took a deep breath and fought against it. The show is almost lost, he thought. His anger, like fire that consumes itself and everything around it, would burn the already-thin chances. It would be used later, he thought, when it would decide success and failure, when it would be a deciding factor.

When they got to the next studio, Banty frowned. It was locked and guitars and drums were placed on a small yard in front of it. Besides, there was no place where he could hide from the sun. As he and Thomas came to stand beside the instruments, a woman and two children emerged from a room beside the studio. When they saw Banty, they stopped, stared at him as if he were an evil spirit, then dashed back into the room. A moment later, a tall man came out of the room, stared at Banty, drew aside the curtain shielding the doorway, and looked inside.

"Are you people crazy?" he shouted. "It's an albino, not an evil demon."

After a few moments, Banty saw the curtain of the room shift aside, and the woman and the two children came out. Banty watched them as they gave him a wide berth and moved towards the street.

"What do you people want?" the tall man asked Thomas and Banty.

"The owner of these instruments," Thomas said. "We want to rent the guitar."

Banty saw the man grow thoughtful for a few seconds, snap his fingers, and enter his room. As they waited for him to return, Banty felt his skin burn from the relentless heat of the sun. Once again, he looked along the sidewalk of the house for shade where he could take refuge, but the sun was high in the sky, and the shade created by the eaves of the roof was small. Sighing with disappointment, he stared at the back of his palms. Freckles, like dirt, had sprouted out on them. Some were red, others were yellow, many were in indecipherable colors. As Banty thrust his hands into the pockets of trouser, the tall man emerged with another man.

When Banty saw the other man, he turned away. Gbenga Idubor, sadist band leader; he thought. Gbenga Idubor, the animalistic band leader. Gbenga Idubor, the biggest bigot in Benin City. Banty knew if Gbenga owned the instruments he wouldn't be able to rent them. Gbenga had a band that played highlife music. Banty was told that an albino had once gone to meet him about playing bass drums for him and Gbenga had told him: "I'd rather die than allow an albino play for me."

"Let's go," Banty told Thomas.

"No, wait."

"Are these the people who want to hire my guitar?" Gbenga asked the tall man in a booming voice.

The latter nodded.

"How can you bring an albino to me, Samuel?" Gbenga said. "Don't you know a curse will come upon me if they use my guitar?"

Not bothering to listen to any more, Banty began to walk away, ignoring Thomas as he called out to him. As Banty walked down the street, his heart beat furiously. Why? he thought, as he swore under his breath. Why the hatred for the albino? Were they the ones who starved themselves of the black skin? Were they the ones who starved themselves of melanin? The tone of the booming voice he had just heard sending tongues of anger to flicker through the chambers of his soul, he took in a deep breath and forced down the anger. Not now.

Thomas caught up with him at a corner leading to the street in which Kimayo's studio was located. But Banty did not break his stride, so Thomas grabbed his hand and tried to make him to stop.

"There's another place I know," he said.

Banty blinked his eyes then squinted at him; his eyes had become apertures of strain and blood. He felt the heat of the sun, like burning coal, hot on the scalp of his head, and his face squirmed. Like trekking through a desert, he thought. Can't go on through this hell. Looking about him, he saw a mango tree standing in front of a bungalow that was about six houses from Kimayo's, an umbrella whose spokes sloped down to provide shade on the ground, a place of refuge for lizards and fowls and flies seeking escape from the fire of the November sun. Gasping, Banty branched off to take shelter in the shade. Thomas went to meet him.

"I'm not going," Banty told him, and a reflective look came into his eyes. "It's tough being an albino. We're not black, we're not white. We're like bats: we're not a bird, we're not an animal. Nobody will give such creatures anything."

"Salif Keita went through this and became a musician," Thomas said. "Why not you?" While Banty thought on this, a Volkswagen car, filled with men, swept past on the road and moved down the street. Thomas pointed at it. "That's Kimayo's car. He's back. Let's go and meet him."

Banty shook his head, but when he remembered Thomas' talk about Salif Keita, he hesitated then started to move towards Kimayo's studio. He staggered rather than walked. He could not see anything at a distance of more than ten meters ahead of him; he was an owl thrust into daylight. Damn! He slammed into a small tree in front of the compound next to the studio and grunted. Thomas drew him from the tree, and guided him away. Damn! He kicked his leg against a rock in his path and squirmed with pain. Thomas put his arm around him and ushered him into the studio. Inside, Banty barely made out Kimayo, his manager, and two other men.

"They've come again," said the manager, pointing at Banty and Thomas.

"Why didn't you rent out the guitar to them?" Kimayo, a tall, bushy-haired man, asked.

"I can't do that, Kimayo," his manager said. "Do you want a curse to come upon me?"

"Shut up there!" Kimayo said angrily. "Give them the guitar at once!"

"Wait there," said one of the two other men. A burly man, he wore a shirt too small for him, and his belly bulged under it. "Is this the guitar we'll use tomorrow?"

"Yes, Okojie," Kimayo said.

"Don't rent it to them," Okojie said, venom in his eyes as he stared at Banty.

"Why?" Kimayo asked.

"If he touches the guitar, and I use it tomorrow, my show will fail."

"Why are you talking like this, Okojie?" Kimayo said.

"What do you mean?" Okojie said and stood up. "An albino is a curse from the gods. Devils. They were born of an evil spirit. They put a curse into anything they touch. Besides, they can't sing."

"That's a lie!" Banty shouted, not able to control his anger for once. "I might be an albino, but I can sing. Given the chance, I'll be the hottest star in this crazy city."

Silence fell in the room, a silence as oppressive as the heat of the November sun. Banty was staring at Okojie as if he could tear him to pieces and throw his carcass into the street. His eyes, like those of an angry wildcat, were blinking and squinting with increased frequency. He hated anyone to say he could not sing and was ready to fight even the devil to prove that he was not dumb and that he could sing. Abuse me, he thought, I can take it. Never say I'm dumb. Never, never say I can't sing.

"He can sing," Kimayo said finally. "The crowd loves him."

"I don't care!" Okojie shouted. "If you give him the guitar, I'll never do business with you again." He stamped towards the door, ignoring Kimayo as he tried to grab his hand. Both of them went out.

"Your sort should be sacrificed as they do in other places," said Kimayo's manager to Banty, "then we wouldn't have any confusion."

Thomas, anger in his eyes, stared at him.

"How can you talk like that?" he demanded.

"I can talk anyhow I want to," the manager retorted.

"You're sick!" Banty shouted at him.

"An animal," Thomas put in.

From the corner of his eyes, Banty saw Kimayo and Okojie, like conspirators, slip into the room. Kimayo, a servile smile on his face, had put his hand around Okojie's waist. They have reached an agreement, Banty thought. An agreement between rats, and he swore under his breath. But he felt Kimayo's hand drop on his shoulder and two fingers pinched him. Knowing this to be a signal that Kimayo wanted to have a private discussion with him, Banty followed him out of the studio. They stopped by the Volkswagen car, parked near a kiosk at the yard in front of the studio, a giant beetle that slumbered in the sun. Banty marveled that he could partially see the car now, so he stared at the sky. The sun had started to crawl down through the clouds; the rays, like the receding head of a turtle, shrinking into the core. Good, he thought. He stared at Kimayo and noticed the apologetic expression on his face. Conspirators, after betrayal, wore that look, Banty thought.

"Go and look for Jake Solo," Kimayo told him. "He'll give you a guitar." Jake Solo was the promoter who had slotted Banty into the breakthrough show at Philomena Hotel.

"He traveled out of town yesterday," Banty said. "He's not coming for the show. Majek Jeggs controls the guitar at the show. He'll never give me any."

"This is terrible," Kimayo said. "And I can't give out my guitar again. Okojie will refuse to give me business in future. I can't afford that because I have mouths to feed."

"Don't worry," Banty told him. "I'll sort it out somehow." He turned towards the studio. "Thomas! Let's go."

Thomas came out to the courtyard. "Where?" he asked.

"Let's just go," Banty said. He nodded at Kimayo, passed by the side of the Volkswagen, and stepped into the street.

He took Thomas to the Plaza Restaurant, an establishment that faced a busy road in which cars and lorries zoomed past like Formula One vehicles. The restaurant was a hundred meters from Philomena Hotel. As they walked to the bar, Banty heard Salif Keita's music wafting from the turntable, rising and falling again and again, the sound of an ocean at a beach, its wave lifting and lapping on the sand repeatedly. An albino just like me, Banty thought, taking a seat from which he could stare through a big window at the road outside.

Thomas placed two bottles of beer on the table and sat opposite him. As Banty sipped from the bottle, he reflected that his sight was clearing up. He could see cars 50 meters away on the road. He stared at his palms. The freckles were disappearing. Outside, the sun was dipping down the sky, chased away by the approach of evening.

He thought about the people who refused to allow him to rent a guitar. They were animals, he reflected. They were animals masquerading as men masquerading as women masquerading as people. Someone once told him: "you don't argue with an animal, you must fight with a beast." Playing the gentleman is wrong, he thought. Smile with those that smile and fight with those that fight; especially when there was no option, when there was no choice, when he wanted to be a musician, when he wanted to be like Salif Keita. Winning would make other albinos see him as a symbol.

But who could he fight to get a guitar? Majek Jeggs? The man in charge of the guitar at the show? He flinched when he thought about confronting him. Banty remembered that the previous week Majek had told him: "You're a curse on the crowd when on stage." At another time, he told Banty: "Why don't you pour petrol on yourself, light a fire, burn, and die?" Recollecting these words, Banty frowned, then he shook his head with sadness. Unfortunately, confronting Majek had to be done if he was to get on the show. His eyes went to the big window, and he stared at the road.

A black Mercedes Benz – Jake Solo's car – passed by on the street.

"Let's go," Banty shouted.

"What's happening?" Thomas asked.

"Jake Solo is around," Banty said, getting off his seat.

He ran out of the bar and came out of the restaurant, Thomas following. Disoriented by the swift change to the light outside, Banty almost collided with a man coming into the restaurant. Swearing, he looked all about him. This is no time to make any mistake, he thought. Any mistake about his sight may mean not taking part in the show. He saw a man hawking hats and sunglasses along the street. He ran to the man, bought a hat, bought a pair of sunglasses with the remaining money on him. I'll need this for the battle, he thought as he headed for Philomena Hotel. I'll need this for any showdown. He and Thomas bore down on the gate of the hotel. Banty was oblivious of the passing cars and motor-cycles – his mind was on Jake Solo. I must explain to him how I lost the guitar, he thought. I must explain to him why I need his guitar. He passed through the gates of the hotel, ignoring the gateman who was shouting at him. He tramped to the car-park and looked around. Solo's car was not there. Thomas turned to him.

"His car is not parked here," he told Banty.

"It must be somewhere," Banty said, beginning to go towards the lobby.

Thomas grabbed his hand.

"Are you sure you saw Solo's car?" he asked.

"Of course I'm sure," Banty said.

He snatched his hand away and marched towards the lobby. Two men who passed by him looked at him as though he were mad, but he didn't care. They can go to blazes, he thought. They can go to hell, go to the edge of the world, go to the edge of the world and fall off it – I must get on the show. When he got to the lobby, he stared at the people milling around. He hoped to catch the lithe figure of Jake Solo, but he didn't see him. He didn't see anyone he knew. He didn't hear the sound of the bass drums pounding inside the hall. Two musicians, friends of Banty, came towards him, tapped him on the shoulder, and called his name. He smiled blandly at them, not seeing them. Perhaps it's due to the light in the lobby, he thought. He decided to turn his side to it and view the lobby with the side of one eye. Still, he couldn't see Solo. Solo was not around.

"What are we going to do now?" Thomas asked him. "We're going to open the show. We have less than an hour, yet there's no guitar."

"We must meet Majek," Banty said. "We must get a guitar from him."

"I'll back you up."

Banty and Thomas headed for the hall, walking briskly. No option but the showdown with Majek, Banty thought. As he passed the corridor that linked the hall to the lobby, a man stood in his way and said: "Unfortunate European, what are you doing here?" With a strength he didn't know he possessed, Banty thrust his hand under the armpit of the man and hurled him up. The man went flying past and crashed on the floor. Oblivious of the man's groans, Banty turned a corner and entered the hall. The session men, amidst the beat of music, were putting the finishing touches to the construction of the stage. Majek was not around, and Banty clenched a fist.

One of the session men was passing by, and Banty grabbed him.

"Where can I get Majek?" he asked.

"He's around," the session man said. "He's around." And he dashed out of the hall. As Banty contemplated his next course of action, he saw Majek come into the hall. He wore his customary black jeans and red vest. Banty noticed the look of disapproval that came into Majek's face as soon as he saw him. His mouth was drawn in a tight line and his eyes sparkled with the fire of anger. But Banty, desperate to take part in the show, was not frightened of him as he usually was.

"You're very punctual," Majek said. "This is the way to make the show successful."

"I've been looking for you," Banty replied. "My guitar has been stolen."

"So what do you want me to do?" Majek snapped. "Turn myself into a guitar?" He started to walk away.

Banty stood in his path.

"Solo said you should give me a guitar," he said.

"Liar!" Majek shouted. "Solo has traveled to Lagos."

"I was there when he said so," Thomas put in. "He said you should give him a guitar."

Majek raised his palms as if to stop further discussion.

"All right, Solo said I should give him a guitar," he said. "But I'm not going to. And nobody can change my mind."

"Do you realize we have to go on stage in ten minutes?" Thomas said.

"I realize that," Majek said, his voice contemptuous. "But I've told Banty he doesn't belong in music. Today is the time to prove it."

Watching his face, Banty read menace on it, read resolution as well. Something desperate had to be done to get this man change his mind. When Majek attempted to walk away, Banty lunged forward, blocked his way again, and grabbed him by the trousers.

"Solo said you should give me a guitar," he screamed.

"Will you leave my trousers!" Majek shouted.

"What's happening here?" said a man who had just come into the hall. Immediately Banty heard the voice, he turned his head and stared. Jake Solo! he thought. Jake Solo was truly around. Banty let go of Majek's trousers. He saw Thomas go to meet Solo to explain the situation to him. After listening to Thomas, Solo looked at Banty, a sympathetic look in his eyes, then stared at Majek. "Give him the guitar."

"But..."

Banty saw a look of anger creep into Jake Solo's eyes.

"Are you crazy!?" he shouted. "Do you want to flop my show? I said give him the guitar!"

Banty looked at Majek and saw the look of fear on his face. He turned and began to walk away. Stopping, he gestured to Banty and Thomas to follow him then headed for the changing room. Banty and Thomas followed him and stopped by the doorway of the room. As they stood waiting for Majek to come out, Banty felt his heart hammering with anticipation, and beads of perspiration dropped from his face. Majek came out and handed a guitar to him.

"You've escaped this one," he said. "Next time, I'll get you."

Banty took the guitar but didn't answer him. He put his arm around Thomas' shoulder and both of them walked towards the stage for one last practice before the show.

Adetokunbo Abiola is a prize-winning Nigerian journalist and writer. He has published a novel titled *Labulabu Mask* (Macmillans Nigeria). He has also published in print and online magazines both in Nigeria and internationally.

SKYE BRANNON UNITED STATES

FIREWEED

IT WAS A remembering day for Baluta. It began with laughter, or a dream of laughter. It was Alanso's laugh, flowing like doves out of her bright smiling mouth. It was Alanso's laugh, out from between those cheeks that caught the sun and held it in a warm glow the rest of the day. It was Alanso's laugh, stirred from the dead to wake Baluta. Sometimes remembering began later in the day, but not today. Baluta had to lift from beneath a stone of grief, so heavy with his sister's memory, to get out of his cot. He had work today, after all.

Baluta washed in the shower, cold after his brother and sister-in-law had had theirs. Cold like Kpatawee Falls back home, Baluta thought. Yes. Today would be a remembering day. He pulled a work shirt over his head. The name 'Joel' was simply embroidered over the heart. The name had been his brother's idea.

"Dese Americans," Jato said, "if you tell dem your Mandika name, dey look like you've given dem a riddle. You tell dem your name is Bob, and dey are all smiles." Jato grinned at his younger brother. "But you can't have Bob, dat is mine."

Jato and his wife, Sama, had already gone. Since Baluta had to have the car to go where the bus route didn't, it was Jato and Sama who had to wake at five a.m. to catch buses to work. Baluta felt awful for this, but he had to work to get a car, and needed a car to get to work. So, here he was, walking toward the family vehicle. Jato called it the Swiss Chevy. The old Camero had so many holes in its body, the attempts at duct-tape patchwork had been abandoned, and Baluta heard the wind whistle through them as he drove through the ghettos of his neighborhood, through the factory district, out to the country, past golf resorts, and finally in through a large gate toward his work site.

Just the week before, he'd taken a left at the crossroads in the neighborhood, to work on a banister for Mrs Giles. She'd nodded, pleased at Baluta's work, and as a reward referred him for more work. "This couple has some cabinet problems that are really bothersome, Jim." Even remembering Baluta's fake name was too difficult for Mrs Giles. "I'll give you a call if they want you to come over."

She had and Baluta was on his way. This time, he would take a right after entering the gate, and drive past the large man-made pond. It was only a lip, a small man-made lip on one side of the water's body, but it was just the same curve as the pond where he and Alanso played, splashing and laughing. She could pull fish from that pond, like plucking flowers from a field, and would howl good-naturedly at Baluta's empty handed attempts. When they would get back to their hut, a square in the shanty-town quilt shadowed by a mountain, Alanso would always tell Grandma Awa that Baluta had caught some fish. She'd smile at Baluta, and he'd kick the dirt embarrassed.

Baluta pulled his attention from the pond, from his remembering. He noted the wrought-iron numbers on the mansions he passed. When he was several numbers away, he took his foot off the gas. He hoped he could glide to a stop in front of the correct house, otherwise, the Swiss Chevy would let out a loud squeal when he hit the brake. He had timed it just right to slow to a dead stop just at the start of brownstone path that led to the palatial home.

He saw a lady, pretty, laid back inside the house, behind the glass of a large bay window. In his side vision, he saw her sit up straight at Swiss Chevy's approach. When he got out of the car, he noticed a frightened look on her face and that she clutched a phone in her hand. That posture, that clutching, that frightened look, it made Baluta remember his father's monkey traps. They were just small boxes with a drilled hole and a nut inside. The monkeys could put their hands in the box to grab the nut, but they could not pull their fists out, and refused to let go of the treasures. This lady in the square of the window, she had the same posture, still and frightened, as those monkeys when Baluta's father would collect them.

By the time Baluta had gotten out of the car, she was gone from the window and standing behind the door, opened only slightly.

"Did you need something?" she called out.

Baluta smiled a wide smile, standing still next to his car. "Hello der, Miss! I am Joel, the carpenter."

"Okay." The woman stayed still behind the door, closing it a little more.

"Mrs Giles said you needed some cabinets fixed?"

"Oh!" Suddenly, the woman became comfortable. The scared monkey in her had run away. "That's right. I forgot Cindy had said you were coming today."

Joel nodded, starting up the path.

"Oh, wait." The lady seemed to shout as an afterthought. She pointed out toward where Joel was walking. "Could you please smash down that pile of dirt?"

"Sorry, Miss?" Joel looked around and saw a small mound of earth, piled up around a hole.

"Yes, that. The real-estate agent just left that hole there when she pulled out her sign. I'll have to use someone else next time. Could you go ahead and fill up that hole?"

"Sure, Miss." He didn't know this lady's name, Baluta thought, and was already at work for her. He approached the mound and the remembering began. It was the mound of dirt full of ants that he and Alanso used to torment. He had been stung once, and then twice, and then a third time. Every time he had cried, and watched the welts rise on the bites. These ant stings were more painful than any other, little fire irons on the skin. Alanso told him that it must have been because he was a sweet boy, and she a sour little girl.

It was only a moment, and the dirt was back in its place, a dot of black in the lush green. The lady watched from the steps, pleased. She introduced herself as Tiffany, and moved through the large entry way, into the extravagant kitchen. She teetered on tall, skinny high heels as she walked, stopped at a cabinet above the sink, and opened it accusingly.

"This has *got* to be fixed." She looked at Baluta for confirmation.

Baluta nodded, but saw nothing wrong. The cabinet was of beautiful hardwood. "What is it, Miss?"

"This," Tiffany tried to push the cabinet door back, and it remained straight out. "This, this door needs to go *all* the way back, not just straight out. *All* the way back. All of them. *All* of them should go *all* the way back."

"Okay, Miss. Dis is not a problem. I can fix dis today. Mrs Giles told you of my terms, yes?"

"Yes. Fine." Tiffany waved absently. "She said you were from Africa?'

"Liberia." Baluta clarified.

"Oh, sorry." Tiffany looked at the cabinet again. "Cindy said you were from Africa. How long will this take?"

"Only a few hours, Miss."

"Fine. I'll just be right there." Tiffany pointed her slender finger toward the granite counter tops. The sunlight bounced from her diamond ring and danced dazzles across Baluta's face. Diamonds.

"They think they've found diamonds in our mountain." Baluta's father, Idirissa, had once told him gravely. "The war will be coming our way soon." Baluta remembered; it was the first time he had seen fear behind his father's strong eyes.

Tiffany scooted up to the granite counter while Baluta began his work. Slick magazines splayed in front of her. Pouting models wearing high skinny heels. Grand dining room and kitchen displays. A collage of movie stars caught in the act of living, with the byline 'who got fat, who got skinny, who got married, who got surgery'. She flipped through the magazines absently while Baluta lost himself in the work, the sawdust, and the remembering.

Tiffany's cellphone rang. It was a custom ring of a song called 'I still haven't found what I'm looking for' by U2. She flipped the phone. "Yes?" She turned a page absently, and then slammed her fist on the counter. "What do you mean they don't have it? It said right there on the website that it was in stock! Have you gone to the paint store on 78th Street?" Baluta tried to shut his ears to this woman's trill. "Are you sure you are asking for the right color? F-I-R-E-W-E-E-D? Fireweed?" The word hit Baluta right in the heart. It knocked his breath from his lungs, and stilled his hands. Fireweed.

"Go! Go you! Go get de fireweed now! You are a very bad boy!" Grandma Awa had caught Baluta with his hand in the cassava pile. He had been so hungry and wanted only a small slice, but Grandma Awa, her eyes usually full of kindness, was irate at this. She never spanked him, no, but ordered something far worse – fireweed. Even in mouths long used to hot peppers, sucking on the bitter red leaves would make your eyes water in pain.

"Fireweed!" Tiffany screeched. "That's the only one that will work. Chet, what are we going to do? We already have two walls painted fireweed in the second guest bedroom? Are we going to have two fucking mismatched walls? Not in my house we aren't. Go to the store on 78th. I don't care. The painters will be here tomorrow and then are booked up for a month with the Tremmel's renovation. Chet, get that paint or I swear to God. Just go."

"Just go! Go now!" Grandma Awa had said, looking down at her mortar, smashing the rice.

"Can I go with him?" Alanso had chimed in, her eyes sparkling.

"Do you want de fireweed too?" Grandma raised her eyebrows to Alanso, who looked down silent.

Baluta's hands stopped working on the cabinets. The remembering had captured him. That day, the day he went to get fireweed. He never wanted to remember that day. With this woman's screaming about paint, it was accosting him now. His trip, past the ant pile, past the pond where Alanso caught her fish, past his father's monkey traps to the small fireweed bush stretched out in his mind. He'd picked the largest leaf he could find. The larger the leaf, the less the sting, he and Alanso had decided.

He held the stem of the fireweed gingerly, ready to hold it up to Grandma

Awa for inspection when he returned, before putting it in his mouth. Past the monkey traps, past the pond, he stopped still at the ant pile. Fear had frozen him. From the ant pile, he saw the dust surrounding their shanty. He saw the jeeps and men with guns and machetes. He saw his father, swinging from a tree, on a rope. He saw a hill on the ground the same colored pattern as Grandma Awa's dress, still, in a growing circle of red.

"Are you there, Chet? On 78th? Do you see the fireweed?"

Baluta held tightly to the fireweed stem, he could not move even though troupes of ants attacked his feet. Sting, sting, sting, he stood still, holding tightly onto his fireweed. He saw little Alanso's ten-year old body, limp, naked in the sun, being passed from one soldier to another, his pants mingling with the dust. Sting, sting, sting.

"Chet, if I don't get that fireweed, I'm just going to die!"

Skye Brannon, a former Peace Corps volunteer, is an American living in Dallas, Texas. She has written two novels, a play, many poems, and several short stories. Samples of her writing and visual art may be found at www.skyebrannon.com

WADZANAI MHUTE ZIMBABWE

COW HEARTED

THOUGH THE SUN shone behind clouds, its rays still beat on the browning patches of grass. My 12-year-old mind tried to repress the image, yet I still cannot forget that man.

The April holiday before that day, Mbuya, my grandmother, sat breaking hard groundnuts with her hands. My 14-year-old sister Rutendo and I sat next to her, strenuously opening the nuts and adding the oval insides to a blue plastic bowl. At times one of us would throw a nut into our mouths then glance at Mbuya to see if she had seen us. She pretended not to have noticed but now and then would comment on the nuts in the bowl that seemed to stay at the same level.

"I wonder what is happening," she'd say. We tried to look innocent.

"We don't know, Mbuya, some may be falling out," I responded, as if they were bits of half-ground maize in the bottom of the pounding bowl that flew out as you put more in. We couldn't blame the chickens. Although they freely roamed around us, they wouldn't venture near the nuts – if they tried we shooed them away. So they cluck-clucked around the grass near their coop, taking advantage of the freedom they enjoyed from dawn to early evening.

We could feel the heat rising, so we covered our faces with hats even while we sat in the shade. It was early morning though it felt later because we had been awake since the sun had peered out from the distant hills. We usually slept early, soon after supper, which was served at sunset so we had ample time to rest from a tiring day. Before dawn, while the mist was still hovering above the grass, the three male farmhands would be up to milk the cows and open the stall for them to search the 4,000 acres of farmland for chewable grass. Mbuya and Sisi, her housemaid, woke up shortly before the farmhands returned with the milk. They had our breakfast ready for us, which was fresh eggs from the chicken coop and bread which, when Mbuya felt like it, would be warm and homemade. Otherwise it would be stale, bought on the one shopping day in the week, which was Thursday.

Visiting the farm was not a choice. It was forced on us by our parents and we braced ourselves for the drudgery of farm life. Of course, a few days after we arrived, we would be running around the extensive fields, chasing nervous black-and-white-patched cows. It was an adventure to be there, away from the noise and chaos of our city life. And for me, it was an escape from him. Our days were long and busy. After breakfast we could go to the *minda* and till the soil, assisting the cows which pulled plows ahead of us. We followed, our small feet plunging into the dirt, our hands pulling the errant weeds that remained, stubborn and clinging to the earth. On particularly hot days we helped Mbuya shell the nuts or went to the garden. The garden was a small one with a fence boundary to protect it from prying chickens. The cows didn't bother since no cow was small enough to fit through the gate, let alone turn in the confined space. We would spray her plants using the water from a well that was so deep you could only hear the water in the darkness.

"It's big enough to fit a grown person, so be careful," Mbuya always warned. So we took extra care, taking all morning if necessary. In the afternoon we walked to the river, passing through tall, parched grass that scratched our exposed legs. We squirmed through the trails to reach the stream and marvel at the sparkling pebbles that shone beneath the green, sometimes brown, water. From there we would head to the water pump five minutes away, where our drinking water came from. We would grow tired from the continuous spinning of the wheel that facilitated the travel of water from its *minda* location to the bigger storage tank closer to the farmhouse. In the evening we would heat some water on the open fire outside the kitchen hut and bathe in the brick structure beside the farmhouse by candlelight, nervously turning at each movement that sounded like a mouse. The darkness of the bathroom and the outhouse was lit by two candles balancing precariously on the windowsill. Some light from the stars would poke its way into the cracks in the corners.

Those were times I enjoyed being at the farm. But when my uncle's gardener was there, I hated the openness and possibilities of the farm. I disliked everything about him: his height – he was nearly as tall as the toolshed – his light yellow skin that always looked sunburnt and red, the three black line scars on his right cheek, his eyes that were a dark contrast to his jaundiced skin. He always wore overalls, even when he wasn't working. Bright green and torn somewhere or the other. His hair clung desperately to his head – although it never saw a comb, it refused to become dreadlocked and clumps of hair just formed on top of his head. He was straight-backed and unsmiling. My 15-year-old brother

Gwinyai, my 14-year-old cousin-brother Tawanda and my 6-year-old cousin-sister Anesu joined us during the August holidays, together with the gardener who was needed at the farm to assist with the maize planting before the crucial rains in October. Each time we visited my mother's brother and my cousins, I stayed close to my brother, afraid of the gardener who had once brushed his hands against my breasts while we were in the garden the previous year. He had not apologized, he had merely grinned, showing the yellowed teeth that matched his complexion. I remembered feeling uncomfortable at his constant scrutiny. For the most part I avoided him.

On this particular day, market day Thursday, Mbuya and the farmhands had driven to the monthly cattle sale in the town center to buy some beasts. Sisi had left a week earlier to visit family in her village. That day we decided to look for stones among the big rocks that formed hills near the river. We climbed the loose rocks, scraping our legs but continuing nonetheless in the adventure. The two boys ran ahead, leaving us girls to navigate our way through the ever-steep hills. We could feel the heat of the sun behind the clouds. When we finally made it over the hill, we ran among the brown, dry grass, playing hide and seek. By mid-morning we were hot, tired and hungry.

We returned to the farmhouse and sat in Sisi's bedroom, which was the coolest room in the house because it wasn't carpeted. The boys sat on the bed while we sat on the floor next to it, sprawled out eating the uninspired butter sandwiches that the gardener had left for us. We ate and read the old books on the bookshelf that dated back to my uncle's university days. Medical books and cattle magazines were our main reading materials, with a few authors like Hemingway and Fitzgerald hidden amongst them. I was deep into *The Sun Also Rises* when I noticed that I was the only one still awake. Hemingway's bulls were running through Pamplona when I spied a shadow outside the window. I stiffened as the front door rattled open. I turned to look at the bedroom door that was a few meters away from the front door. The gardener's frame emerged through the doorway as he lowered his head to fit through the entrance. He glanced around at the sleeping bodies on the bed and the floor. The bookshelf that was across from the bed creaked. He settled his gaze on me and motioned me to the door with his head. I moved closer to my sister.

"Mmm," she complained in her sleep.

He walked up to the bookshelf and sat down, grunting as he did. He opened a Bovine magazine and spread it across his upper legs. He bent one leg as he proceeded to unzip his overalls. His hand pulled something out and my eyes widened with fear. His eyes lightened as he looked from me to the inside of the magazine. I shook and gripped my sister, afraid to open my mouth in order to awaken my brother and cousins. I shakily got to my feet and edged my way to the door, passing the bed and bumping my seemingly comatose brother. The gardener watched me as, with a knowing grin on his face, he continue to stroke whatever was beneath the magazine.

I made my way to the bedroom door then the front door and ran outside to the shed about 20 meters away. It was a small shed which housed a small tractor and some tools. I found a hiding place in the back amongst a plow and some farm tools. There was darkness around me when I had finished covering myself. Although the heat in the shed was stifling and uncomfortable, I tried to not make a sound. At first I heard my own quick breathing and the moo of cows in the distance, then suddenly the ground was moving as his feet thundered across the yard. No words escaped his mouth as he overturned some tools looking for my hiding place. My head was hidden in my hands and I dared not lift it. After a few seconds and some quick breaths, light flooded me and I realized that he had found me. He grabbed my right arm and nearly wrenched my collarbone from its socket with the force. I screamed as he dragged me behind him. He roughly pushed me onto the hard ground in the opposite corner and shed his open overalls with impatience, letting them hang just below his knees. As he lowered himself I watched his eyes darken as they turned from menacing delight to recognition then horror at the realization of his own death. He fell to my side and for a moment I did not know what had happened. Gwinyai and Tawanda were standing in the entrance, my brother holding a hunting rifle. The ringing in my ears left me unable to move.

My brother and cousin turned the stiff gardener over while Rutendo and I stood on him to prevent his falling forward. The four of us dragged his body into a wheelbarrow while my little cousin Anesu followed. We pushed and pulled it past the house, past the kitchen hut and along the trail leading to the garden well. He was heavy and with the sun finally out from behind the clouds, our skins had a sheen of moisture. We pushed his body, now covered with flies, into the well. I drew some water, hearing a thud as the water bucket connected with some part of his descending body. My sister threw sand on the wheel barrow and scrubbed while I poured water on her efforts.

We heard the rumbling of Mbuya's pick-up truck dragging its trailer full of cattle along the red dirt road leading to the farm gate. We ran as my brother and cousin pushed the wheelbarrow back along the trail to the shed. The three of us ran to meet my Mbuya and the farmhands as they drove into the yard and parked in front of the house. Mbuya slowly climbed out on the passenger side. We each hugged her. She didn't question my holding on tightly to her a little longer.

"Where are the boys?" she asked.

"Avo," Anesu pointed to their guilty-looking faces as they emerged from the shed.

"Did you bring us sweets, Mbuya?" Gwinyai asked. Rutendo looked at him curiously.

"Yes, Mbuya, you promised us sweets," I echoed. She patted my head and handed me a small packet of Crystal Assorted sweets. I yelled a hasty thanks while heading for the *minda*. The other four ran after me.

We sat amongst the sprouting maize stalks and ate. The sweets tasted different; they were not as good as I remembered.

Wadzanai Mhute is a Zimbabwean writer whose writing focuses mainly on the plight of women. Her articles and stories have been published in *Afrique, MethodX, MIMI Magazine, Per Contra* and the *Philadelphia Weekly*. She is the recipient of the Leeway Art and Change Grant.

MARYANNE CLOUDS TODAY

HER NATIVE NAME was Kumga, meaning Crow – because that's what she sounded like when she got stuck up a tree as a girl and one of her uncles had to climb up and help her down.

She grew up on one of the West Coast missions, and spent her days hunting and fishing – one day she was introduced to tennis and fast became a champion player. She also played netball some too – but then she got married, had a couple of kids and that was the end of that.

I met her many years later, at the Community College – and remember her as a sedentary older lady, but with a quirky, lovely sense of humor.

My first week at the college, as the new whitefella teacher, she tilted her head to one side, grinned, and started to sing aaawhaannghaaawhaaayayayahhhnn...

"What you doing, dear?" I asked.

"Oh", she pursed her lips, "...nothing."

The others told me later – you know she likes you, she's singing you.

"Thank you, dear, but I think my missus might object to this."

"Tsss," she sucked her lip with mock disappointment. "I like you anyway." And her whole face lit up with an enormous grin.

The other time I heard this was when she played cards – she would hum and rock, and proceed to obliterate the opposition in gin rummy. And grin like a bear the whole time.

Time went on, and Maryanne would paint her clouds and trees: "Not 'llowed to do dot-dot style, you know. Get us a cuppa tea, would you dear?"

And later, as we got to know each other, she'd ask my opinion. "What you t'ink, this tree here, should it have friens?"

We looked at a lot of art-books together, but Utrillo was a favorite of hers. Maybe it was his life – "he done a good job of this street here, din't he; musta rolled down this gutter often enough, eh?" And she'd quake with laughter.

But she refined her methods, and her skies grew luminous and her trees had many friends.

As she got older, her weariness often got in the way – as a long-time dialysis user, she would come away from the hospital drained and sad – but still at least managed to draw while she had to sit there. She took time out, but always came back with loads of paintings under each arm – later on, it would be a whole convoy of nieces and nephews, bearing boards and canvases – one time, as she sat there painting, she stopped to rest, rocking to and fro gently. It had been a particularly bad session at the hospital, and she was deathly tired.

The studio had three windows and a door, and in each of these a head would appear every couple of minutes: "Just checking Mum's OK, she paintin' still? Yah, hi Mum."

She'd apparently raised a passel of kids as well as her own sons and daughter, so there was always someone around to look out for her.

The last time I saw her was this : she'd been in hospital, one of her uncountable stays, when I got the message – she's asking for you, go see her, she won't last the weekend.

So we went, and there she was, a tiny little head on the pillow, surrounded by all her family. "Hello dere, nice you could come. They taken me off that machine, finally."

So what do you say in that situation – do you say "you lookin' good, you'll be up and about in no time..."? What crap.

I looked out the window instead: "Hey Maryanne, look at them clouds, girl, wow!"

She looked, turned her head back to me, and there was that great grin, all over her face. "Gimme some of that Pepsi, dear" – and the daughter said, "Not too much now Mum... Oh, what am I saying?"

Maryanne lapsed in and out of consciousness for the rest of the visit, so we eventually left quietly.

She finally went to sleep and didn't wake up, a few days later.

But she's still with us, you know. Like every morning, I look up at the sky – yep, she done a great job there: Maryanne clouds today!

Ivan Gabriel Rehorek is an expatriate Czech living in Australia. He works with both aboriginal and wider communities on various art projects. He lives with his beautiful wife, children, dog, saxophones, puppets and books.

OVO ADAGHA **NIGERIA**

HOMELESS

"WILL MOTHER FLOG me today, Nne?" enquired my seven-year-old brother, Ebuka, as we walked home from school. He was holding my hand – his small head arched expectantly towards me.

"Of course," I said and made a face at him. "The way you are looking, one could mistake you for a pig."

His chubby face clouded as he digested this unpleasant piece of information. Mother's remonstration was not an event to look forward to. Her outbursts were extremely emotional, and were usually characterized by heart-rending sobs.

He stared down at his crumpled clothes and made a futile attempt to appear presentable. There were several dirt stains on his school uniform – a tell-tale account of his afternoon indiscretions. It was obvious he had engaged himself in a rowdy playing session during break time.

"But Nne, it was not my fault; my friend, Munachi, is responsible. He kept grabbing me with his dirty hands while we were playing. I told him to stop but he wouldn't listen. He even poured sand in my eyes, and when I told him to stop..."

Ebuka went on and on. He was fervently trying to present his case as he half-jogged and half-trotted to keep up with my long strides. His voice trailed off in my ears. I was walking fast and wasn't paying attention to what he was saying. He was in the habit of getting into trouble and always blamed his friends for his woes.

Angry car horns honked right and left. The midday sun was at its harshest, blazing down from the skies with unrestrained hostility. It was a busy time of day and navigating the traffic was a challenge. I held Ebuka firmly in my hand as we got set to cross yet another road. At his age, he still hadn't realized that motor cars could kill someone. Once I had caught him running after a truck that was ferrying goats and squealing with delight.

Good thing I held him on leash because at that moment, one of his friends – being ferried home in his father's car – called out to Ebuka as they sped past us. My brother almost started after the car but I was able to restrain him firmly. He started jumping and waving at his friend with glee.

I looked at him as he jumped up and down on his bare feet, obviously overjoyed at seeing his friend. His tattered-looking uniform, like mine, had seen better days. Mother couldn't afford to buy us new uniforms. To us, going to school with footwear was a luxury. The only pairs we had were reserved for Sundays and other special occasions – to ensure their longevity. But my brother was untroubled by these details. He was yet to know the difference between being poor and rich.

Several cars bearing other schoolchildren drove past us as we trudged home, accompanied by the familiar irritating pressure and burning sensation on the soles of our feet. When, after a while, Ebuka became silent, I knew from experience that his feet were hurting. I would have carried him on my back, as I used to do in the past, but he was too big for me now.

To distract him from his travails I spoke softly to him:

"We are almost home. I will tell Mother that it wasn't your fault that your clothes got so dirty."

His face brightened at this suggestion. He looked at me and winked conspiratorially in that unique manner of his that reminded me so much of our father. Ebuka and I were the only children borne by our parents, but we were more than brother and sister. Even though the age difference between us was just six years, I had a strong matronly attachment towards him – maybe because I had been taking care of him since the day he was born. On his part, he treated me rather deferentially, as if I was his junior mother.

The death of Father two years ago was a cruel blow to mother and me. Father was my friend. We shared a close kinship and affinity which was not uncommon between father and daughter. Ebuka didn't know what it was like to be dead. And, to parry his endless questions about Father's whereabouts, we had told him that father had traveled 'overseas'.

Ebuka often reminded me of Father, because they were so alike, especially in certain mannerisms. Father used to wink at me that way whenever he and I colluded to keep something from Mother.

We trudged on under the scorching attention of the afternoon sun. I was hungry and my stomach grumbled repeatedly in protest. I hadn't had breakfast because the leftover food of the night before wasn't enough for me and Ebuka. Most times, mother and I had to forsake food so that Ebuka could eat.

We lived in a sprawling neighborhood which consisted of shanty houses, zinc tents, and mud contraptions. It was always pervaded by a steady ooze of odor that emanated from the slime-drenched gutters, putrefying carcasses of dead animals and other disagreeable elements of life. There was the occasional cement building in a few areas, but their smoke- and dirt-drenched exteriors had yellowed with age and misuse.

Our home was a rag-tag assembly of wood, zinc and misshapen clay bricks. Mother had ingenuously draped a lengthy portion of tarpaulin cover over the roof and it extended outwards over the frontage. This was the reason we didn't get drenched during the rainy seasons. Under the frontage extension, she had nursed a small kiosk into life – our only source of livelihood.

I had learnt long ago not to be proud of my home. On my first day in school, I had naively exposed myself to open ridicule when during routine personal introductions I had unwittingly told the class where I lived with my parents. To this day, I can still hear the raucous notes of derisive laughter which greeted my pronouncement.

We had moved to this place some years ago when Father lost his job as a railway worker. It had been a shocking departure from the railway quarters where we used to live. It was as if we had fallen from grace and Father took it very hard. Several times before he died, I caught him gritting his teeth in sadness. We all struggled to adapt to the new environment. But it was my home nonetheless, and there was nothing I could do about it – at least not while I was still in school. I lived for the day I would be able to start work and earn enough money to relocate my family to a more conducive environment.

We were already in the neighborhood when we heard the first loud crash.

Ebuka and I tensed, and then sprinted the last few blocks to our home. We were just in time to witness what would perhaps become the darkest episode of our lives.

❖ ❖ ❖

It was with shock that we beheld the scene.

We met a pack of people running about frenziedly. The objects of their distress were three menacing-looking bulldozers. I had seen similar machines before at construction sites, only this time, they were being used as agents of destruction. The three of them swung around in a vicious circle, pulling and knocking down buildings.

There were shouts of anguish and confusion. I watched with horror as a middle-aged woman stripped naked and threw herself on the ground before her dingy zinc hut.

"Kill me!" she shrieked. "Kill me, what are you waiting for?"

Some men of the neighborhood hurriedly draped a cloth around the struggling woman and carried her away. She was kicking and cursing with all her might.

"Cursed be the day you were born! You all are cursed from this day!" she cried, her eyes flashing in anger.

The unheeding bulldozer rammed into her hut and crushed it to pieces.

People were running around in a frenzied manner, trying to salvage properties from their doomed buildings. Mother was one of them.

There was a fierce wild look about her – like that of a hen whose brood of chicks were being threatened by an external force. Her wrapper was almost falling off her waist as she bustled. She herded us into the house and started throwing things around. I joined her. Ebuka stood and watched us, as if he could not comprehend what was happening.

It was happening at last – the threat of demolition which had hung over our heads for the past few months. It all began to make sense – Mother's weird behavior over the past few days. She had been irritable, snapping at me and Ebuka and talking in her sleep. She must have known that they were coming and yet her unflinching hope had left her unprepared for this moment. The few families who had the means had moved away from the neighborhood. We only stayed because we had nowhere to go.

Mother was whimpering, "Oh my goodness, oh my goodness," and something unintelligible in her dialect as we desperately shuffled clothes and other household items into bags, battered boxes and suitcases.

We heard another loud crash outside. The shanty buildings were crashing on all sides. Dust, debris and startling sounds of collapsing buildings intensified the terror of the moment. It was all too much for Ebuka. He started to cry.

Mother turned and yelled at him. "Pack! Pack something!"

It was a miracle how we managed to get our belongings out of the shack before the bulldozers swung in our direction. Mother drew us to her bosom and her hands trembled as she gripped us tightly. I opened my mouth in a soundless scream as one of the rampaging bulldozers shoved our makeshift shack aside.

❖ ❖ ❖

A few hours after the bulldozers had done their bit and gone away, it started to rain. Dusk was fast approaching. Solemn-looking clouds hung low and mournfully from the skies. A few hopeful vultures, in defiance of the rain, waited and flapped their wings in earnest expectation. I heard moans of despair and grief.

Ebuka and I clung to each other on a nearby bench – shivering. We still hadn't had our lunch. We watched apprehensively as Mother moved about in the rain, gathering pieces of our belongings that were scattered everywhere. It was an unpleasant sight: clothes, cooking utensils, books, earthenware and pieces of furniture were strewn across what used to be our front yard.

It looked like a place flattened by war. Our ghetto neighborhood had been turned into a tragic exhibition ground of twisted wreckage, battered fragments of wood and piles of broken bricks. Thick layers of dust and plumes of smoke rose from the smoldering ground, in the midst of which stood the occasional wardrobe, kitchen cupboard or iron bed-frame, all that remained of family homes.

A few distressed-looking figures picked among the debris like the vultures that were waiting patiently by the corner, while others gathered in small dazed groups with folded arms.

Mother hadn't spoken a word since the bulldozers brought our shack down, but her demeanor spoke volumes.

My fear of the dark and unknown seemed to encircle me, but as I watched Mother moving about in the rain, her back hunched in despair, I knew that I could never name the color of her pain.

Ovo Adagha is a poet and fiction writer from Nigeria. His short stories and poems have appeared in several online and print journals. He is currently living in Aberdeen, Scotland, where he is working on his debut novel.

THE THIRD AND FINAL CONTINENT

I LEFT INDIA in 1964 with a certificate in commerce and the equivalent, in those days, of ten dollars to my name. For three weeks I sailed on the SS Roma, an Italian cargo vessel, in a cabin next to the ship's engine, across the Arabian Sea, the Red Sea, the Mediterranean, and finally to England. I lived in London, in Finsbury Park, in a house occupied entirely by penniless Bengali bachelors like myself, at least a dozen and sometimes more, all struggling to educate and establish ourselves abroad.

I attended lectures at LSE and worked at the university library to get by. We lived three or four to a room, shared a single, icy toilet, and took turns cooking pots of egg curry, which we ate with our hands on a table covered with newspapers. Apart from our jobs we had few responsibilities. On weekends we lounged barefoot in drawstring pajamas, drinking tea and smoking Rothmans, or set out to watch cricket at Lord's. Some weekends the house was crammed with still more Bengalis, to whom we had introduced ourselves at the greengrocer, or on the Tube, and we made yet more egg curry, and played Mukesh on a Grundig reel-to-reel, and soaked our dirty dishes in the bathtub. Every now and then someone in the house moved out, to live with a woman whom his family back in Calcutta had determined he was to wed. In 1969, when I was 36 years old, my own marriage was arranged. Around the same time, I was offered a full-time job in America, in the processing department of a library at MIT. The salary was generous enough to support a wife, and I was honored to be hired by a world-famous university, and so I obtained a green card, and prepared to travel farther still.

By then I had enough money to go by plane. I flew first to Calcutta, to attend my wedding, and a week later to Boston, to begin my new job. During the flight I read *The Student Guide to North America*, for although I was no longer a student, I was on a budget all the same. I learned that Americans drove on the right side of the road, not the left, and that they called a lift an elevator and an engaged phone busy. "The pace of life in North America is different from Britain, as you will soon discover," the guidebook informed me. "Everybody feels he must get to the top. Don't expect an English cup of tea." As the plane began its descent over Boston Harbor, the pilot announced the weather and the time, and that President Nixon had declared a national holiday: two American men had landed on the moon. Several passengers cheered. "God bless America!" one of them hollered. Across the aisle, I saw a woman praying.

I spent my first night at the YMCA in Central Square, Cambridge, an inexpensive accommodation recommended by my guidebook which was within walking distance of MIT. The room contained a cot, a desk, and a small wooden cross on one wall. A sign on the door said that cooking was strictly forbidden. A bare window overlooked Massachusetts Avenue. Car horns, shrill and prolonged, blared one after another. Sirens and flashing lights heralded endless emergencies, and a succession of buses rumbled past, their doors opening and closing with a powerful hiss, throughout the night. The noise was constantly distracting, at times suffocating. I felt it deep in my ribs, just as I had felt the furious drone of the engine on the SS Roma. But there was no ship's deck to escape to, no glittering ocean to thrill my soul, no breeze to cool my face, no one to talk to. I was too tired to pace the gloomy corridors of the YMCA in my pajamas. Instead I sat at the desk and stared out the window. In the morning I reported to my job at the Dewey Library, a beige fort-like building by Memorial Drive. I also opened a bank account, rented a post-office box, and bought a plastic bowl and a spoon. I went to a supermarket called Purity Supreme, wandering up and down the aisles, comparing prices with those in England. In the end I bought a carton of milk and a box of cornflakes. This was my first meal in America. Even the simple chore of buying milk was new to me; in London we'd had bottles delivered each morning to our door.

In a week I had adjusted, more or less. I ate cornflakes and milk morning and night, and bought some bananas for variety, slicing them into the bowl with the edge of my spoon. I left my carton of milk on the shaded part of the windowsill, as I had seen other residents at the YMCA do. To pass the time in the evenings I read the *Boston Globe* downstairs, in a spacious room with stained-glass windows. I read every article and advertisement, so that I would grow familiar with things, and when my eyes grew tired I slept. Only I did not sleep well. Each night I had to keep the window wide open; it was the only source of air in the stifling room, and the noise was intolerable. I would lie on the cot with my fingers pressed into my ears, but when I drifted off to sleep my hands fell away, and the noise of the traffic would wake me up again. Pigeon feathers drifted onto the windowsill, and one evening, when I poured milk over my cornflakes, I saw that it had soured. Nevertheless I resolved to stay at the YMCA for six weeks, until my wife's passport and green card were ready. Once she arrived I would have to rent a proper apartment, and from time to time I studied the classified section of the newspaper, or stopped in at the housing office at MIT during my lunch break to see what was available. It was in this manner that I discovered a room for immediate occupancy, in a house on a quiet street, the listing said, for eight dollars per week. I dialed the number from a pay telephone, sorting through the coins, with which I was still unfamiliar – smaller and lighter than shillings, heavier and brighter than paisas.

"Who is speaking?" a woman demanded. Her voice was bold and clamorous.

"Yes, good afternoon, Madam. I am calling about the room for rent."

"Harvard or Tech?"

"I beg your pardon?"

"Are you from Harvard or Tech?"

Gathering that Tech referred to the Massachusetts Institute of Technology, I replied, "I work at Dewey Library," adding tentatively, "at Tech."

"I only rent rooms to boys from Harvard or Tech!"

"Yes, Madam."

I was given an address and an appointment for seven o'clock that evening. Thirty minutes before the hour I set out, my guidebook in my pocket, my breath fresh with Listerine. I turned down a street shaded with trees, perpendicular to Massachusetts Avenue. In spite of the heat I wore a coat and tie, regarding the event as I would any other interview; I had never lived in the home of a person who was not Indian. The house, surrounded by a chain-link fence, was off-white with dark-brown trim, with a tangle of forsythia bushes plastered against its front and sides. When I pressed the bell, the woman with whom I had spoken on the phone hollered from what seemed to be just the other side of the door, "One minute, please!"

Several minutes later the door was opened by a tiny, extremely old woman. A mass of snowy hair was arranged like a small sack on top of her head. As

I stepped into the house she sat down on a wooden bench positioned at the bottom of a narrow carpeted staircase. Once she was settled on the bench, in a small pool of light, she peered up at me, giving me her undivided attention. She wore a long black skirt that spread like a stiff tent to the floor, and a starched white shirt edged with ruffles at the throat and cuffs. Her hands, folded together in her lap, had long pallid fingers, with swollen knuckles and tough yellow nails. Age had battered her features so that she almost resembled a man, with sharp, shrunken eyes and prominent creases on either side of her nose. Her lips, chapped and faded, had nearly disappeared, and her eyebrows were missing altogether. Nevertheless she looked fierce.

"Lock up!" she commanded. She shouted, even though I stood only a few feet away. "Fasten the chain and firmly press that button on the knob! This is the first thing you shall do when you enter, is that clear?"

I locked the door as directed and examined the house. Next to the bench was a small round table, its legs fully concealed, much like the woman's, by a skirt of lace. The table held a lamp, a transistor radio, a leather change purse with a silver clasp, and a telephone. A thick wooden cane was propped against one side. There was a parlor to my right, lined with bookcases and filled with shabby claw-footed furniture. In the corner of the parlor I saw a grand piano with its top down, piled with papers. The piano's bench was missing; it seemed to be the one on which the woman was sitting. Somewhere in the house a clock chimed seven times.

"You're punctual!" the woman proclaimed. "I expect you shall be so with the rent!"

"I have a letter, Madam." In my jacket pocket was a letter from MIT confirming my employment, which I had brought along to prove that I was indeed from Tech.

She stared at the letter, then handed it back to me carefully, gripping it with her fingers as if it were a plate heaped with food. She did not wear glasses, and I wondered if she'd read a word of it. "The last boy was always late! Still owes me eight dollars! Harvard boys aren't what they used to be! Only Harvard and Tech in this house! How's Tech, boy?"

"It is very well."

"You checked the lock?"

"Yes, Madam."

She unclasped her fingers, slapped the space beside her on the bench with one hand, and told me to sit down. For a moment she was silent. Then she intoned, as if she alone possessed this knowledge: "There is an American flag on the moon!"

"Yes, Madam." Until then I had not thought very much about the moon shot. It was in the newspaper, of course, article upon article. The astronauts had landed on the shores of the Sea of Tranquility, I had read, traveling farther than anyone in the history of civilization. For a few hours they explored the moon's surface. They gathered rocks in their pockets, described their surroundings (a magnificent desolation, according to one astronaut), spoke by phone to the President, and planted a flag in lunar soil. The voyage was hailed as man's most awesome achievement.

The woman bellowed, "A flag on the moon, boy! I heard it on the radio! Isn't that splendid?"

"Yes, Madam."

But she was not satisfied with my reply. Instead she commanded, "Say 'Splendid!'"

I was both baffled and somewhat insulted by the request. It reminded me of the way I was taught multiplication tables as a child, repeating after the master, sitting cross-legged on the floor of my one-room Tollygunge school. It also reminded me of my wedding, when I had repeated endless Sanskrit verses after the priest, verses I barely understood, which joined me to my wife. I said nothing.

"Say 'Splendid!'" the woman bellowed once again.

"Splendid," I murmured. I had to repeat the word a second time at the top of my lungs, so she could hear. I was reluctant to raise my voice to an elderly woman, but she did not appear to be offended. If anything the reply pleased her, because her next command was:

"Go see the room!"

I rose from the bench and mounted the narrow staircase. There were five doors, two on either side of an equally narrow hallway, and one at the opposite end. Only one door was open. The room contained a twin bed under a sloping ceiling, a brown oval rug, a basin with an exposed pipe, and a chest of drawers. One door led to a closet, another to a toilet and a tub. The window was open; net curtains stirred in the breeze. I lifted them away and inspected the view: a small back yard, with a few fruit trees and an empty clothesline. I was satisfied.

When I returned to the foyer the woman picked up the leather change purse on the table, opened the clasp, fished about with her fingers, and produced a key on a thin wire hoop. She informed me that there was a kitchen at the back of the house, accessible through the parlor. I was welcome to use the stove as long as I left it as I found it. Sheets and towels were provided, but keeping them clean was my own responsibility. The rent was due Friday mornings on the ledge above the piano keys. "And no lady visitors!"

"I am a married man, Madam." It was the first time I had announced this fact to anyone.

But she had not heard. "No lady visitors!" she insisted. She introduced herself as Mrs Croft.

My wife's name was Mala. The marriage had been arranged by my older brother and his wife. I regarded the proposition with neither objection nor enthusiasm. It was a duty expected of me, as it was expected of every man. She was the daughter of a schoolteacher in Beleghata. I was told that she could cook, knit, embroider, sketch landscapes, and recite poems by Tagore, but these talents could not make up for the fact that she did not possess a fair complexion, and so a string of men had rejected her to her face. She was 27, an age when her parents had begun to fear that she would never marry, and so they were willing to ship their only child halfway across the world in order to save her from spinsterhood.

For five nights we shared a bed. Each of those nights, after applying cold cream and braiding her hair, she turned from me and wept; she missed her parents. Although I would be leaving the country in a few days, custom dictated that she was now a part of my household, and for the next six weeks she was to live with my brother and his wife, cooking, cleaning, serving tea and sweets to guests. I did nothing to console her. I lay on my own side of the bed, reading my guidebook by flashlight. At times I thought of the tiny room on the other side of the wall which had belonged to my mother. Now the room was practically empty; the wooden pallet on which she'd once slept was piled with trunks and old bedding. Nearly six years ago, before leaving for London, I had watched her die on that bed, had found her playing with her excrement in her final days. Before we cremated her I had cleaned each of her fingernails with a hairpin, and then, because my brother could not bear it, I had assumed the role of eldest son, and had touched the flame to her temple, to release her tormented soul to heaven.

The next morning I moved into Mrs Croft's house. When I unlocked the door I saw that she was sitting on the piano bench, on the same side as the previous evening. She wore the same black skirt, the same starched white blouse, and had her hands folded together the same way in her lap. She looked so much the same that I wondered if she'd spent the whole night on the bench. I put my suitcase upstairs and then headed off to work. That evening when I came home from the university, she was still there.

"Sit down, boy!" She slapped the space beside her.

I perched on the bench. I had a bag of groceries with me – more milk, more cornflakes, and more bananas, for my inspection of the kitchen earlier in the day had revealed no spare pots or pans. There were only two saucepans in the refrigerator, both containing some orange broth, and a copper kettle on the stove.

"Good evening, Madam."

She asked me if I had checked the lock. I told her I had.

For a moment she was silent. Then suddenly she declared, with measures of disbelief and delight equal to the night before, "There's an American flag on the moon, boy!"

"Yes, Madam."

"A flag on the moon! Isn't that splendid?"

I nodded, dreading what I knew was coming. "Yes, Madam."

"Say 'Splendid!'"

This time I paused, looking to either side in case anyone was there to overhear me, though I knew perfectly well that the house was empty. I felt like an idiot. But it was a small enough thing to ask. "Splendid!" I cried out.

Within days it became our routine. In the mornings when I left for the library Mrs Croft was either hidden away in her bedroom, on the other side of the staircase, or sitting on the bench, oblivious of my presence, listening to the news or classical music on the radio. But each evening when I returned the same thing happened: she slapped the bench, ordered me to sit down, declared that there was a flag on the moon, and declared that it was splendid. I said it was splendid, too, and then we sat in silence. As awkward as it was, and as endless as it felt to me then, the nightly encounter lasted only about ten minutes; inevitably she would drift off to sleep, her head falling abruptly toward her chest, leaving me free to retire to my room. By then, of course, there was no flag standing on the moon. The astronauts, I read in the paper, had seen it fall before they flew back to Earth. But I did not have the heart to tell her.

Friday morning, when my first week's rent was due, I went to the piano in the parlor to place my money on the ledge. The piano keys were dull and discolored. When I pressed one, it made no sound at all. I had put eight dollar bills in an envelope and written Mrs Croft's name on the front of it. I was not in the habit of leaving money unmarked and unattended. From where I stood I could see the profile of her tent-shaped skirt in the hall. It seemed unnecessary to make her get up and walk all the way to the piano. I never saw her walking about, and assumed, from the cane propped against the round table, that she did so with difficulty. When I approached the bench she peered up at me and demanded: "What is your business?"

"The rent, Madam."

"On the ledge above the piano keys!"

"I have it here." I extended the envelope toward her, but her fingers, folded together in her lap, did not budge. I bowed slightly and lowered the envelope, so that it hovered just above her hands. After a moment she accepted it, and nodded her head. That night when I came home, she did not slap the bench, but out of habit I sat beside her as usual. She asked me if I had checked the lock, but she mentioned nothing about the flag on the moon. Instead she said:

"It was very kind of you!"

"I beg your pardon, Madam?"

"Very kind of you!"

She was still holding the envelope in her hands.

On Sunday there was a knock on my door. An elderly woman introduced herself: she was Mrs Croft's daughter, Helen. She walked into the room and looked at each of the walls as if for signs of change, glancing at the shirts that hung in the closet, the neckties draped over the doorknob, the box of cornflakes on the chest of drawers, the dirty bowl and spoon in the basin. She was short and thick-waisted, with cropped silver hair and bright pink lipstick. She wore a sleeveless summer dress, a necklace of white plastic beads, and spectacles on a chain that hung like a swing against her chest. The backs of her legs were mapped with dark-blue veins, and her upper arms sagged like the flesh of a roasted eggplant. She told me she lived in Arlington, a town farther up Massachusetts Avenue. "I come once a week to bring Mother groceries. Has she sent you packing yet?"

"It is very well, Madam."

"Some of the boys run screaming. But I think she likes you. You're the first boarder she's ever referred to as a gentleman."

She looked at me, noticing my bare feet. (I still felt strange wearing shoes indoors, and always removed them before entering my room.) "Are you new to Boston?"

"New to America, Madam."

"From?" She raised her eyebrows.

"I am from Calcutta, India."

"Is that right? We had a Brazilian fellow, about a year ago. You'll find Cambridge a very international city."

I nodded, and began to wonder how long our conversation would last. But at that moment we heard Mrs Croft's electrifying voice rising up the stairs.

"You are to come downstairs immediately!"

"What is it?" Helen cried back.

"Immediately!"

I put on my shoes. Helen sighed.

I followed Helen down the staircase. She seemed to be in no hurry, and complained at one point that she had a bad knee. "Have you been walking without your cane?" Helen called out. "You know you're not supposed to walk without that cane." She paused, resting her hand on the banister, and looked back at me. "She slips sometimes."

For the first time Mrs Croft seemed vulnerable. I pictured her on the floor in front of the bench, flat on her back, staring at the ceiling, her feet pointing in opposite directions. But when we reached the bottom of the staircase she was sitting there as usual, her hands folded together in her lap. Two grocery bags were at her feet. She did not slap the bench, or ask us to sit down. She glared.

"What is it, Mother?"

"It's improper!"

"What's improper?"

"It is improper for a lady and gentleman who are not married to one another to hold a private conversation without a chaperone!"

Helen said she was 68 years old, old enough to be my mother, but Mrs Croft insisted that Helen and I speak to each other downstairs, in the parlor. She added that it was also improper for a lady of Helen's station to reveal her age, and to wear a dress so high above the ankle.

"For your information, Mother, it's 1969. What would you do if you actually left the house one day and saw a girl in a miniskirt?"

Mrs Croft sniffed. "I'd have her arrested."

Helen shook her head and picked up one of the grocery bags. I picked up the other one, and followed her through the parlor and into the kitchen. The bags were filled with cans of soup, which Helen opened up one by one with a few cranks of a can opener. She tossed the old soup into the sink, rinsed the saucepans under the tap, filled them with soup from the newly opened cans, and put them back in the refrigerator.

"A few years ago she could still open the cans herself," Helen said. "She hates that I do it for her now. But the piano killed her hands." She put on her spectacles, glanced at the cupboards, and spotted my tea bags. "Shall we have a cup?"

I filled the kettle on the stove. "I beg your pardon, Madam. The piano?"

"She used to give lessons. For 40 years. It was how she raised us after my father died." Helen put her hands on her hips, staring at the open refrigerator. She reached into the back, pulled out a wrapped stick of butter, frowned, and tossed it into the garbage. "That ought to do it," she said, and put the unopened cans of soup in the cupboard. I sat at the table and watched as Helen washed the dirty dishes, tied up the garbage bag, and poured boiling water into two cups. She handed one to me without milk, and sat down at the table.

"Excuse me, Madam, but is it enough?"

Helen took a sip of her tea. Her lipstick left a smiling pink stain on the rim of the cup. "Is what enough?"

"The soup in the pans. Is it enough food for Mrs Croft?"

"She won't eat anything else. She stopped eating solids after she turned one hundred. That was, let's see, three years ago."

I was mortified. I had assumed Mrs Croft was in her eighties, perhaps as old as 90. I had never known a person who had lived for over a century. That this person was a widow who lived alone mortified me further still. Widowhood had driven my own mother insane. My father, who worked as a clerk at the General Post Office of Calcutta, died of encephalitis when I was 16. My mother refused to adjust to life without him; instead she sank deeper into a world of darkness from which neither I, nor my brother, nor concerned relatives, nor psychiatric clinics on Rash Behari Avenue could save her. What pained me most was to see her so unguarded, to hear her burp after meals or expel gas in front of company without the slightest embarrassment. After my father's death my brother abandoned his schooling and began to work in the jute mill he would eventually manage, in order to keep the household running. And so it was my job to sit by my mother's feet and study for my exams as she counted and recounted the bracelets on her arm as if they were the beads of an abacus. We tried to keep an eye on her. Once she had wandered half naked to the tram depot before we were able to bring her inside again.

"I am happy to warm Mrs Croft's soup in the evenings," I suggested. "It is no trouble."

Helen looked at her watch, stood up, and poured the rest of her tea into the sink. "I wouldn't, if I were you. That's the sort of thing that would kill her altogether."

That evening, when Helen had gone and Mrs Croft and I were alone again, I began to worry. Now that I knew how very old she was, I worried that something would happen to her in the middle of the night, or when I was out during the day. As vigorous as her voice was, and imperious as she seemed, I knew that even a scratch or a cough could kill a person that old; each day she lived, I knew, was something of a miracle. Helen didn't seem concerned. She came and went, bringing soup for Mrs Croft, one Sunday after the next.

In this manner the six weeks of that summer passed. I came home each evening, after my hours at the library, and spent a few minutes on the piano bench with Mrs Croft. Some evenings I sat beside her long after she had drifted off to sleep, still in awe of how many years she had spent on this earth. At times I tried to picture the world she had been born into, in 1866 – a world, I imagined, filled with women in long black skirts, and chaste conversations in the parlor. Now, when I looked at her hands with their swollen knuckles folded together in her lap, I imagined them smooth and slim, striking the piano keys. At times I came downstairs before going to sleep, to make sure she was sitting upright on the bench, or was safe in her bedroom. On Fridays I put the rent in her hands. There was nothing I could do for her beyond these simple gestures. I was not her son, and, apart from those eight dollars, I owed her nothing.

At the end of August, Mala's passport and green card were ready. I received a telegram with her flight information; my brother's house in Calcutta had no telephone. Around that time I also received a letter from her, written only a few days after we had parted. There was no salutation; addressing me by name would have assumed an intimacy we had not yet discovered. It contained only a few lines. "I write in English in preparation for the journey. Here I am very much lonely. I sit very cold there. Is there snow. Yours, Mala."

I was not touched by her words. We had spent only a handful of days in each other's company. And yet we were bound together; for six weeks she had worn an iron bangle on her wrist, and applied vermilion powder to the part in her hair, to signify to the world that she was a bride. In those six weeks I regarded her arrival as I would the arrival of a coming month, or season – something inevitable, but meaningless at the time. So little did I know her that, while details of her face sometimes rose to my memory, I could not conjure up the whole of it.

A few days after receiving the letter, as I was walking to work in the morning, I saw an Indian woman on Massachusetts Avenue, wearing a sari with its free end nearly dragging on the footpath, and pushing a child in a stroller. An American woman with a small black dog on a leash was walking to one side of her. Suddenly the dog began barking. I watched as the Indian woman, startled, stopped in her path, at which point the dog leaped up and seized the end of the sari between its teeth. The American woman scolded the dog, appeared to apologize, and walked quickly away, leaving the Indian woman to fix her sari, and quiet her crying child. She did not see me standing there, and eventually she continued on her way. Such a mishap, I realized that morning, would soon be my concern. It was my duty to take care of Mala, to welcome her and protect her. I would have to buy her her first pair of snow boots, her first winter coat. I would have to tell her which streets to avoid, which way the traffic came, tell her to wear her sari so that the free end did not drag on the footpath. A five-mile separation from her parents, I recalled with some irritation, had caused her to weep.

Unlike Mala, I was used to it all by then: used to cornflakes and milk, used to Helen's visits, used to sitting on the bench with Mrs Croft. The only thing I was not used to was Mala. Nevertheless, I did what I had to do. I went to the housing office at MIT and found a furnished apartment a few blocks away, with a double bed and a private kitchen and bath, for 40 dollars a week. One last Friday I handed Mrs Croft eight dollar bills in an envelope, brought my suitcase downstairs, and informed her that I was moving. She put my key into her change purse. The last thing she asked me to do was hand her the cane propped against the table, so that she could walk to the door and lock it behind me. "Goodbye, then," she said, and retreated back into the house. I did not expect any display of emotion, but I was disappointed all the same. I was only a boarder, a man who paid her a bit of money and passed in and out of her home for six weeks. Compared with a century, it was no time at all.

At the airport I recognized Mala immediately. The free end of her sari did not drag on the floor, but was draped in a sign of bridal modesty over her head, just as it had draped my mother until the day my father died. Her thin brown arms were stacked with gold bracelets, a small red circle was painted on her forehead, and the edges of her feet were tinted with a decorative red dye. I did not embrace her, or kiss her, or take her hand. Instead I asked her, speaking Bengali for the first time in America, if she was hungry.

She hesitated, then nodded yes.

I told her I had prepared some egg curry at home. "What did they give you to eat on the plane?"

"I didn't eat."

"All the way from Calcutta?"

"The menu said oxtail soup."

"But surely there were other items?"

"The thought of eating an ox's tail made me lose my appetite."

When we arrived home, Mala opened up one of her suitcases, and presented me with two pullover sweaters, both made with bright-blue wool, which she had knitted in the course of our separation, one with a V neck, the other covered with cables. I tried them on; both were tight under the arms. She had also brought me two new pairs of drawstring pajamas, a letter from my brother, and a packet of loose Darjeeling tea. I had no present for her apart from the egg curry. We sat at a bare table, staring at our plates. We ate with our hands, another thing I had not yet done in America.

"The house is nice," she said. "Also the egg curry." With her left hand she held the end of her sari to her chest, so it would not slip off her head.

"I don't know many recipes."

She nodded, peeling the skin off each of her potatoes before eating them. At one point the sari slipped to her shoulders. She readjusted it at once.

"There is no need to cover your head," I said. "I don't mind. It doesn't matter here."

She kept it covered anyway.

I waited to get used to her, to her presence at my side, at my table and in my bed, but a week later we were still strangers. I still was not used to coming home to an apartment that smelled of steamed rice, and finding that the basin in the bathroom was always wiped clean, our two toothbrushes lying side by side, a cake of Pears soap residing in the soap dish. I was not used to the fragrance of the coconut oil she rubbed every other night into her scalp, or the delicate sound her bracelets made as she moved about the apartment.

In the mornings she was always awake before I was. The first morning, when I came into the kitchen she had heated up the leftovers and set a plate with a spoonful of salt on its edge, assuming I would eat rice for breakfast, as most Bengali husbands did. I told her cereal would do, and the next morning when I came into the kitchen she had already poured the cornflakes into my bowl. One morning she walked with me to MIT, where I gave her a short tour of the campus. The next morning, before I left for work she asked me for a few dollars. I parted with them reluctantly, but I knew that this, too, was now normal. When I came home from work there was a potato peeler in the kitchen drawer, and a tablecloth on the table, and chicken curry made with fresh garlic and ginger on the stove. After dinner I read the newspaper, while Mala sat at the kitchen table, working on a cardigan for herself with more of the blue wool, or writing letters home.

On Friday, I suggested going out. Mala set down her knitting and disappeared into the bathroom. When she emerged I regretted the suggestion; she had put on a silk sari and extra bracelets, and coiled her hair with a flattering side part on top of her head. She was prepared as if for a party, or at the very least for the cinema, but I had no such destination in mind. The evening was balmy. We walked several blocks down Massachusetts Avenue, looking into the windows of restaurants and shops. Then, without thinking, I led her down the quiet street where for so many nights I had walked alone.

"This is where I lived before you came," I said, stopping at Mrs Croft's chain-link fence.

"In such a big house?"

"I had a small room upstairs. At the back."

"Who else lives there?"

"A very old woman."

"With her family?"

"Alone."

"But who takes care of her?"

I opened the gate. "For the most part she takes care of herself."

I wondered if Mrs Croft would remember me; I wondered if she had a new boarder to sit with her each evening. When I pressed the bell I expected the same long wait as that day of our first meeting, when I did not have a key. But this time the door was opened almost immediately, by Helen. Mrs Croft was not sitting on the bench. The bench was gone.

"Hello there," Helen said, smiling with her bright pink lips at Mala. "Mother's in the parlor. Will you be visiting awhile?"

"As you wish, Madam."

"Then I think I'll run to the store, if you don't mind. She had a little accident. We can't leave her alone these days, not even for a minute."

I locked the door after Helen and walked into the parlor. Mrs Croft was lying flat on her back, her head on a peach-colored cushion, a thin white quilt spread over her body. Her hands were folded together on her chest. When she saw me she pointed at the sofa, and told me to sit down. I took my place as directed, but Mala wandered over to the piano and sat on the bench, which was now positioned where it belonged.

"I broke my hip!" Mrs Croft announced, as if no time had passed.

"Oh dear, Madam."

"I fell off the bench!"

"I am so sorry, Madam."

"It was the middle of the night! Do you know what I did, boy?"

I shook my head.

"I called the police!"

She stared up at the ceiling and grinned sedately, exposing a crowded row of long gray teeth. "What do you say to that, boy?"

As stunned as I was, I knew what I had to say. With no hesitation at all, I cried out, "Splendid!"

Mala laughed then. Her voice was full of kindness, her eyes bright with amusement. I had never heard her laugh before, and it was loud enough so that Mrs Croft heard, too. She turned to Mala and glared.

"Who is she, boy?"

"She is my wife, Madam."

Mrs Croft pressed her head at an angle against the cushion to get a better look. "Can you play the piano?"

"No, Madam," Mala replied.

"Then stand up!"

Mala rose to her feet, adjusting the end of her sari over her head and holding it to her chest, and, for the first time since her arrival, I felt sympathy. I remembered my first days in London, learning how to take the Tube to Russell Square, riding an escalator for the first time, unable to understand that when the man cried "piper" it meant "paper", unable to decipher, for a whole year, that the conductor said "Mind the gap" as the train pulled away from each station. Like me, Mala had traveled far from home, not knowing where she was going, or what she would find, for no reason other than to be my wife. As strange as it seemed, I knew in my heart that one day her death would affect me, and stranger still, that mine would affect her. I wanted somehow to explain this to Mrs Croft, who was still scrutinizing Mala from top to toe with what seemed to be placid disdain. I wondered if Mrs Croft had ever seen a woman in a sari, with a dot painted on her forehead and bracelets stacked on her wrists. I wondered what she would object to. I wondered if she could see the red dye still vivid on Mala's feet, all but obscured by the bottom edge of her sari. At last Mrs Croft declared, with the equal measures of disbelief and delight I knew well:

"She is a perfect lady!"

Now it was I who laughed. I did so quietly, and Mrs Croft did not hear me. But Mala had heard, and, for the first time, we looked at each other and smiled.

I like to think of that moment in Mrs Croft's parlor as the moment when the distance between Mala and me began to lessen. Although we were not yet fully in love, I like to think of the months that followed as a honeymoon of sorts. Together we explored the city and met other Bengalis, some of whom are still friends today. We discovered that a man named Bill sold fresh fish on Prospect Street, and that a shop in Harvard Square called Cardullo's sold bay leaves and cloves. In the evenings we walked to the Charles River to watch sailboats drift across the water, or had ice-cream cones in Harvard Yard. We bought a camera with which to document our life together, and I took pictures of her posing in front of the Prudential Building, so that she could send them to her parents. At night we kissed, shy at first but quickly bold, and discovered pleasure and solace in each other's arms. I told her about my voyage on the SS Roma, and about Finsbury Park and the YMCA, and my evenings on the bench with Mrs Croft. When I told her stories about my mother, she wept. It was Mala who consoled me when, reading the *Globe* one evening, I came across Mrs Croft's obituary. I had not thought of her in several months – by then those six weeks of the summer were already a remote interlude in my past – but when I learned of her death I was stricken, so much so that when Mala looked up from her knitting she found me staring at the wall, unable to speak. Mrs Croft's was the first death I mourned in America, for hers was the first life I had admired; she had left this world at last, ancient and alone, never to return.

As for me, I have not strayed much farther. Mala and I live in a town about 20 miles from Boston, on a tree-lined street much like Mrs Croft's, in a house we own, with room for guests, and a garden that saves us from buying tomatoes in summer. We are American citizens now, so that we can collect Social Security when it is time. Though we visit Calcutta every few years, we have decided to grow old here. I work in a small college library. We have a son who attends Harvard University. Mala no longer drapes the end of her sari over her head, or weeps at night for her parents, but occasionally she weeps for our son. So we drive to Cambridge to visit him, or bring him home for a weekend, so that he can eat rice with us with his hands, and speak in Bengali, things we sometimes worry he will no longer do after we die.

Whenever we make that drive, I always take Massachusetts Avenue, in spite of the traffic. I barely recognize the buildings now, but each time I am there I return instantly to those six weeks as if they were only the other day, and I slow down and point to Mrs Croft's street, saying to my son, "Here was my first home in America, where I lived with a woman who was a hundred and three."

"Remember?" Mala says, and smiles, amazed, as I am, that there was ever a time that we were strangers. My son always expresses his astonishment, not at Mrs Croft's age but at how little I paid in rent, a fact nearly as inconceivable to him as a flag on the moon was to a woman born in 1866. In my son's eyes I see the ambition that had first hurled me across the world. In a few years he will graduate and pave his own way, alone and unprotected. But I remind myself that he has a father who is still living, a mother who is happy and strong. Whenever he is discouraged, I tell him that if I can survive on three continents, then there is no obstacle he cannot conquer. While the astronauts, heroes forever, spent mere hours on the moon, I have remained in this new world for nearly 30 years. I know that my achievement is quite ordinary. I am not the only man to seek his fortune far from home, and certainly I am not the first. Still, there are times I am bewildered by each mile I have traveled, each meal I have eaten, each person I have known, each room in which I have slept. As ordinary as it all appears, there are times when it is beyond my imagination.

Jhumpa Lahiri is a US author of Bengali descent. Her début short story collection, *Interpreter of Maladies* (1999), won the 2000 Pulitzer Prize for Fiction, and her first novel, *The Namesake* (2003), was adapted into a popular film with the same title, directed by Mira Nair. Her latest collection, *Unaccustomed Earth*, won the Frank O'Connor Prize for 2008.

CPSIA information can be obtained
at www.ICGtesting.com
Printed in the USA
JSHW052220190521
14984JS00007B/66

9 781906 523138